PHYXE
GODDESS OF FIRE
by Stacia D. Kelly

CatKlaw, Inc.

Manufactured in the United States of America

Cover by My Creative Pursuits
Interior Design by Stacia D. Kelly
Edited by Jennifer Parkinson
Cover Art by My Creative Pursuits ©2011

Published by:
CatKlaw, Inc.
www.catklaw.com
Virginia

ISBN 978-0-9852837-1-1
Print Version
Copyright© 2012 by Stacia D. Kelly

Dedications

To the Ladies
To my mother, for teaching me to read and write at such
an early age. To my grandmother, for allowing me to fall
in love with romance and the story. To the Sparkling
Hearts - JT, E Tate, and Cat - for keeping me moving
forward.

To the Guys
Hal, thank you for the ever patient alpha, beta, and
gamma reads.
Lil Man, for understanding all of my late night writing.
For Cat, for helping me plot & being supportive no matter
what I choose to do.

To Coach Tom & Team Infinity
Thank you for pushing me to focus on my dreams and
talents.

I love you ALL!

From the Private Goddess Chronicles of Phyxe, Goddess of Fire

I've had better days. Trust me, in the several millennia I've been alive, none can compare. This one?

Sucks.

And I'm tired. I want to do something. Seriously, DO something.

Wreak havoc, cause fires, maybe resurrect a planet or two. Whatever has to be better than this, right?

I kicked my feet up on the table daring Zhanne to say something.

I've been listening to her drone on for about an hour now. The Goddess of Energy carried a soothing and focused sense about her, but she sets my teeth on edge with a look. We get along, sort of. Every thousand years or so we actually agree on something. And yes, I still keep to Old Earth time, makes the most sense since we spend a lot of eras on that particular planet. But this? This is the same old, same old. I've been itching to do something. Anything, even if it means starting another war on one of my planets.

My sister Goddesses frown on that. No, not Gaian. The Goddess of Earth loves my temper. She's my hunting partner right beside me causing chaos and resurrecting souls every step of the way. But, the Goddesses of Air and Water? Well, Wystin and Glacial vibrate at a different frequency than I do. They hate my emotional outbursts. And I don't always understand their softer ways. Who the hell wants to meditate when you can spar full on?

Truth be told, they're pretty successful with their beliefs. Not my style.

"Phyxe, pay attention." Electricity danced over my skin raising the hair on my arms.

I tilted my head and let my eyes settle on the blue-skinned, white-haired one standing at the head of our obsidian conference table. It never failed to amuse me, the holographic map shimmered and cast a slivery outline around her as it always did. I wondered if she made it dance, or if it was a by-product of her nature.

"I was. I'd rather be doing something." I was listening. Just because I hadn't had my head turned towards her, eyes focused on her, didn't mean I hadn't heard her.

Can we tell? Meetings bore me.

Shivers danced along my spine, and I cast Zhanne a look. The energy ramped up in the room. I lifted an eyebrow. Oh, I definitely need a diversion, but the Goddess of Energy and I clashing in our war room? Bad idea if we wanted to keep the technology intact. Rebuilding was such a pain and suffering through Wystin's glares over all her precious tech stuff, well, unnecessary.

Seriously. She can be a baby about her gadgets and circuits.

I dampened down my fire. Zhanne's energy retreated, so I returned my gaze to my boots. I'd kicked them up on the table, mostly to annoy her, but also to give myself some room to stretch out. The chairs fitted the smaller Goddesses. Gaian, who stretched out like I was, and I were a little longer and larger than the other three. I didn't fault them their slightness, but the furniture should adjust for all of us.

I think they did it out of annoyance. Hell, I knew how to create ones far better suited for Gaian and I, but neither of us had done it yet. Showed how much we didn't want to be here.

Zhanne refrained from snapping at either one of us for our boots, although she eyed us both, so I left them. I listened and let my eyes trail over the edges of my boot. The seams were frayed. I should repair them, or make new ones. I tried to concentrate on Zhanne while she droned on and contemplated setting down on a planet and wreaking havoc. The Goddess of Energy had nothing new. I had too much power bottled up, and I couldn't release it in our realm, not without resetting our alignment between the realms. We were prohibited from using the full force of our abilities in the sacred space Zhanne created to house us. She played an intricate game to keep us all balanced in such close proximity to each other. She claimed it was for safety and stability.

Some days, I wondered.

I half listened as Zhanne continued with her review of the state of the Universe. Fire flared as a different energy began to race over me when I stared at the holographic map. Across the known galaxies, 232 registered as habitable planets, only 42 acknowledged remembering their base elemental deities, and even those seemed to be confused. Then again, every so often the Powers That Be went around them, birthed a new galaxy for them to learn while crushing an old one. Our creators served as a constant reminder that we were not all powerful nor the only ones playing across the cosmos. As the Goddess of Fire, those planets radiating higher on the heat scale–those pulsing red on the map called to me. I bit back a hiss of dismay at the meager six denoting realms with even a passing interest in worshipping the fire element.

"There's meaning here, sister we must seek out the patterns." Glacial smiled a soft smile at me when I cut my gaze to her. Her deep blue eyes were large with understanding.

The fire retreated. I can't get mad at the pixie-sized water goddess when she radiates warmth and love. A rush of calmness wafted over me. Damn her for her intuitive skills. She knew how to balance me out.

Across from me, Gaian, Goddess of Earth smirked. "I don't know. I think I kinda agree with Phyxe. I'd rather be out doing something." She toyed with a dagger, rolling it from hand to hand across and through her fingers.

Wystin sat perfect in stillness, listening, her dark hair flowing around her face, her back straight, her hands folded in front of her, as she was wont to do. I thought about rolling a fireball across the table at her, to stir things up. The Goddess of Air, after all these years, still wasn't sure how to deal with my pure physical response to the realms.

Sucked to be her.

Oh stars, I needed to get laid, or set something, someone on fire. I sound bad even to myself. No wonder they were all out of sorts with me. I need action. I haven't been this much of a bitch in decades.

The point between my shoulder blades began to itch. I rolled my shoulders back and took a deep breath. The sensation didn't leave.

We've been un-worshipped for centuries on many of our planets. I can't remember the last time one of us had been called. The years blended together.

Although, if I asked, Wystin would spout off the facts and statistics until we all died from boredom. Even in the few times in recent centuries, when we'd touched down, we'd been unrecognized. Stars, we'd all forgotten how to interact with the races under their protection. Hell, each of our names were garbled and changed thru the eons and universes. The humans on Earth called me phys-ed instead of fix. I stopped correcting them after the first six times. I'd ignored many requests through the years, but answered several hundreds. I was almost ready to respond to the next best thing. Yet only Gaian seemed to sense my unease, the restlessness.

Zhanne returned to her hologram. "Issues begin to brew in Sector Four. Gaian, two of the upheavals are yours."

I smiled when Gaian's eyes lit up at the idea of upheaval.

"Wystin, Glacial, one each. Your markers are here." The hologram grew in size, zooming to fit only the planets in question over the table.

I shifted in my seat, dropping my feet to the floor. Pinpricks of unease swept down, over my neck and across my shoulders. I moved, sliding forward in my chair, shaking them off instead trying to focus on Zhanne and what she was saying.

The hair on arms stood up, a tingling swept over me. I glanced away from Zhanne and my sisters. I checked in with my body, my intuition. Premonition? I closed my eyes for a split second and focused, but no, visions remained hidden. My eyes snapped open, and I gazed around the room. My sister goddesses of Water, Earth and Air sat unaware in their seats at the monstrosity of a table. Had no one else sensed the power shift?

I leaned forward and dug a dagger out of my boot, restless with the energy snaking through my body, which I'd begun to attribute to my restlessness instead of any outside influences. The fire rose in me, a wave of nausea passed over me. My vision swam. I replaced the dagger, shifted forward even more and tried to curl my fingertips into the obsidian stone in front of me as a steadying action. My fingers sunk through the edge.

I saw my sister of Earth shift and move. Gaian almost reached me in time. She actually leapt across the table as if to grab me. "Phyxe, no ... wait."

"I am not doing it," I whispered. My sight darkened, a large black tunnel reached out before me, spiraling. My reality splintered.

It hurt like the nine hells of the Voids.

❧ONE ❧

"Mother of the universe...I am going to kill whoever did this..."

The energy where her chest should have been expanded as she tried to take a deep breath. Electric shocks arced throughout her nervous system as it rebuilt, impulses only. Then, in a matter of seconds the pulses coalesced into a physical form. One minute she was electrons and neutrons, in another, flesh and blood. Images flashed past her mind's eye as she did a quick review of the million and one ways she'd ignite the person who'd pulled her. Electrical sparks flared in response.

They could have asked. They should have asked. Then again, she'd ignored requests before. Perhaps she'd flay them to the bone and resurrect them and then do it all over again for her own entertainment and the sheer rudeness of yanking her through time and space.

The dark tunnel lightened as her body assembled into shape. Phyxe crouched, her left knee buried in the sand, her right foot planted flat. Her arms extended on either side of her bent leg, balancing her on the shifting sands beneath her. Her palms sunk deep; the grains tickled her skin. She struggled to ignore the pain as she adjusted to the dimensional shift. The tiny pinpricks of flesh and muscle as they awoke were easy to deal with when she was the one who moved herself through space. She rolled her shoulders. Her back arched up in the smallest of stretches. The weight of her weapons settled into place, the familiar heaviness of the daggers in her boot sent satisfaction winding through her. The scent of desert, sands, dry heat, and latent fire beneath the surface wafted past her nose.

Bless it all, one of her worlds.

Ah, so whoever pulled her didn't have the finer art of yanking goddesses around the known universe. A smile started deep in her body.

Taujan. Good.

Perhaps she'd wait to fry the person who'd ripped her across space and time. Then again, the fires within flared hot and bright. Massive destruction might be good for the soul. She'd done worse in her youth. This wasn't the first instance she'd been pulled across the dimensions because someone demanded her presence instead of asking, but she'd sure as hell make it one of the last. She didn't recall the other times being this painful, this hard on the reconstruction. She would hunt down every incantation, in each book, computer, any piece of technology, anything anyone ever used to call her in the known and unknown Universe and make sure they were dust when this was all over.

"*Thats.* Focus." She whispered the curse.

Nighttime sounds of desert life descended on her as her hearing restored itself. Her body began to demand she move. She stifled a sigh. They'd better have a damn good excuse for it. Here she'd been restless after eons of inactivity and dormancy, so many had forgotten her, several planets continued on their paths, alone. She knew the laws. She'd asked for this.

It didn't mean she had to like it.

The mists clouding her vision retreated. She took stock. Solid again. She curled her hands in the sands, bit by bit. Sheer physicality of becoming made her hum. Her muscles protested the prolonged crouch after being pulled between realms. Something warm and rigid settled around her wrists as her body became whole again.

Click. A heaviness descended on her. Her eyebrow twitched.

Only her eyes moved, hidden still from anyone watching her, as she remained crouched, looking down, her hair flowing down over her face. She bit back a growl. Golden bracers circled her bare forearms extending from the edge of her wrist to mid arm. She didn't wear jewelry. She left that to Glacial and Wystin. She rotated her right arm in a small, slight, imperceptible motion. Shiny. Lightweight. Interesting and imprinted with strange symbols–hieroglyphics? No. Before. She frowned. An oddity, and she'd been around long enough to know oddities were rare.

A masculine chuckle washed over her, and Phyxe surged to her feet. Her muscles rippled, warmth snaked along her skin. She flipped her hair back over her shoulder as she planted herself in the sands. One hand dropped to the hilt of her sword, the other settled around the grip of the laser pistol. The nerve. Energy crackled along the edges of her entire being. Her height and stature she knew would give any man pause. She was not a tiny woman. A fever snaked over her, lighting every cell in her body. She growled low, energy swirling within her.

"That was far too easy. Are you sure you're a Goddess?"

"Choose your words with care, human," she said, adapting to his language without thought. She swept a look over the dark creature before her. Scars slashed from eyebrow to jawline marring the perfect symmetry of the tattoos on his cheek. Ebony hair hung in a disheveled mess. His eyes glowed like embers in the night. She memorized the markings on his chiseled bare chest. Dark complexion, almost as black as night, made the black on black emblems barely discernible. His skin crawled with the lines. She couldn't tell if they were tattoos or brands.

"Oh, I'm no more human than you are, lady." The flash of his white teeth startled her.

She sniffed to test the air. Burning flesh, ash and a hint of sulfur burned the back of her throat and beneath that a layer of lavender. She eyed him as red swirled in his eyes.

"You trifle with powers beyond your control, demon." Phyxe flipped her hand over to call the fire from within her, but only a small spark flickered to life in the center. She stared down at her empty palm. "What the hell?"

His laughter flowed over her. "Not so all powerful, Lady Fire, are you?"

Her power pooled behind the metal, unable to surge forward as it desired. It flared down her arm and stopped, a wall. Her chest tightened. Anger swelled up, threatening to burst forth. "Remove this, *knullare*."

She should have known. Ask for action and get yourself trapped until you figure it all out. *Krite.* Hadn't she learned that damn lesson eons ago? Stupid, stupid, stupid.

Krite.

Phyxe knew she glowed. Her body heated up. Her golden aura of trapped heat danced around her. The energy lines tripped over her skin. Red and gold arched over her, rippling, chasing, ready to surge forward. Light spilled out in every direction as her aura lit up the night.

She clenched and unclenched her hand. Nothing, only a spark. She would have incinerated the entire world in that second if she could have. Damn wall. Anger scorched a trail inside her, writhing, wanting to break free. Few ever lived to tell about angering the Goddess of Fire. In centuries past, she'd roasted most of them without thought.

"Get these trinkets off of me," she said, each word clipped.

"I cannot, until you've completed the task you were called to do." The demon's smile flashed in the darkness again. He folded his arms over his chest. His silver tipped claws glimmered.

"Task? You pulled me through dimensions for a demonic task?" She laughed. "I don't do jobs for demons. You're looking to die, aren't you?"

She shifted her weight in the sand. She memorized, theorized. He was not in fear of her. This demon held more power than he should. He looked amused, as if he knew exactly what her limitations were. Gods, what a good fireball right about now would do. Her fingers twitched. Killing him the old-fashioned way, the idea offered some satisfaction. Rip his head from his shoulders, bare handed, that sounded even better.

"I have a name, Lady Fire, I'm called Rais. Just as I am quite aware of all the names you go by across the Universe. And, yes, you'll do this one task, or one of your precious planets will cease to exist." He smiled. His pointed teeth gleamed white in the night.

Phyxe lifted her chin and settled her tongue against an incisor, refraining from issuing another growl. Demon. Rais. She toyed with the idea of burying a dagger in his chest. It would be easy enough to do especially from this distance. But, then, she'd remain clueless as to why and how he pulled her. And, he knew what would release the bracers.

Oh, she'd come a long way from her fledgling years.

9

Lucky demon.

"You think to threaten one of my worlds? You're not powerful enough to affect any kind of upheaval all on your own." She stepped closer to him.

The vision of resurrecting him within the flames over and over and over again for the next few thousand millennia flitted past her mind's eye. Roasting him, she filed the thought. It held promise.

He laughed. "No one said I was alone."

Phyxe let the fire coil through her, and she leapt. Sparks lit off her. Her dagger settled in her hand as she slammed into the demon. He howled in anger as the heat of her palm burned into him. She smiled as the small bits of fire landed on him. Maybe she couldn't throw a fireball, but she'd use flashes of fire here or there. He reared back as she sliced him open. Embers followed sinking into the open wound.

His howl turned from anger to pain. "Bitch Goddess."

He moved. His silver nails elongated even more, and he sliced back at her. Her body swayed, and she danced out of the way. She flipped her dagger from palm to palm. She didn't trust what poisons he had laced in his claws.

"You got the Goddess part right, hell hound." She darted back a little further as he drew closer again. "Well, yeah, you got the Bitch part right, too. Now, why don't you be a good demon and tell me why you're playing planet side. You're supposed to be hell realm bound, not cavorting around on my planets."

"You'll have to figure it out, lady."

She smiled as he sneered the word lady. Shadows shifted around them as if waiting to help or hinder. She feinted right and then leapt towards him again, fire urged her forward, burning through her, dancing with ferocity.

The silver glint out of the corner of her eye distracted her, blinding her for the moment. She gasped in pain when his claws slashed across her bare mid-drift. She barely registered the hiss of a sword as it cut past her, slicing deeply into the demon's arm. Her empty hand clamped down over the gashes, sparks tripping off her, impeding the progress of the dark poison. Her legs gave way, and she dropped to her knees, the sands shifted around her as if to shelter her from the battle.

On one level, she heard the demon's howl as he

flashed away from the scene. On the other, she realized, she may have traded one demon for another, but she couldn't bring herself to care. She fought the poison. Damn the bracers. What the hell had he laced his claws with? She bit down her teeth. Her eyes clamped shut as she tried to focus. Pain rampaged through her, splintering, shattering, and leaving chaos behind. She could do without the lesson in mortality. Been there, done that, several centuries ago. It hadn't been any fun then either.

"*Krite.* Now I'm going to have to hunt him down." She panted. The poison oozed down her veins, but her fire cascaded along behind repairing as much as it was able within her current limits.

"Lady, you're not fit to be hunting anything on this planet." The deep baritone flowed over her. The sparks lit higher. Fire stirred, banking hard against the bonds. "Not that either of you seem to be from here. Mind telling me how the hell you got on my world?"

She pried open her eyes. Lethargy threatened to overtake her as the fires within tried to scorch the poison. In her full power, the demon would have never broken through her personal barrier. The damn bracers ... stars, she needed them off her.

Darkness shifted and parted, her vision switched, and it was if the faint light of sunset swept over the desert sands. She eyed the warrior before her when he turned back to face her. Tall, stars, he was tall and muscled. His face set in stone. Strong jaw covered in dark stubble. Gods, he was gorgeous. Someone had crafted his body and energy pattern as if by hand paying exquisite attention to each detail, but who? Despite the black sludge attempting to reach her heart, she ached to move closer, the fire in him calling to her.

"He pulled me," she said, forcing her tone and breathing to even out. "What planet?"

He stared at her. "He pulled you? With what? Some sort of ship? Why would he pull you?"

She moved her hand away from her stomach and glanced down at it. Her nose wrinkled at the foul smell. "I have no idea how he did it, or why he did it other than I am the ruler of the Elemental Flame. What planet am I on?"

The tall warrior shook his head, a lock of dark hair

fell in his face even as he dropped down next to her, laying his sword at his side. "According to our legends, our history, the Elemental Fire is male. He is a warrior, a weapon of destruction, a God. He can fell cities with a thought, decimate planets."

"You've got your stories." She clamped her hand down on her stomach again and went to sit up. His reached for her.

"Let me see." He said as he pushed her back down.

Startled, she let him. She'd start to heal at any moment now. *Krite,* she'd better. She'd annihilated cities, planets even, when called to do so. "I am the reality, warrior."

Warrior, she was the damn warrior. She'd always been. She'd fought the battles, won the wars, destroyed the planets and resurrected those that were worthy. She'd loved. She'd lost. She'd dealt. She just was.

"You don't look like a ruler of anything at the moment." He moved her hand.

Her head reared back as his energy collided with hers. He'd touched her. Stars, every molecule in her body took notice. Her heart rate leapt. She looked up at him. A hazy sense of awareness swept through her. Blackness hovered at the edges of her vision.

No, no, no ... she wanted to stay with him, figure out how he'd connected with the fire in her.

"His claws got too close. I'm going to have to shut down and rest." She took a deep breath forcing herself to stay focused. Belatedly, she realized she was staring rather pointedly at his face as if memorizing the hard lines, the faint beard, the disheveled, uneven black hair and the even darker than dark eyes. Sexy, powerful. She liked, very much so. Too bad she couldn't focus enough to do anything more than stare at him for the moment. *Halja,* she had to be gone. Her sisters would have a field day with this one.

"You're badly wounded." His large hand wrapped around the arm not clasped down on her stomach. She bit her lip to keep from crying out, in surprise or pleasure, she wasn't sure which. "I thought you merely ducked out of the way for me to get a better strike."

She mentally shook herself and tried to shake his hand off. Men didn't touch her unless she allowed them to. She needed him to let go. He was clouding her vision. "As if. Let go."

"Let me see the extent of your wound." He ignored her and gently began to pry her fingers away from her abdomen.

She halted, looking down to where his hand was. Fire licked her flesh everywhere he touched, but black puss seeped at the edges of the gashes. Shock rippled at the contact of his hand on her bare skin. Pure heat and sparks raced over her. Every cell in her body stilled. Her gaze trailed down the length of his arm, back to his face. It'd been so long since she'd been touched, few dared. Her head dipped towards him, warmth spread desire ricocheting through her.

She stopped him from touching any closer. "Don't be foolish. The poison will work its way out on its own. Don't get any on you. I can barely heal myself at the moment. I don't need you poisoned, too."

Her stomach tightened, and he moved back as if burned. His eyelids dropped, shielding his thoughts from her view.

"Poison?" He frowned down at her. "I need to get you to a healer."

"Excuse me? I told you. I'll heal. All demons have poison in their claws. And apparently, Rais dipped his even more so to pull and hurt me." She turned her eyes up to him as if she hadn't heard him correctly. She took a deep breath. Was the man not listening? She could heal herself. She just needed a moment or two.

Her vision swam. Ok, perhaps three or four moments.

Tempted, oh, so tempted to tussle with him since she couldn't call the flame regardless of the liquid darkness rolling through her. Gods, he was bigger than her and made her feel ... feminine. She bit her lower lip, for the first time in millennia, undecided. She was at a distinct disadvantage. Yes, she wanted to follow the demon's trail, but she needed to rest.

Not like she'd moved from the sands where she'd fallen yet either. Some goddess she was. Good thing her sisters couldn't see her now.

The damn bracers were leaden weights around her wrists, a heavy reminder for patience. Her power pooled.

A look of resignation crossed his face as he forced

himself to remove his hands. "You're going to the healer before you fall on your face. And then, you can explain this word, demon, to me."

"Oh, for the love of ..." She started and then the darkness swept over her.

Strong arms gathered her close. A smiled drifted through her body before she succumbed. Get pulled by a demon, land in the arms of a sexy male. She'd say she'd come out ahead in the deal.

But the *Ubilin* would pay for the poison. She relaxed into the warrior's body, letting him and the healing process take over.

Maybe, just maybe, he'd survive it all.

❧ TWO ☙

If anyone tried to tell Lord Truant Marius, Marius to most, and Tru to his closest friends, he'd hike across the nighttime desert sands with the self proclaimed Goddess of Fire in his arms, he'd have told them the smell of Falavian flowers muddled their senses. Fire was male and elemental, and yet pure beauty, heat and sensuality nestled in his arms. Her mass of red gold hair spilled over his arm. Black lashes, tipped with gold, formed crescents against the smooth tanned skin of her cheekbones. He bit back a growl of annoyance as her sword scabbard dug into his arm. He should have removed taken the blade from her, but he worried more about her passing out than her weapons.

He knew better than to think she was who she claimed. Off-worlders crafted many stories to get on his planet wanting to negotiate with their trade routes. Gods and goddess didn't exist. If they had, his planet wouldn't have endured the hell it had for the last few hundred years.

No god was that cruel.

He walked, carrying her through the night across the Shifting Sands. He carried her east, to Raiche to summon the boat for the Haven. The island caverns housed the Matrons, the closet healers, and thankfully, the best on the planet. He hoped they knew enough to help fend off the black puss oozing from her wound. In all his years of existence, even this dark poison was new to him. He refrained from touching it worried she'd been serious about it harming him as well. He didn't have time to be down. His warriors waited for him at the Watch Tower to the south. He'd gone off on his own to recon, confident in his ability to travel the Sands without them. Firon watched over him. The unplanned battle deep in the desert delayed him, even more so now with the slight detour.

Someone summoned her, the demon? One of his own? She certainly wasn't a Fironian woman. And, in truth, his warriors couldn't be everywhere across the lands any longer. No technology, limited numbers of warriors. He bit back a growl of frustration. He blamed his faulty, hazy memories. He knew they once lived with far more technology, but he couldn't remember where it all went or why. Every time he tried he thinking about it, he encountered mind-numbing pain setting him back days.

Damn his father.

The woman in his arms shifted and groaned.

He cast a quick glance over her sleeping facade. Heat coiled deep within him as she snuggled in, closer to him. He'd memorized every line, curve, and angle of her face in the last hour. She was beauty and strength incarnate. His entire body lit when she moved out of the sands and leapt towards the ... Demon. The term rolled around his head. He itched to head out and destroy the thing. No woman should have to battle, much less such a creature.

He tried to dampen his response to her shifting closer to him, but every cell, every muscle tensed and focused on her. He hadn't thought when he'd leapt into the middle of her battle. She darted into battle and instinct took over.

Something in her called to him. He knew damn sure he didn't want it to.

This attraction would fade. It had to. He'd been too long without a woman. He needed to rectify that. His work, duty, required no distractions.

An off-worlder, a deluded one, and thinking she was a Goddess, but still an obvious off-worlder needed to hold no sway over his actions. He didn't desire the headache that came with keeping a woman, no matter how much his body lit next to hers. He'd been too long without a bed or a bedmate. That had to be it. She was nothing like the women of Firon.

Nothing.

The world exploded in light and sound around them. Sand kicked up in a whirlwind to his right. He curled her into him and dove to the side. Her body tensed in his arms as if she sensed the attack even deep in her slumber. Tru snarled in outrage. He dropped into the sands, protecting, shielding her as he tried to work their way behind the nearest sand dune.

16

He struggled a bit with her weight and weapons. Trying to balance a woman of her stature and weapons, he realized she was larger than he'd expected, pure muscle and strength. Nothing about her made a response easy or common.

He'd thought it wise to travel without his warriors? Gods, what the hell had he been thinking?

Once he had her well covered, he pulled his sword from the scabbard on his back. He glanced over her. His gaze fell on the weapon in a holster on her side. She lay nestled in the sands as if Firon protected her. "Lady, you're unlike any woman I know, but you have an arsenal on you I'd kill for."

Not expecting a response, he reached over and unlatched the laser from its place. He looked down at the weapon as it settled in his palm. His hand curled around the metal. This would even the odds. "Do you know how long I've wanted one of these back in my hands?"

No. Of course she didn't. Hell, she didn't know what planet she was on. He might think she was delusional, but even he didn't have a good explanation for what he'd seen her do against the dark one in the desert. No woman on Firon fought like that, much less radiated such power. He'd have sworn he was hallucinating, but he knew full well the sparks of fire had drawn him across the sands to her. He'd make her explain it all when the darkness no longer taunted her.

He dropped low in the sand, moving in minute slowness away from where she lay. He'd draw them away from her before he attacked. Already wounded, she didn't need to be caught in the crossfire. He didn't want to chance anymore damage to her than she'd already taken. He had no idea how long it would take her to recover from the poison. He wasn't sure whom to even ask.

He eyed the desert night and stared deep into the shadows. He demanded his body blend into the darkness. Damn it all, he should have worked to make better time and brought his warriors with him. He knew better than to go alone. However, no one ever accompanied him in his travels. It was safer and easier to keep his travels secret for himself, the mission and his men. He preferred to use the planet to his advantage—alone and without distraction.

Now he walked into an ambush. The woman sidetracked him, and he hadn't sensed her or the demon.

He turned back to the sands. His vision adjusted to the shadows, the distances. He felt the two beings not too far from him, trying to use the darkness for cover. He swallowed and tasted the bitter scent of the fear and adrenaline in the air. Anticipation rolled through him; fury ran a close second. It was getting old, this dance in the night. More off-worlders. Every cell of his body vibrated with their metallic taste and scent.

He ran his tongue across the back of his teeth and stared into the darkness. The last few years left him with nothing to do but study and hunt the ones killing their men and stealing the women from the planet. Each one carried the same stink as if they'd been crafted or molded at the same time.

It was high time it ended. He'd had enough. His people deserved their lives back, not continued life dwelling below the sands for safety. Hell, his planet Firon suffered because of them. He wanted their waters back. He wanted their cities and homes resurrected.

This hiding underground grew tiresome.

He crawled through the sands, letting the winds carry his scent away from his movements. He moved as a desert creature. A shadow crossed his vision to the left. He flattened himself against the sands and waited, watching. He wanted a movement, a hint. None hunted his deserts as well as he did. His arm holding the laser stretched out slowly in the sands. He settled himself in to wait.

There.

He squeezed the trigger and light arced out across the night sands. The shadow before him screamed in pain. Tru pulled himself up and rolled. His dagger appeared in his hand before the thought even crossed his mind. The metal arced out and sliced, the sound of the cry cut off.

He moved before the second shadow realized what he'd done. Shifting with the shadows and the sounds of the night, moving slowly over the sands. These off-worlders hunted at odds with the planet. He'd been born to hunt with it, even if Firon wasn't responding.

When the second shadow dared to dart across the sand, Tru was ready for him. The laser flashed. He focused on wounding rather than killing this time. While he hadn't used the weapon in decades, its familiar response settled well in his hand.

He wanted answers. He shoved the laser into the waistband of his pants and strode across the sands sensing no other threats.

He sighed and wrapped his hand in the man's uniform. He ignored the gurgling groans coming from the man's shredded throat. Hell, he'd been aiming for his shoulder. His aim was off. He blamed his lack of practice over the years.

He dragged the struggling man over and dropped him next to his unconscious so-called Goddess and kneeled down, removing all weapons, pocketing a few, and casting others aside. Regardless of the danger, for some reason, he didn't want to stray too far from her side. His skin twitched as if a million fire ants nipped at him when he'd been too far away. He glanced over at her. She rested quietly in the sands, looking completely at peace, her breathing normal. The fire ants stopped. He turned his head to check on the first off-worlder, who lay still in the sands, his life force halted. Tru felt no remorse. Too many lives stolen from him. This was, well, this was *sajako*, war.

He wrapped a hand in the man's hair and lifted his head so he could see him. Hells, useless. The man held no answers. His throat incapacitated, fear widened his eyes. Only the tell tale tattoos on the side of his face gave Tru any indication that he was part of the others he'd battled elsewhere on his planet.

The damn off-worlders invaded every piece of land they found.

He dropped the almost dead man in the sand again. Leave him for the creatures of the night to finish off. The man was useless, no longer a concern. He needed to move the woman to safety. He didn't care how steady her breathing measured out. Her lashes never flickered. He stepped over the inert form and leaned over to gather her up in his arms. He paused long enough to work the sword from her back and placed it over his own. He didn't need it biting into him for the rest of the trek.

A howl echoed over the sands.

Tru gathered her close, attempting to shield most of her as he lifted his head and let a howl rip from his throat in answer. Her height made her hard to shield. He might be the tallest of their warriors, but she wasn't far behind him. He curled her into his chest as shadows emerged from the sands around him. He tucked her head into the crook of his arm, hiding her from his men.

"Lord Marius. We saw the fire. Devos sent us to check on your safety." A low voice whispered across the sands, barely audible.

"Two down. I am fine. Bury the dead one, take the other one to Devos. I need to get this woman to the caverns. She's been injured." He bit back a groan as her hand unconsciously curled into his chest.

"There are six of us, m'lord. Two can return with the bodies." The man moved to step closer. Tru straightened realizing one of his Lieutenants stared at him, watching him. "We will escort you."

"I don't recall asking for your escort, Eriaku. I do believe I said to return with the bodies." He lifted his chin and his eyebrow at the same time. He wasn't above putting the Goddess of Fire back on the sand and trouncing one of his warriors for disobeying him. He hadn't tussled with any of them in a long while. It might be time to renew their respect for his leadership. Hell, he realized, he wanted none of them near her.

Where the hell was this possessiveness coming from? He didn't have time for a tryst. He should hand her over to Eriaku and let him take her to the Matrons.

Something in him snarled in protest. His arms tightened around her. He wasn't letting her out of his sight.

Gods, he had to be tired. There was zero chance in history he was that concerned about one female. Especially, one deluded female.

"No disrespect intended, m'lord. You'd said she was injured. I thought only to help." Eriaku stepped back, melting back into the darkness with the other warriors.

"None taken, Eri. Get the one back and use whatever methods you need to get the information out of him. Ask the others to report in about a dark skinned male warrior with strange black tattoos. He is the one who hurt this female. He will be put to ground." Tru curled her as close as he could get her. His body heated.

"Yes m'lord. Where was he last seen?"

"Check my trail. I wasn't hiding it. Firon might have done so in my stead. We've traveled for the last hour. You can track back. She is not ours. He brought her here. I want to know how and more importantly, why." Tru bit back anything more. The invaders had been stealing women, but this one, they'd brought to him. He trusted his closet warriors with his life. But, for some reason, he wasn't so willing to do so with hers.

He gazed down at her sleeping facade. What was it about her?

"Yes, m'lord."

Tru watched until they disappeared into the night with the aliens' bodies before he turned back to make his path to Raiche.

Across the planet, hidden deep within the snows of the northern hemisphere, Rais smiled as he observed the satellite feed on the screen in front of him. He'd kicked back in the communications room with his feet up on the desk when he'd returned to the keep Marius' family had left so long ago. Abandoned, shielded by Lord Riske by the very technology hiding the planet, it proved to be the perfect home during his stay—or his imprisonment—as he'd started to think about it. Dark and dank suited the demon in him just fine. The inability to leave irked him. He quashed the whisper from his non-demon half, the half writhing in pain from the bonds of the markings on his skin. He shoved it aside. No need for any of that now. He had a mission. He couldn't be sidetracked from his survival. Every beat of his heart depended on this. He wasn't about to die because of the whim of some bored god.

Since he couldn't remain near Tru, he'd wanted to watch the first skirmish with the goddess. The tattoos along his body burned for a moment when the cameras finally revealed them and then settled to a steady hum. A perverse sense of pleasure washed over him as the pain hit her, guilt followed closely on its footsteps. Whispers swirled around him, some more insistent than others. He ignored them all. He had to. Some of the whispers threatened to over take him, seep into his well being.

He couldn't afford that now.

He'd known she'd been bent on his destruction when she appeared. The fire of her anger reached out to feed his soul. Half of him had wanted her to take a shot. He hadn't realized how well the bracers would keep her in check. Better that they had, he wasn't done here, yet.

He grinned when his wraith hit her. She'd been surprised, but not weakened. She would prove a worthy adversary. Hopefully, she'd keep Tru sidetracked enough to finish his job here on the planet, a plan started to form, one that would keep them all alive.

This might be getting fun.

❧THREE ❧

"He expects us to get that out of her?" A slender finger poked the right side of her abdomen, staying far enough away from the open wound, but close enough to cause a ripple of discomfort. If Phyxe could have growled, she would have, but lethargy wrapped around her, kept her from moving, reacting. "It's like tar from the lava pits."

A shift and rustling came from her left. A whispery soft voice flowed over her. "He said heal her, keep her hidden, and he'd be back."

The first voice snorted. "Always the way he talks to us. As if he thinks the healing process is easy."

"Shush, he protects us all the best he can. He only knows what we let him know about our ways here. And, the poor boy is tired."

"Poor boy nothing. It's his responsibility like his father's before him. He knew it."

Phyxe hovered between awareness and tracking the trails the sounds waves made across the backs of her eyelids. Pretty colors. She focused as well as she could. Bitch One. She'd name the pissy one, Bitch One. It suited the sound of her voice.

She could have named her something worse, but something in the air hinted at a place of worship, so she didn't let her thoughts venture too far into the realm of blasphemy in case she upset the tenuous balance.

Of course, being bound and poisoned, she should upset it all. *Krite*.

"Yes, Seirreana. Lord Marius knows it as we know our responsibility. It doesn't mean we can't be compassionate about his plight, about all our plights. We are in this together. Now, how are we going to heal her?" A cool hand settled light as a feather on her brow. "She's colder than she should be. Her lips are starting to turn blue. Perhaps the poison is slowing her body's natural healing process, making her cold?"

Phyxe softened her outlook, some. Ok, so her name wasn't Bitch One, but it suited her far better than Seirreana. Of course, if Bitch One had to deal with her in full power, she'd be a whole lot less of a shrew. The warrior who'd stepped into her fight deserved more honor than she gave him. Lord Marius. Not many humans would dare to throw themselves into battle between a demon and a goddess. And, he had. Maybe not the smartest thing she'd ever seen a human do, but damn brave and sexy to boot.

A shiver raced through her body at the thought of the warrior and every spare inch of chiseled body she'd been able to glimpse before folding into the sands. A lord, that meant he held power here. No wonder he'd been so sure of himself in the sands and declaring this place his world.

"Well, she's not one of ours, who knows how she responds to anything, much less whatever that is in her."

"Seirreana."

Phyxe willed her eyes to open so she could see the two hovering over her, but her eyes steeled shut. The poisonous sludge crept through her body trying to dampen whatever hint of flame it could find. If she could peal her eyes open and dislodge her tongue from the roof of her mouth, she'd tell the crotchety one to stuff it and bring her flame.

"What? She's obviously an off-worlder. Never seen a single woman who looked like her, even before we shut down the ports. She's as tall and muscled as the men, and ..." The women's voice lifted and a startled gasp caused her words to stop. "Ah, Etheria?"

Heat played around her abdomen, bounding and rebounding against the poison.

"Yes?"

A finger prodded her side again, well away from the open wounds. "Do you see what I'm seeing?"

The hand lifted off her head. "Oh, heavens."

"Do you?"

A rustling sounded around her again. Blankets piled over her. Warmth. Heavenly warmth. If Phyxe could have sighed she would have. The cold began to retreat from the first layer of skin. Perhaps in a few hours, she'd be able to move again, if she didn't set the blankets on fire. Oh hell, setting them aflame would be a blessing in disguise. She longed to say thank you, but remained hovering between awareness and oblivion.

"We tell no one, just as he asked."

"He didn't ask."

"Enough. She is to be kept hidden. We'll need to warm her up. The blue in her skin can't be a good sign."

"If we keep her mostly covered, can we send in one of the young ones to keep an eye on her? I don't trust that she showed up here. The men can't be everywhere, and some of the elders should monitor what they can. It's a trick."

The soft sigh flitted past her ears. "We'll have to trust one of the young ones. They haven't been taught to monitor, yet. We'll send Firiea to her. She has a good head on her shoulders. I don't think this woman's a trick, but I don't trust the events around her arrival. We must keep to the plan at all costs, but if we keep her mostly covered."

"And hide all the weapons?"

"Yes, the weapons cannot remain, they'll go with the others, and her clothes will have to be switched. She might pass if we keep her garbed as we are. We'll have to think of something to hide her hair. No one on the planet has ever had such color. And, if we keep a close eye on her, there's no telling what she is, not with ..."

"Agreed."

Phyxe wanted to protest as the voices trailed off. No one would be taking her weapons, much less her clothes. She would not pass as one of them. Even though she couldn't shift herself to blend in better, she was a goddess. And, she'd be damned if she let them get away with hiding her. She had a demon to hunt.

She could feel them moving away from her but was powerless to do anything about it. She bit back a mild curse. Damn that *knullare* and his trinkets from hell. Next possible chance she had, she'd be spending some ass kicking time in the hell regions, if only to remind them of the balance of power. *Ubilins* and the hell regions, they knew better. Fire and brimstone were under her domain. She wasn't beyond reminding every last demon which goddess ruled Fire.

Krite.

At least the poison wasn't killing her. She didn't want to resurrect. She had one particular male to seek out, understand. Why the hell had he jumped into the middle of the fight?

Sparks still flickered throughout her body, limited and focused on eating at the dark sludge. If they'd bring her fire, she could do so much more. Instead, she shut down. Safe enough for the time being to let the embers work their magic.

All she needed was a spark.

She drifted in the darkness behind her eyelids. Heat beckoned to her. Lava pulsed deep within obsidian walls. Energy stirred, sleepy, lethargic. Heat swept through her body and surged fiery fuel along her core.

"Mistress?" The voice faint, tired reached out to her.

Fire raced along her skin, pooling at her wrists. She took a deep breath and willed it under control even in this hazy, between realms space. Energy coiled. The lava within the walls shifted as energies began to awake. Power swirled and bubbled. It itched to be called.

The image blurred and changed.

A room appeared with black walls, flames dancing in the depths. A copper basin balanced on unseen tethers in the middle of the room, fire flared from its center. Phyxe set a bare foot on the edge. The flames leaned into her and captured her foot. She smiled in relief and delight as the fire welcomed her. Without hesitancy, she stepped into the flame and balanced herself in the basin. Flames licked up her body. She let them swirl up and cocoon her from sight. Her head dropped back in ecstasy as the fire cleansed her body.

Zhanne? She cast the thought out and attempted to use the energy dancing along her body. She sensed nothing further than the planet. There were no voices beyond the planet. She could faintly hear the inhabitants all across the planet, the planet itself, but beyond, beyond ... silence.

It was never silent.

Mistress? The sleepy voice of the planet called to her.

Yes, Ancient one?

You called to me. I heard you. It has been so long since anyone has called.

I know the feeling, Ancient One.

How long?

I'm not sure. It has been thousands of years since I've been called myself.

Shock rippled through the planet. The earth shifted. *The ungrateful little ...*

No. Phyxe shouted. Her body tensed in the flame. *Do not harm them. They do not understand.*

But to dishonor and forget our creators? Unacceptable.

I am not your creator, Ancient One; I am your protector, nothing more, nothing less.

You are the source of all Fire.

No, I am the ruler of Fire, not the source.

Phyxe turned in the basin. Her movements slow, lethargic since she merged with the flames. She stopped with a quick intake of breath.

Her warrior stood before her, hovering in the door. Heat flared deep in his eyes.

She swallowed the smile threatening to escape as his eyes traveled over her naked, flame-licked form. She was used to the adoring gaze of men and women, but with his, she wanted the appreciation to be real.

"You are not..."

She smiled, "Human?"

"Obviously."

"On fire?"

"Obviously."

"What then? That doesn't cause you pain?"

Phyxe shook her head. The fire tickled her skin as the edges of her hair brushed against her naked back. "No, the flames feed me. They are my essence. They heal me. "

She took a step and reached out to move from the basin. The flames pulled back from her body, a trail of heat left in their wake.

"Lady Phyxe." A dark figure darted out of the edges of the dream to help her, a robe in hand.

His eyes flashed with anger. "You dare to reveal yourself to one of my own?"

Phyxe cut him a glance as the flames licked higher.

"Your people were mine long before they were ever yours, Warrior." She hissed. "You'd do well to remember that."

The flames flared around her and fed her soul, renewed and invigorated. She held out her palm, a small spark, a fledgling flame struggled to burst forth. Her hand closed with a snap. She heaved a frustrated sigh.

"I am bound here for the time being." An unladylike 'this sucks' echoed in her head. It was Old Earth slang, but it fit.

"We are going to set some ground rules until we figure out how to get you out of here," he swore.

Phyxe smiled. The warrior lord was disgruntled in the dream realm or not, either ticked off over an ill-conceived power struggle, or there was something more. Universe above, she wanted him in the flame with her to see how hot they could burn.

"Young one, leave us please."

"Yes, m'lady." The girl darted a look at Lord Marius. Then she deposited the robe in front of the basin and scooted between him and the entryway. Her form turned to mist, blending back into the dream before she faded through the doorway.

He continued to scowl. His arms crossed over his chest. She'd almost wished he'd remained bare-chested, but the willowy shirt he donned since he'd picked her up in the deep desert hinted at the strength she knew lay beneath. She dropped the robe and smiled as his scowl deepened.

"Is this the problem, warrior?" She ran her hands down her naked sides and a well of satisfaction sprung forth as he growled at her.

"Knock it off. You are not human." He stood his ground. A muscle in his cheek twitched.

That had never stopped her before. She was flesh. She was blood. She was also ... more.

"You're not quite sure what I am, warrior." She stepped out of the flame and over the robe pooled at the base. "You see a woman, but so very unlike the others on your planet. I am a warrior, like you. So, here, I am other."

His body tensed as she drew closer. She leaned into him, leather against skin. Her nipples harden as they came into contact with the sensuous fabric. Her fingertips trailed up his chest, and tugged on the collar of his shirt so she could reach the warm flesh. She needed his heat.

This close to him, this time, she took what she could get. Centuries had passed since she'd shared any kind of closeness with another being. His body called to hers. She wanted him. Wanted him deep inside her. Wanted to share the edge of insanity with him. Wanted his heat. She knew he would make her burn.

Could he handle it?

He groaned as her hands hit flesh. She watched as fire flared deep in his eyes. His arms curled around her and trapped her against him.

"You ask much, lady."

She smiled. "I ask nothing."

A hard smile crossed his face. "You are too used to getting what you want."

He dropped his arms and set her away from him. An inner struggle crossed over his face.

Phyxe frowned. He wanted her. Even in this dream realm, she could feel it. Hell, she could taste it in the air. His body reacted to hers anytime he drew near. Hers did the same.

"I will be back in three days time to check on you. Do not corrupt the Matrons in my absence. And do not leave this sanctuary."

He turned on his heel and vanished in a wisp of smoke.

Phyxe stared at the lingering haze. For a brief moment, the fire of passion flared into anger. Dissatisfaction. Yet, a smile crept across her face. Her anger disappeared as mirth threatened to overtake her. He was lucky she wasn't in a temper or had full use of her powers. Frustrated? Hell, yes. She wanted to play. Pissed off? No. He'd have had a fireball on his ass out the door.

Well, hell.

No one ever turned her down. Even in her dreams.

❧FOUR ❧

Truant jackknifed up in the bed of furs panting. Sweat dripped down his bare chest. His heart beat in triple time.

A growl of frustration ripped from his throat. She'd been bathing in the flames, fire caressing every lean inch of her bare skin. He'd wanted nothing more than to strip down and join her, even if the heat flayed the skin from his body. He'd have died a happy man, dream or no dream.

It all seemed so real. Gods. He should be taken out into the desert sun and left to die for his stupidity. His body lusted after the Fire Goddess, not a god, but a woman who played with fire and who had a body to die for. He'd never met his match in all his time, and he'd been alive a long time, but there she was, naked, on fire, and standing toe to toe with him.

Phyxe. Her name rolled through his brain. Somehow, it seemed appropriate.

He ran a hand over his face. Leave it to him to be lusting after a Goddess awake or asleep. Women were to be taken care of, helped to pursue their artistic creativity, allowed to challenge in intelligence and arts, yet sheltered and adored. This one, this one would want adoration, but on her terms, and she'd be damned if she wouldn't give as good as she would get. He might have met one he could play with and play hard. She'd expect it, and then, she'd leave when all was right on the planet again. She'd walk away or he'd send her back. Either way, he'd be on Firon making sure all was right in the world.

He grunted and threw off the covers. So much for thinking he'd get some much needed rest in the few hours he could delay. He had no time to play, no matter how tempted. He pulled on the clean clothes that had magically appeared at the foot of his bed. He'd known the

Matrons would take care of them both. As much as he needed to be back with his men, he'd figured he could spend a few hours to recover and recuperate.

He was wound up but hadn't realized how much so. He had an unknown source trying to overtake his planet. Thousands of women and children had been lured to their deaths or scurried off planet to who knew where. Now a sexy Goddess hid deep within the caverns, probably corrupting the Matrons and their students.

It all served to piss him off.

He wanted his calm desert sands back. He wanted his warriors to hunt the dunes again and return to the soft havens of their homes deep within the shifting sands. He wanted them participating in galactic interactions as a power, not hiding and retreating as the universe went on without them.

Instead, they'd retreated to the sands and caverns and ventured out at night to hunt trapped by the very technology his father had put into place to keep the people of the planet safe. Little could be done against the invaders. Somehow, they knew almost before he did what his next steps were.

Like every time they'd known before.

He threw on his weapons and strode out of the room and into the hallway. Firon was off limits to the galaxy unless a special request came to the Council. The House of Marius had not approved any requests in hundreds of years. He wasn't about to start now, not after the last few years of dealing with these invaders. Hell, he didn't even know how to let them in even if he wanted to. Once the invaders were dealt with, he'd damn well figure out how to open access back up and set up the trade routes—on his terms—the way it should have been done in the first place. Of course, it all hinged on him finding the tech his father had hidden and erased from their minds. Damn the old man. He'd wanted them hidden, safe. Now, Tru needed a level playing field.

He needed to know who these alien fighters were, and how they were getting onto the planet. These new ones were different, harder, and darker than those who'd caused Firon's current isolation. Too many of his people died in recent battles with these dark ones. He'd created the Havens and hidden the women and children the best he could while Firon's warriors set out to cleanse the planet's surface of intruders once again. The heat from the lava swells deep beneath the surface confused the aliens and kept his people well hidden.

He was tired. He wanted to find a safe place of his own and lay down to sleep for a week, a month, a year, but he couldn't.

He wouldn't.

He hadn't slept soundly ... in a very long time. Light naps didn't count, not when if he fell too deeply asleep, he could hear the people crying out to him. His people expected his protection, his guidance. They expected him to keep them safe. He'd traveled the nights from city to city to check in and prepare the families for the battles to come.

The aliens would be hunted. He'd suffered their actions long enough and attempted to be defensive in nature. All because he'd refused the Galactic Council's request to reopen trade routes and negotiations. Hell, he didn't even know how to open the trade routes, but he'd figure it out. And now, it had taken a few years, but somehow, they'd snuck onto his planet and were attempting to bring his power down around him.

It had been far too long since his warriors engaged in serious battle. Yet, not a single one faulted him for refusing to reopen negotiations. Their memories of the reasons were long and sharp, even if most complained of a hazy point. They all missed Lady Gisele Marius and her soft and gentle healing ways.

Tru's breath hitched at the thought of his mother and her large dark eyes and musical voice. When the Negen kidnapped and killed her, his father refused to negotiate, instead, closing their borders to the other realms.

No, he needed to focus on the current situation. Eventually, he would avenge his mother. Now, their skills needed to be reawakened. It had been years since they'd battled others rather than toyed with battle amongst themselves. They'd needed little time to sharpen their senses, re-hone the skills that had been in such demand by the other worlds.

Tomorrow, the Fironers alien hunts would begin. If it required annihilation and all out war, Tru was ready to put it to the test to make a point to the Galactic Council. His people would not be bought, sold or traded for their abilities. He refused to allow their women to be sold as sex slaves around the galaxy. Their refined ability in the arts and dance had drawn many to their planet in the past. And, he refused to allow the men to be sold into wars, most especially wars that were not of their creation.

If the galaxy wanted Firon, then Firon would have equal say on the Council. Until the offer was made, he intended to keep his people protected the best way he knew how. Keep them hidden. Let the planet defend them. Few races other than theirs could handle the desert sun, the heat or even find water where there was none to be found.

And now, he had the woman to deal with. He couldn't ever recall having met a female warrior even when the trade routes had been open. Of course, he'd been hunched over his studies for the most part, learning all the diplomacy he needed to know, so who knew if other planets had women hunters and fighters.

Apparently, they did. The sword on her back looked at home, the hilt battle worn. He ran his hand over his eyes and continued to wind his way through the Haven. No matter she set off sparks and heat in a desert battle. It was a trick of some sort. She couldn't be a Goddess, perhaps the lord's consort? But a Goddess? How could a woman, softer, more nurturing in nature be ready to battle?

She met him eye to eye. Her body honed to perfection, a seasoned warrior. She moved with fluid grace, her long red and blond locks swung with each sway of her hips. Her golden eyes flamed with roused passions.

He couldn't turn her loose among the population. Men would fall and women would harm themselves thinking they could do as she did. Their women were known for their beauty, artistry and healing. Their bodies not honed and crafted for battle.

Hell, he didn't want to share her with the others. Since she'd appeared in the darkness before him, he wanted nothing more than to cart her off to the safest place he could find and lock them in for days. His body almost demanded it.

She'd glowed in the desert. She'd glowed, and his body, his skin hummed in response.

He had responsibilities.

He had a hunt to plan. Sex with a woman who seemed determined to rule him was out of the question. He had enough of his own women who vied for the spot as his lady. He didn't have time for the games, the drama.

Gods. She was Fire. It had taken all his willpower to set her down in the soft furs and turn away to let the Matrons tend to her.

When she'd stepped naked from the basin in his dreams ... hell, when she'd turned in the flames, his internal temperature shot through the roof. When she'd pressed her naked skin up against him, his body responded as if it were real, and he were nothing more than a young one near his first female. If she hadn't demanded, he'd probably have sunk to the floor with her, dream or no dream. He wanted to call her alien, but he couldn't. She was other, and she was more.

He shook himself mentally as he strode through the maze of corridors of the Haven.

He stopped suddenly. He'd been wandering without direction, without thought, and the obsidian corridor ended at a dark wall. A hazy memory flitted past his mind's eye as he stared at it. He frowned, a slight pain starting midway between his eyes. He forced it away and reached out and ran his hand over the wall. His fingers found a deep crevice and curled into it. A soft click opened the wall with a hiss.

He remembered. He had forgotten about this room and something cleared in his mind and he remembered the secret passage.

He bit back a growl and stared into the darkness waiting for his eyes to adjust. Lights flickered to life before him and bathed the hanger in a soft red glow. Lava light illuminated the cavern through the walls. A whistle of appreciation escaped his lips before he could stop it.

Dear Dad. Screw you.

His breath hissed out. He knew it. He knew he'd forgotten something or been told to forget. Damn the old man. He knew his father had powers ... did the old man have the ability to make them all forget things? He, or someone he'd had on his council must have. As much as Tru would swear his mind was his own, the gapping holes, the flitting memories and now this. Unreal.

Fifty gliders lined the floor. They gleamed red in the soft light; their metal casings look undaunted by the lack of use. He strode over to the closest one. The glider's panels lit as he drew near. A gentle whir lifted the glider from its resting place on the deck.

"Lord Marius. How may I serve you?"

His hand halted in mid-air. He clenched his fist and pulled it back to his side. Interesting. His father left more than a few things out when passing on Warlord reports. He didn't remember the gliders talking. What else hadn't he been told? Hell, what else had he forgotten?

"M'lord?"

"How do you know who I am?" It seemed silly to be talking to a machine, but what else was normal about his day.

"Your insignia m'lord, it carries your activation code." The metallic voice chirped back.

Tru gazed down at the ring on his hand, the one marked with the House Marius. His fingers curled and uncurled. He was leery of what else he'd uncover with his plan. This technology was not the same as he hazily remembered. They'd never been this far advanced. What else had the old man accomplished in the years they'd been hidden before his death? What else had he been made to forget?

"Are all the gliders programmed thus?"

"Yes, sir, Lord Marius the Fourth, your father, placed the encoders in the cache behind you. There is one per glider for your men."

"How many other cache's are there?" At least the machine was more than forthcoming with information than his father had been. He made a mental note that if he ever had children, he'd skip naming them Marius, maybe he'd let them choose their own house name.

"Fifty-three caches at last inventory, m'lord."

"What?" He turned, looking around the hanger. Where the hell were they all stashed?

"There are fifty-three bases such as this one. Two others contain as many gliders as you see here. Four others contain gliders, devices and more technology."

He did the math. He should have known about these things. Why had his father kept this from him? Distant images danced past his mind's eye. Memories bubbled to the surface as if a lock opened.

"M'lord. Your central AI, Zen, is at the Old Palace in Tian. She is hidden in a console room. You'll find the latch a few meters down the main hall on the left, near the picture of your parents. She maintains connections across the planet with the devices and technologies buried in the caches. She also helps maintain the status in the Havens."

Gods, it kept getting better and better.

In the years since his father's passing, someone, somewhere should have mentioned the technology his people had hidden. More than a few of his men had to know of these things and the Matrons ... how had it all been hidden, wiped from so many of their memories? He and Devos should have known about this, remembered it and known where it all was.

What happened to his simple desert existence? He was a man of sands and dunes, some simple machinery, not wires and voices, technology, doing things for him that his council should have been doing.

Gods, he needed sleep, uninterrupted, dreamless sleep. He couldn't remember the last time he'd lain down to regenerate and succeeded.

"I think it's going to be a long night."

The glider responded, "M'lord, there's exactly two hours and forty-two minutes and ten-seconds left of darkness."

He groaned. Tian wasn't on his list of places to visit. Home. He'd left it long ago with a promise to return only when things had been set right again.

His schedule, and his promise, had been rearranged.

Phyxe stared up at the ceiling, unmoving for the moment, taking stock. The last remnants of poison had seeped out hours ago. Her body and mind wide were awake after the intense fire dream with her sexy desert warrior. It had somehow fueled her, accelerated her healing. She knew without a doubt, he'd stepped into her dreams. Based on his exit, he wasn't too happy about it either.

For the moment, she ignored the sleeping body beside her in the chair. The young one, called Firiea, wouldn't sense her until she was ready to let her know she was awake.

What were her Sister Goddesses doing? If she couldn't contact them, she was certain they had no idea where she'd been pulled. They'd be livid. Perhaps the void she created on the planet would be an indication? She couldn't tell with her powers dampened. She wasn't used to being on her own. As much of a loner as she considered herself, she was never without her sisters. At any given time since she'd been formed into creation, she'd been able to reach out to them. Even if she did want to ignore Zhanne on most occasions, her influence now wouldn't be unwelcome. She was part of the five, and together they balanced the universe. Apart, they could and would wreak havoc. The rules kept them in balance.

Krite.

She sighed to herself. Without Glacial's water or Wystin's air influences, her fiery nature could flame unchecked. Zhanne, as the Goddess of Pure Energy, was the one who could function unchecked, yet she preferred the relative safety of their inter-dimensional home. In fact, in the last 5,000 years, Zhanne ventured out only once, that Phyxe could remember, because Gaian had been trapped while saving her earth-worshipping people.

Damn the demon for pulling her here.

And for the hell of it, damn the warrior for turning her down. Her fist landed with a soft thud on the furs. He could have helped her take the edge off her nerves, dream or not. Hell, she could have relaxed him some, too. The man was wound up.

She stared up at the obsidian ceiling. No, she would do better than she had in the past. She could remain on her own for a while, even if it meant she had to be hyper vigilant about the flames. She would familiarize herself with this Haven as they called it. Unconnected from her very nature and her sisters, she couldn't call on her powers to help her research the planet's past. She couldn't see the path to the future. *Krite*, these bracers! Even in times of testing, when she'd forcibly limited herself, she still had her connection to her sisters, her knowledge.

She'd be damned if she were staying stuck underground, even if they were the closest things to fire caves she'd ever seen. Tomorrow. Sleep first, reconnaissance later. Tomorrow, she would take stock of the Haven and decide her best approach to the planet. She could do this without the full use of her abilities. She forced the muscles in her body to relax. She'd trained for this, subjected herself to harsh realities through her years.

The desert warrior needed help for something. His sentient planet slumbered for far too long, and the planetary sleep shifted the natural order of things on the surface. Hopefully, the changes wouldn't occur too rapidly for the inhabitants to adjust.

Sleep, Mistress. I will warn you of any impending danger.

Phyxe smiled, her eyes closed at the now familiar voice. Dreams were never just dreams. *You should be resting as well.*

I have rested long enough. It is time to see what my beings have been up to. The balance here needs to be restored. I'm honored you woke me and came to my aid.

It was not my doing, ancient one. If I had only known, I would have made it my goal.

There is no fault in not knowing, there is only fault in knowing and not doing.

You are wise, ancient one.

I am a Mother.

Phyxe gave a sleepy laugh. *Something I will never be, I am honored you allow me to share in your re-balance.*

Sleep, Goddess of Fire. I will wake you when you are recovered enough to deal with the information I gather.

Protect the warrior, Ancient One. He does not know you slept. He does not believe I have the power to help him.

He will learn. His family is a powerful one.

Good. I like him.

Sleep.

Phyxe drifted off as images of warming fires swept over her. The ancient essence of the planet wrapped around her, glowing, protecting as she re-gathered her strength.

The dark figure stayed as still as possible in the chair until she heard the lady's breathing even out. With quiet footsteps she darted around the room making sure everything rested in the proper place and was easy to reach in case the lady needed something in the night. Etheria warned her the lady who traveled with Lord Marius was unusual. The Matrons seemed to alternate between worrying the newcomer would bring him harm, or she was the harbinger for change.

Firiea knew the lady brought them salvation.

She'd read the ancient texts in the databanks. She knew the histories. She'd devoured them. She'd seen the inconsistencies, the name changes, and the incantations calling to a woman. For a long time, she'd believed their Fire God, Phyron, was not a God at all, but Goddess. The Lady was the Goddess incarnate. She knew it. The Lady glowed with it, and while she wanted to shout to the Matrons her studies proved her right, she'd made a promise to herself and to the only one who mattered now, the Fire Goddess, even if unheard of yet. The Matrons gave her shelter and love. The Goddess of Fire would give her purpose and life.

She would be the Fire Goddess' priestess, a warrior, like her for her planet. She would help them heal, hunt and fight. The other students laughed at her musings in their studies while the Matrons smiled. From the texts, she'd known the possibility existed. However, she hadn't been sure how it was going to become a reality.

Now, she knew. She'd vied for position of handmaiden to the newcomer, nervous, yet somehow unafraid. She'd been certain there was something different. Although the eldest among the uninitiated, she had not taken the vows the Matrons had, nor would she. She was determined to be both wife and mystic.

She retreated to her portion of the room and settled into her furry bed with her clothes on. If the Lady stirred, she would be right at her side for every step. She would watch and learn.

Beneath the Haven, lava stirred. Bubbles welled up and burst. Wave after wave of molten rock rippled along, cascaded along the planetary ley-lines. Energy surged, shifted, balanced, redistributed at the core, and the sentient nature within the shell pulled herself from her centuries of slumber.

Tendrils swept out, searched and sought answers. The planet Firon found her inhabitants, her children, in pockets around the world. Some resided in the cool desert of the night, traveling, living, laughing, loving. Others slumbered under the harsh light of day. Her planet pulsated with sand dunes. Centuries ago, she'd had oases, havens above ground offered respite. Waters, while infrequent above grounds, cleansed and purified below. Now, pockets remained. A shell encased her outer reach.

Firon struggled, pushed and prodded against the barrier and then growled in frustration when it refused to move. How dare it. Her reach extended beyond her own being. In the past, she'd been able to talk to the neighbor planets, shared in the activities within their realm. She had neighbors. She had friends. Someone and something blocked her.

No wonder her Lady Goddess landed here.

And, no wonder her irritation reached new levels. Together, they would find the remedy for the blockage. She needed to restore the balance. She sensed too little water topside. She'd either wandered off her gravitational path, or her axis titled in the wrong direction through the years she'd slept. Something was off.

And it needed to be repaired.

❧FIVE ❧

Rain lashed at her in torrent. The smell of wet fur assaulted her nose. If there was anything the Goddess of Earth hated more, it was the smell of wet cat, especially when she was said wet cat. It pissed her off. Almost as much as her unsuccessful search for her sister. She rolled her shoulders and bit back another growl. You'd think finding the Goddess of Fire would be an easy task. She sparked at every turn, like a gemstone.

But no. This grew more and more ridiculous with each planet. She'd landed in the middle of a heat-drenched jungle. Two minutes later, she was soaked to the bone, wet fur plastered to her head, and ready to take someone's head off. This was supposed to be a fire planet. Who had jungles on fire planets? Hell, who'd forgotten to update the planetary database?

"It's ok, kitten." A masculine voice drifted over her, warm and slow.

Her feline head lifted and tilted. Kitten? She was the largest, most gorgeous tiger she'd been known to create and someone dared call her kitten? She dropped a paw on the ground, hard. Water splashed up and around her ankle.

"The rains will stop soon. Then, father sun will come out and dry us both off." Deep, male, it washed over her, tantalizing and yet, soothing.

Gaian scanned the jungle floor, yet no one hovered near. Her gaze lifted to the trees. Vines draped from tree to tree forming random patterns. Thick foliage blocked the sky from view yet somehow showers of rain fell through to mark her fur-lined face.

Gods, this sucked.

There. Her vision narrowed. A dark figure huddled against the trunk of a tree halfway up the thick greenery.

"Ah, you found me." He sounded amused.

"You're a beautiful creature." Awe laced his tone

now.

She preened. Of course, she was. She was a Goddess after all. It was part of the job requirement. Who'd heard of an ugly goddess?

"Tigers are rare here. We had so many long ago."

His heartfelt sigh wrapped around her. She stepped closer, watched him, and tried to make out his features in the haze. Water pooled in her eyes, and she blinked and tried to clear her vision. Even her sense of smell refused to cooperate with the rains.

"I don't think I've ever heard of your coloring in our region though."

No. She was pretty sure he hadn't. Her coloring was rare on any planet, no matter how much she tried to match the local species. She always remained more golden and white than the rest. It was her mark. She was a Goddess after all, unique.

She wanted to leap up to his perch, but doing so would show off her abilities too much. No normal tiger could make such a leap. The man was too high up. But damn it, she wanted to see who spoke to her. The slow, sexy voice enthralled her. She hadn't been this entranced in centuries.

"Many will try to hunt you, if I tell them I saw you," he said.

She growled and shook her head. Let them try. She was on a mission, no matter how much she was entranced by the voice. She'd be damned if some planetary fascination with tigers would delay her from finding her sister.

"No worries, kitten. I will not tell. The balance here is off kilter. Too many focus on profit and less on their internal balance."

She cocked her head at him and listened.

"As their priest, I can do nothing but guide them if they come to me."

Priest? Ah, an explanation for the calm, hypnotic effect of his voice. And his seemingly total lack of fear from her form. She should leave. Phyxe was not here. An Earth-based worship, this was her planet, not Phyxe's. She was loath to leave the voice though. He sounded hurt, yet peaceful.

"You're not sure whether to stay or go, are you

42

kitten?" The weight of his stare immobilized her for a moment as he watched her, gauging.

Startled, she stared up at him. Her nose lifted as she tried to gather a scent from him. Nothing, but wet fur and rain. Damn the rains. She shook her head. Focus. Phyxe was not here. Duty called to her across the dimensions. She had to continue on.

"Our paths will cross again, kitten. Get yourself out of the rains. This has to be far more unpleasant for you than it is for me." His tone softened, knowing and sure.

She sat on her hunches, ignored the rain and looked up at him through the branches. She made the decision once she found Phyxe, she would return whether the people of this planet called her or not. She would return for the voice.

Gaian growled. It was the best she could do without revealing herself. She lifted a paw at him and then turned and disappeared into the rains beneath the foliage. When she was a safe enough distance away, she faded into nothing as she transported herself into the dimensional rifts again.

She made a mental note of the coordinates. She would return.

And she would find the owner of that voice.

Phyxe groaned in her sleep, thrashed among the furs covering her. Hazy tendrils of memories reached out and captured her in its web.

The whip raised high in the air and strained to break free from its wielders grasp. Her hands tied, outstretched along the bar in front and above her. Her feet strapped to the floorboards. Her muscles screamed in denial, the position they'd kept for hours pulled her in uncomfortable directions. Knives prodded her open flesh as the thick leather tore at her back, skin melted apart at the whip wielders' will.

Millions of eyes turned towards her. She stood on the slaver's block high above the crowd. Her body wanted to quiver under the heat of their stares, but she would not. She would not show them the fear they were all so hungry to see. In fact, she wasn't afraid. In truth, the real fear she bit back involved lashing out in anger and frustration and hurting the unsuspecting souls who'd done nothing more than turn out with curious stares. To them, this was their culture.

Nine? Ten? She lost count on the number of times the whip slithered across the raw flesh of her back. Flesh, gone after the first two strikes. In this form, she would have none for a long time to come. Scars would be her constant reminder.

The crowd hushed as she refused to wilt under the beating. She imagined a steel column up the center of her back. She refused to sink to the hardwood floors beneath her bare feet.

Blood trickled down the back of her leg and stained the wood. Numbness swept over her. She didn't care. The demon of a man could go on forever, with the sea of watching eyes; she wouldn't show any weakness. As the Goddess of Fire, she'd be damned if she showed the minions before her weakness. Bring the fires close enough to her to grasp. She needed her hands free, then, let these men learn the word 'fear'.

"Jarden, let us take her back to the holding pens." The young, masculine voice halted the whip as it began to snake her way. "She won't bring in any money this way. People will be too afraid to buy her."

She refused to blink. The whelp thought she would be civil now. Furious, she memorized the details of the men who'd brought her to this place. They would pay for every drop of her life-blood as it seeped from the various wounds they inflicted. The idea of revenge kept her from swaying as the pain arched through her body. She would roast them over an open flame, in full view of the same eyes watching her now.

They would pay.

Phyxe woke with a start. Her hands clenched in the furs beneath her. Her legs twisted in the covers as if she'd thrashed about for several hours.

It never failed. The old memories returned to haunt her whenever her guard was down. Memories, never dreams. She groaned and stared up at the dark ceiling, seeing the minute details in the stone. Energies abounded, why now?

She'd been trapped before. That time, she'd gone through an evolution cycle in her powers. Each of the goddesses had one. She'd been dumb enough to be on a planet rather than in their inter-dimensional home when her cycle hit. PMS was a bitch whether human or Goddess. She was thankful hers were every few thousand years, and predictable.

She gave up staring at the ceiling and pulled herself upright in the bed. Blankets pooled around her waist. Her internal clock told her she hadn't slept long. The fires of the earlier dream renewed her. She survived for years without sleep, so long as she had fire. She didn't want to test the longevity with the bracers wrapped around her wrists.

"M'lady?" A sleepy voice whispered through the doorway.

"Go back to sleep, young one." Phyxe eyed the clothes the Matrons left at the foot of the bed for her.

She got up and let her hands run over the materials, softer than they looked, serviceable. So many layers. Apparently, the good women of Firon did wear pants, under their skirts. Phyxe grinned. She'd make do. She left the skirts in a pile on the bed, instead, pulling on the under layers, the pants and the shirt. The cloak she left as well. Thankfully, her boots still rested at the foot of the bed. She'd go barefoot before wearing in new footwear on this planet. She'd made the boots to withstand the heaviest of fires. She glanced around. No weapons. She hadn't been dreaming when they'd taken those away. She would make do and find some along the way. They couldn't all be under lock and key.

"You're not."

Phyxe smiled.

"No, I am done. You, however, need more sleep than I do." She let her voice drop low and hypnotic to urge the girl back to bed. She would have to work more with her other skills rather than using pure fire.

The sleepy girl would slow her down in her curiosity. She wanted to investigate, which meant not being seen until she was ready for it. Every surprise, every potential terror needed to be found. She needed to know why the demon pulled her here and where the hell here was.

She sniffed and tilted her head. Smoke? The young one hadn't built her a fire, there shouldn't be smoke with this heavy of a scent crossing her path unless there was a blaze of infernal levels somewhere nearby.

Her entire body lit. She leaned over and shook the young one awake.

The girl blinked up at her and then bolted upright, "M'lady?"

"There's a fire blazing. How many are here and below us?" She asked, quickly throwing the room apart searching for her weapons.

"There are 42 total in the Haven, mistress. And the nursery."

Phyxe stilled and only her head turned. "Nursery?"

"Yes, m'lady. The nursery is below us, in the most protected space. We have only two there at the moment ... what is that?" The girl's eyes widened as the smoke intensified. "M'lady!"

"I know. Get the warning out and get the Matrons moving outside but into the shadows. This could be a trick. Use alternate routes out of the caverns. Are there any?" she asked. Damn it, where the hell where her weapons? Every fiber of her being knew this was a ruse, but now that she was planet-side she couldn't leave two innocent souls to the flames. She may not recognize each soul across the galaxy, but once she was in their realm, she took each on as her responsibility.

"Yes m'lady. We know the drills, but I must get the young ones," she said.

Phyxe lifted a brow. "If I'm correct, and I usually am, we'll need to travel through the fire to get them. Can you walk through fire?"

The girl didn't flinch at her this question, but bowed her head. "No, Mistress."

"Then get moving on what you can do. I will go after the children. Only two, yes?"

"Yes."

Two she could save, limited powers or not. Phyxe turned and strode out of the room. She took a moment to get her bearings, which way was up, which way went down, further into the earth.

"Mistress, I sense distress?" The planet flared to life

46

in her mind.

"Yes. There's a fire in the Haven, children below it," she answered.

She sensed Firiea bolt out the door behind her, heading to more level ground as she'd asked the girl to do. The planet shifted and rolled beneath her feet. *"I cannot get to them, Mistress. Something is blocking me."*

"That's fine. It can't block me. I will rescue the children. Keep the Matrons as safe as you can. I know you're bound." Her gaze narrowed through the haze of smoke.

Phyxe let the planet and her senses guide her. She tuned out the cries of the Matrons as they darted here and there above her in the cavern. Instead, she focused completely on the two heartbeats she could sense, faintly from the caverns below. The heat threatened to overwhelm her, and she half smiled. Bring it. Fire she could handle, bound or not. Her body, mind and spirit were built for it. Other had tired to bring her down in flames and suffered the consequences.

Fire could not harm her.

She wound down the pathway, the heat intensifying. Energy rippled across her skin. She smiled. Well, hello, flame. Smoke filled the hallway, she strode forward, unconcerned. She heard the cries of small ones echoing against the walls. Her stride lengthened. She may be able to handle the smoke and flames, but she'd neglected to ask Firiea how old the children were. Their body size would gauge how long they could last in the flames. Her teeth clenched. Damn the ones causing upheaval on this world. Had she been in full power, she'd have teleported to the children, laid low the fire and hunted the one who'd started it. She was certain that this was not a natural flame. Someone had flared it on purpose and for harming the small ones, the innocent, she would make certain they paid.

"Two meters to your left, Mistress."

"Thank you." Phyxe took the measured steps and halted, the children's cries directly near her. She bent down, under the haze of smoke.

"Little ones, you need to get as close to the floor as you can, if you can hear and understand me," she whispered. She sensed two bodies lowering to the floor.

"Stay there, let me absorb what I can."

She slowly began to focus and draw what smoke and flames she could into her body, hoping against hope that her powers cooperated. She knew she couldn't push her powers, but so far, she'd been just fine pulling them. She closed her eyes and centered herself, tuning out the soft mewing of the children. She needed to focus.

Her skin tingled. The smoke flowed over her body, teasing, taunting, and dancing around her before pulling into her. The room around her cleared. The children's cries dimmed. Her lungs filled. She took a deeper breath. She refused to allow the children to die.

The room cleared some.

"Mistress, the fire is in the back of the nursery. Several others are on each level of the Haven."

"Deliberately set then," Phyxe commented. *"He has a traitor in his midst."*

Phyxe crossed the room as the smoke cleared more, rolling into her rather than spreading through the air in the room. In a matter of seconds, she had the blaze contained, letting the flames lick her skin for a few moments before she extinguished them in their entirety. She stumbled as two small bodies crashed into her, latching their strong little arms around her legs.

"You have magic. We knew someone would come to save us." The little girl was about five years old. Her big blue eyes sparkled up at Phyxe.

A matching set of blue eyes looked up at her from her other leg in a slightly older identical face but with the features of a boy. "I was dreaming that the shadows came alive and then it got really, really hot."

Phyxe let her hands rest lightly on each child's head. "I am very glad you both woke up and had enough sense to drop to the floor when I asked. How about we see about getting out of here? There seem to be a few more fires to put out before we can find the Matrons. Can you walk with me?"

Two heads nodded in sync.

"Wait a minute!" The girl darted away from her before Phyxe could stop her. In a flash she returned with an arm wrapped tightly around a small stuffed horse. "Now there's no fire, I don't have to leave Beauty behind."

Phyxe smiled. "No little one, you don't. What's your

name?"

"Narissa. This is my brother Sethen."

"Good to meet you. I'm Phyxe."

"Are you an angel?" This from Sethen.

She laughed. "No Seth, I'm no angel. I am something more. But right now, we need to get you out of here and make sure the others are safe, too. You both can help me do that, right?"

They nodded again.

"Right, let's go then. We've got people to take care of." She took each small hand in one of her own and began to retrace her steps. Someone would be roasting in an eternal flame of hell when she figured out who'd put them all in danger.

Phyxe stepped out in to the cool night air of the desert with a sound asleep Narissa in her arms and Sethen staggering to stay on his feet at her side. Her eyes adjusted to the dark night.

"Mistress, you were able to rescue them!" Firiea darted to her side, her arms sweeping out to catch Sethen as he tumbled forward.

Another dark form stepped from the shadows, reaching for the burden in her arms. She tightened her hold a minute before releasing Narissa to the other woman. They'd been so very brave for her, staying close behind as she'd methodically put out the flames. Seven mini-fires in all set to do nothing more than smoke them out.

"Is everyone accounted for?" She attempted to count the shadows in the dark.

"Yes, Lady. All accounted for now that you've brought us the children." Etheria stepped from the shadows. "How did you brave the flames?"

Phyxe opened her mouth to answer the elder and then stilled. Her ears strained to make out the sound. She turned on a foot, searching the darkness.

"Take cover. Hide!" she cried out.

A shadowy form ripped through the darkness, tumbling her to the ground. She sunk her nails into hardened skin and raked as she flipped over and finally away from him.

"Demon boy," she growled.

"Goddess bitch." He grinned back at her. "I see my poison didn't work."

Shadows began to dance around him. Dark figures crawled out of the darkness towards them. Stars, no weapons, no flame. She started tracking the shapes, using all her senses. These creatures the demon had with him were humanoid, not otherworldly.

"It's going to take more than a demon pup to bring me down." She whirled as a dark figure darted out at her, sword slicing down. She lashed out a foot and smiled when she heard the pop that was his knee. The man howled in pain and dropped to the sands.

"Nicely done." If the demon's smile could have gotten any wider, it did.

A scream echoed out through the sands.

Her teeth clenched. Out numbered and without her weapons or her powers, sneaky bastard.

"I see my men are finding what they were looking for." He bowed. "I'll leave you to see if you can save any of them."

He launched himself vertical and with one giant flap of the dark leathery wings on his back, disappeared into the night sky. Phyxe growled in the darkness, another scream forced her into action. She stole through the night making quick work of the men as she could. A neck snapped beneath her bare hands for the one trying to make off with Firiea. A rib cage shattered for the one dragging Etheria.

"M'lady, they're gone," a voice whispered out across the darkness.

Phyxe halted. "Are all accounted for?"

Firiea's wail of grief pierced the night. "No, No, No."

She raced across the sands back to the young woman. "Firiea?"

"They're gone," the girl wailed. Her dark hair fell over her face in dishevelment. "They're gone. Those evil creatures took them."

Phyxe froze. "Are you telling me they took the children?"

"Yes." The girl's cries began to subside. "I hid them as fast and best I could. They're desert born. They know

50

not to cry out during battle. They know how to hide."

Fire flared to unstable height within Phyxe. It boiled with nowhere to go. "This was no accident. Those fires were set to flush you out. To flush the children out. And I, oh, *Krite*, I let everyone walk into it." An uncomfortable feeling welled up inside of her.

"Mistress?" Firiea looked up at her, eyes wide. "Your eyes. "

Phyxe glanced around as the women began to appear around her. "What about them?"

"They're on fire."

"Not surprising. As ticked off as I am, all of me should be on fire ... a fire so high and bright that it would blind the planet." She closed her eyes and took a few deep breaths, pushing the uncomfortable feeling aside. "Get yourselves back into the Haven. I'm going to track those men. The fires are out. You're obviously safer underground than out."

Maybe, she thought. Were they safe? Someone had obviously set the fires from within. She lifted her head and took another deep breath in. A faint hint of embers reached her. She had to believe they'd be safer in the Haven than out of it.

"Lady?"

Phyxe turned ready to growl at the Matron who stopped her. She needed time to think, to plan. With her powers bound she was operating at a loss. Outstretch arms holding a bundle of tightly wrapped leather stopped her.

"We had no right to take these away." Etheria set the bundle on the ground before her and stepped back.

Phyxe leaned forward, making quick work of the ties that bound the bundle together. Could it be? Yes. Fire lit through her body. Her weapons, holsters and sheaths.

"No worries, Matron. I understand completely. But I thank you even more for their return." She could hunt without them, but meting out justice with them, would be so much the sweeter.

She didn't even take note when the Matron melted back into the darkness as enthralled as she was with having fire-forged steel in her hands again. Demon boy was about to learn his lesson. She would get those children back and find out who'd put the Matrons in danger if it was the last thing she did in this incarnation.

The children.

Phyxe settled the scabbard across her body. The sword fell into place. Her belt she strapped around her hips. The lasers fitted into their rightful slots. The daggers dropped into their homes in her boots. A smile started deep within her body. Weapons were a good start. Her powers back would be better. But she'd take what she could get for now.

"Lady?" The whisper came from behind her, the entryway to the Haven.

She turned her head ever so slightly, an eyebrow lifted.

Firiea stepped forward, a bundle in her arms. "I brought you provisions. I gathered them as quickly as I could."

The girl flipped open the bundle. "A cloak to keep you covered from sands and heat. Food rations, a map. The cloak has hidden pockets, water pockets. The map marks where to find the water caches."

Phyxe stared down at the supplies laid out before her. "You were very thorough."

"You don't survive our planet by being unprepared. There is enough to last you till you get to the next cache. Supplies will be laid out there as well."

She would have walked the desert without a thought to prepare. She was used to relying on her powers, her abilities. She'd been focused on only one thing, retrieving the children. Not that the desert or lack of water would kill her, it would slow her down.

Mistress?

Yes, Ancient.

I can aid you in your search.

Phyxe looked up at Firiea. "I am in awe of your speed of thought and actions."

Mistress, you need to go. Now.

Phyxe moved lightning fast, whirling the cloak on her body, with the rations placed and hidden.

Lead me where you need me to be.

You can walk among the fires. It will be faster and safer.

"Thank you for the supplies." Phyxe looked over at

Firiea. "But I fear I need even more from you. I'm going to change the game, the tactics. You're going to have to keep some secrets."

"M'lady, I am yours. You have more than proven yourself. You saved the children from the fires," she replied.

Phyxe nodded and walked back into the Haven, pulled towards her rooms. She strode in, sure of herself. Firiea to trailed behind.

A crevice opened in the wall to the far right of her room. The whisper of a crack expanded wide enough for her to step through the layer of protective obsidian, which sealed the caverns from the volcanic activities deep below. Lava cascaded through the open portal, a blinding orange and yellow waterfall of liquid fire. The heat seared Phyxe's skin, and she relished the burn. Familiar. Intoxicating. Powerful.

Phyxe laid a hand on the black glass of the wall, tilted her head and cast a glance over her shoulder to make sure Firiea understood she was not to follow. She smiled when the girl nodded at her and stepped back outside her room.

Close this behind me. I do not want the young one stumbling through. She can't protect herself from your heat, yet.

Yes, Mistress.

Phyxe stepped between the walls, and the fissure sealed behind her. With steps surefooted and fleet, she followed the path the planet opened for her. Heat pounded over her, coming from everywhere, and nowhere at once. It fueled her, even though the internal flames of the planet lived several leagues below where she strode. She wanted to stop and take in the beauty behind the black walls and floor. Slick and clean, the lava danced in rivers below her feet and called out to her. Black on black shadows flickered behind the walls and sparks flared up, shot up and streaked behind them. She had her own private fireworks display in red, orange and gold.

There is an issue with my balance, Mistress.

What do you mean? Phyxe withdrew her gaze from the fiery show taking place behind the walls and floors and focused on the path as it opened before her. Cracking and creaking threatened to shatter her eardrums as the earth ripped open before her, quickly filling in the with the obsidian layer. Heat washed over her in waves—hot, heavy, and pulsating. A new corridor formed and the intense heat lessened then surged forth again as the process repeated. A lesser being would have died with the first wave of heat. Phyxe let it roll over her, feed her. She absorbed each hit of heat and stored it deep inside.

There is a shield around me, preventing me from following my natural, variable path. Instead, it steers me on a fixed course through my days.

A shield? The shield bound her to this place as well perhaps ... she glanced down at the bracers on her arms.

Yes, Mistress. I found it earlier when I checked the balance of nature on my surface and realized the levels of desert and water are out of sync. Above has always been more sand than anything else, but I did have mini pockets to which my people could retreat. Now, these oases are more rare to find and disappearing rapidly.

They're dying. Pain sliced through her stomach at this revelation. Phyxe frowned. She couldn't let Tru and his people die.

Yes, and I don't think they know it.

Another knife-like pain, this time, close to her heart. What connected her to this place and these people? Sure it was one of her fire planets, but it seemed deeper than that.

She sighed. *Can we fix it?*

Yes, if we can dissolve the shield and restore my path.

We will do it.

She would set it all to rights, then figure out the why of it. As much as she wanted to roast the demon over an open spit, she'd wait, like the dormant volcano, then spread destruction if she needed to rebuild everything— while keeping the people safe. They were innocents. They didn't deserve to die. The demon and his invaders would suffer her wrath instead.

Yes, Mistress. I have not figured out how or from where the shielding stems.

Phyxe nodded to herself. Figure out shielding, check. Find the children and return them to the Haven, check. Figure out how to kill the demon and why his minions were stealing women and children, check. Get bracers off her body, check. Her 'to do' list kept growing, and she hadn't even been on this planet for a full cycle, yet.

What else did you want to show me? She asked.

The ground below her feet rumbled. She took a few quick steps to steady herself and threw a hand against the nearest wall. The walls rippled underneath her palm. The lava swelled higher beneath her feet.

Ancient? How imbalanced are things here?

Run, Mistress, run. I am trying to contain it, but my energy is low.

Phyxe darted forward then slowed her steps and waited for a new tunnel to open up and form another path. She lifted her arm to protect her head from falling rock. A large piece of obsidian sliced through her forearm. She started at the sharp tingling. Mental note, no running underground on an unstable planet without her normal body armor.

I'm sorry, Mistress!

Forget it. Focus. A few cuts and bruises aren't going to stop me. Keep that tunnel open. She forcibly ignored the stinging in her arm and the blood dripping down her skin.

The tunnel formed a longer passageway, and she maintained a steady sprint. She coughed when she inhaled a rather powerful cloud of black ash. Next time, she'd stick to the sands.

Mother of—. A large rock glanced off her head. She staggered. *Krite!*

She could do this. She and Gaian played this way, testing each other numerous times. This should be no different. Her ability to shield herself wouldn't be too much to ask, would it? She lifted her fingers to her head and took a deep breath when her hand came away coated in blood. At this rate, the planet would kill her on accident before the demon ever could.

Less than half a mile, Mistress. It's now all aftershocks. I contained the deepest break. I'm not sure how much longer I can hold it. You need to put me back on course before this becomes commonplace.

Working on it. A large section of the tunnel's ceiling tumbled down around her. Phyxe danced aside. Heat surged forth as the lava crested closer. Her skin burned. The tips of her hair crackled. Sparks flew.

Another crevice ripped open before her. Phyxe dove

through to cooler, more regulated air. The wall shattered beside her. The lava rolled forth and slammed into the black glass serving to funnel it back into place. She collided with the wall on the other side of the hallway, her hand holding her ribs. She lay there for a moment and took stock. The crevice sealed behind her. Lights flipped on overhead.

Krite. Her ribs hurt. Her head hurt. She glanced down at her arm. Blood crusted sealing the wound. Okay, so thank the fires that tried to kill her for also starting her healing process. She probed the injury on her head. The blood stopped there. At this rate, she was going to need a bath in water rather than fire. She shuddered. No, thank you.

Are you okay, Mistress?

I've been worse.

She took a deep breath and pushed herself up the wall to her feet. The hallway lay in ruins around her. Paintings shredded or unhinged, lights askew from their fixtures, and rugs covered in debris and dust. Well, even that could have been worse.

Welcome to Tian. This was once the capital of the planet. Visitors came from across the galaxies to rest and play among my sands. It has been deserted for centuries.

Phyxe forced the pain to retreat and dropped her hand from her side. She'd find something to wrap her ribs later and somewhere to rid her hair of the blood.

Pristine white walls arched high. Lines of flowing architecture greeted her everywhere she looked. Half moon arches graced the doorways flowing into smooth stonewalls. The floor sparkled with multi-hued blue and green glass tiles adding even more light wherever sunshine spilled in. Crystal pedestals topped with dark wood marked the railings of the main staircase. A carpet of the deepest blue, plush and thick, lined the stairs. Someone loved blending the masculine and feminine into a perfect balance. Phyxe trailed her hand up the wooden banister as she set her feet softly in the carpet.

Up and to your right, Mistress. Down the hall, beyond the largest painting.

Phyxe bit back a curse as her body protested the simple act of walking up the stairs. On the planet less than a cycle and already it was planet one, goddess zero. She wandered down the tiled floor. This had once been the home of royalty, a long time deserted. A fine layer of sand dust lay over everything. If the place were hers, she might never leave it. Luxury, elegance. Through the large crystal cut windows layered heavily with lush curtains, she could see the hint of sun as it started to peek across the horizon. Full daylight would be upon her soon.

This painting? Phyxe stood transfixed for a moment swearing that a slightly younger version of Marius stared back at her in full royal regalia. His jet black eyes glittered. His hair still dark and slightly shaggy, hinted at a mischievous nature, even though the royal uniform informed of his professional and family status. A half smile crossed his face.

Yes, Mistress.

She shook herself and ran her hands over the stonewall under the edges of the painting. Her fingers settled into a natural crevice and pulled. The door slid back with a groan. Again, lights flickered to life as she stepped over the threshold. Computer consoles lined every aspect of the room. Large screens dovetailed on the walls. Electronic images housed in each one, different, yet all showing the various sands of the planet around her.

"Well, I'll be damned," she whispered. Technology, finally, something she could use.

"State your clearance, intruder." An angry feminine voice lashed out as the databanks lit up and came alive.

A smile crossed her face. Oh, a system with an attitude. She laughed then winced. Pain ran across her fractured ribs, yet pure delight raced through her body.

"Phyxe, Goddess of Fire." She strode across the room to a keyboard console and looked down at the lit screen. Clearance? She was clearance.

"Step away from my system or prepare for the consequences."

Phyxe hiked an eyebrow, but couldn't get the grin off her face. Bitchy. Bitchy. "I think you'd be happy someone woke you up."

"You are not House Marius." The system countered the commands Phyxe entered on the keyboard. Her fingers deftly flew through all the known codes in the universe to break into the operating system. Hell, she may be away from Sanctuary, but she could hack computer systems in her sleep. She wasn't a warrior for nothing—on the battlefield or in the cyber realm. Wystin would have berated her for her slowness. Zhanne would have zapped the stubborn AI.

"I definitely am not of House Marius," Phyxe replied. "And Lord Marius is not here. I am. You and I are going to have a talk about what's been happening on your planet, so I can fix it."

"You are not House Marius. You do not have access."

"Yeah, yeah, he keeps telling me what I can't do, too. Shows what you both know." In triumph, she countered the last of the tricks the AI tried to throw at her and hacked through the fail-safes. She set herself up as a superuser for the system.

Take that, ornery computer.

"How did you?" If computers could sputter in shock, this one did.

"As I said, I'm not House Marius. I'm better. Name?" Phyxe asked.

"I am Zen."

"Hello, Zen. I'm Phyxe. We're going to work together now, aren't we?"

"Yes, Lady Phyxe." Was that sarcasm? From a computer system?

"Good."

Demon, off track planet, and now one computer system who'd be wracking her data banks on how to eject her from control of the system. She'd hacked AIs long before Zhanne had taught them Computer Tricks 101. Zen would have to deal.

"Let's see what the last few centuries wrought on your surface. Show me the histories, Zen."

A brief pause, as if Zen thought about it, then images flickered to life on the largest screen in the room. The others dimmed. Phyxe settled into a large over-stuffed chair.

His seat. It had to be, too large to seat anyone else.

A little flare of vindictive pleasure stole over her as she settled in the masculine chair. It served him right. He wouldn't allow her to claim him in the dream, so she'd claim that which belonged to him.

She fell into her task and absorbed the information as

fast as the AI could feed it to her. At the edge of her subconscious, she felt a little tug. Like Phyxe, Firon was also trying to glean from the AI what had happened to cause this imbalance.

At one point, ages ago, the Firon held the status of an interstellar retreat, a playground for travelers, and offered entertainment of various sorts. Phyxe watched the arts and dances fly past on the screen. Desert dances enthralled thousands with shows of whirling silks. Their women knew their arts, their bodies honed to perfection from dance. Their hands perfecting the art of pottery, glass making, jewelry making, anything they could get their hands on ... ended up as a beautiful piece of clothing, jewelry, household item or healing tool.

Firon, the Ancient one, sat in the midst of various interstellar travel paths. It was a well-suited rest point for weary space travelers. Phyxe took note of how the warriors had traveled off planet often. They had been hired for battles due to their sheer size and natural ability to fight and paid well for their skills. Many outsiders came to study at the War College in Fintar. She noticed the Research Labs in Sianan as well. Firon's people were strong, fit, healthy, and intelligent. No wonder visitors flocked here.

Then, a shift, the planet closed down. No reason mentioned, but she caught sight of the passing of Lady Gisele, Tru's mother. Warriors recalled to their homes; travel stations set on standby.

Phyxe frowned. "Zen, what caused the retreat?"

"The information you requested is not in my data banks."

"Run a speculation," she ordered the AI.

"No." A masculine voice ripped across the room.

Phyxe's breath caught and her heartbeat went into overdrive. She swiveled the chair around with one foot; the other one curled up under her. She hadn't been paying attention to anything other than the computer and its scenarios. Where the hell were her protective instincts? This mere human male so effortlessly bypass her self-preservation and snuck up on her ... goddesses, this would not do.

She reminded herself to breathe again. Her warrior stood at the edge of the room. Anger and shock radiated across the hard planes of his face. His entire body tensed as if he wanted to draw his sword and leap across the room at the screen.

"What in the sacred fires do you think you're doing?"

She tapped her fingers in rhythm against the arm of the chair. "Researching. Learning. Finding out what happened, so I can help you."

"You're NOT helping me." He strode into the room. His eyes darted everywhere in quick assessment.

He'd never seen the room. She'd bet an amber fire gem on it.

"It's a computer system. She is an artificial intelligence made to sound and act human while maintaining a more mathematical approach to logic."

"I know what it is. I haven't seen it in a long time," he snapped. A frown formed, his eyes taking it all in.

"Lord Marius. My name is Zen, welcome to Command Central. I wondered when the House of Marius would return."

He looked up, searching for the voice. Anger radiated from every muscle twitch.

"Hello, Zen," he said.

Phyxe kicked herself back around in the chair. "Zen, return to speculation."

"No," he commanded again.

The images on screen paused.

"No?" Phyxe glanced at him, eyebrows uplifted. "Then you know why the planet was shut down."

He nodded. "I do. She doesn't need to speculate."

"Explain then."

He glared at her. "You know, you demand rather than ask."

"So do you, your point?"

"I rule here."

"As do I. Eons before you were born."

"Impossible. You are younger than I."

Phyxe rolled her eyes even though inwardly she preened at the thought she was younger than he. What woman didn't want to appear younger than she was? Yet, why is it people never understood she didn't function on the same timelines as the rest of the known universe?

"I don't think you want to know how old I am, warrior. Besides, I still want an explanation. I can't help you without all the details," she said.

"You're not helping me," he muttered as he ran his hand over his face.

"Yes, actually, I am. You may not want me helping you, being a woman and all." She tried to keep the sneer from her voice. His was not the first planet where women weren't considered worthy of being warriors. "But I'm stuck on your planet because of your demon problem. Therefore, you are going to deal with me doing my job, as you are doing your job. And, by the way, doing my job in a way I don't normally do it."

"You are going to cause more hurt than help," he said.

Phyxe rotated her neck, letting the bones shift and crack, a sure sign of removing her stress. "The women here, if they're happy in their role, won't care that I'm a fighter. If your histories are correct, they know there are other ways of living out there."

She didn't bother to point out just how much they knew about her fighting skills or that she was going to start tracking the children as soon as she understood more about the planet and what had happened. She didn't need to add another worry to his already over taxed body and mind. She'd rather he focus on over taxing her. She would take care of the children, well, hell, she'd take care of the Matrons too.

"Not the point," he said.

"Then explain it. And then, tell me why the hell you closed down the planet to interstellar travel." She turned the chair with her foot to watch him.

"The men here are trained fighters. We are taught from the age of three how to fight, how to lead. Even our scientists studied the art of war, how to make our bodies better, stronger, faster. If I allow you to take such a role here, what is left for our men? The women nurture, they heal, they craft. They create beauty and art." He paced around the room.

"We," his chest expanded as he took a deep breath, "know nothing except battle. It has been bred into us. Strategy, logic, weapons, fighting."

She sighed. "You're warriors. So, what? There is always room for a balance. Women can heal and fight. So can your men." She flipped a hand around as Zen's lights flickered about the room. "There is never only one path."

"You are determined to cause havoc." He cut a glance at her.

She shook her head. No, she was pretty sure havoc found her on most occasions. "I may be Fire. I may be a fighter. But, I am not stupid. I am determined to bring the balance back to your planet. Tell me why you closed the planet off."

"I didn't do it," he said.

She refrained from rolling her eyes at him. "Fine, then tell me why your predecessors did it."

"We didn't agree with the politics leading the galaxy."

And very few people ever agreed with the current politics, so? She lifted an eyebrow and waited. There was more to it ... there had to be.

"Our men were not bred to rape and pillage and take women and children into slavery. We are born to fight and to protect. We hear both sides, we select the side which resonates true. We fight. That is IT. End of story."

"What?" She tensed in her chair. Her hands locked down on the sides of the chair.

Had she not been paying attention in the last hundred years or so? Who the hell had come into power and allowed such atrocities to reign in the galaxy? Slavery? Rape? She and her sisters had dealt with those issues eons ago. The known planets were not supposed to be in that kind of evolutionary cycle. Someone's head was going to roll, and she'd better beat Gaian to the punch.

"If you're a Goddess, you should know this." He said throwing her words back at her.

She snarled and came up out of the chair. "I am a Goddess, but that doesn't make me infallible, warrior. You have one world to look after. I have, or had, several hundred more. Try to keep track and manage hundreds to your one. And, oh yeah, add in the fact when I am called, I have to choose where and when to answer a request."

Ok, she hadn't had any to answer in the last eon. No one had called. Hell, how could things have gotten so out of balance?

"Slavery." She took a deep breath and pulled her anger back into herself, away from him, away from potentially doing damage where it would be least served. It wasn't as if she could fly off the handle and target the nearest head of the galactic council to roast. She was stuck for the moment. She added it to her to do list. As well as visiting her planets regardless of whether they called her or not.

Right after she roasted that damn demon.

"It's not ok ... slavery," he uttered.

She shot him a look. His voice quivered.

"They took my mother."

Well, ... damn. What was left of the fury rushed out of her body in a single breath. "She is alive?"

"I don't know." His body sagged against the nearest table. "My father assumed the worst when he couldn't find her. He shut us down. He lasted several years before walking into the desert to die. Apparently, he'd been working on all this before he did it, too."

One more item added to her list.

"We need to deactivate his shield." She directed her comment to both him and the AI.

"I can't," both man and machine chimed in together.

She rose to her feet. "What do you mean you can't? And yes, either one of you can answer."

Tru answered first, "He didn't tell me his codes, his keys or even where he hid all our technology. Until a few hours ago, I couldn't find the technology. He thought the fewer who knew, the better. My father had the uncanny ability to make people forget things he didn't want them remembering."

Phyxe nodded. For a moment, her heart beat harder as his loss wrapped around her. But she set these sympathetic feelings aside. Energy never died. It only changed form.

She turned back to the console. "We're going to have to find it all. The planet can't stay cloaked."

"Why not?"

"Because his shielding set her on an unnatural path."

He scowled. "What do you mean, unnatural path?"

"She means at our current course, our water supplies will dry up within the next five years," Zen explained for her.

Thank you, Ms. Artificial Intelligence. She shot a scowl at the computer bank and reminded herself to have Wystin program some compassion into the AI before she left the planet.

"You mean, my people are dying?" Shock spread across his features. He turned towards the console nearest to Phyxe.

"Breathe, warrior." Phyxe reached out a hand. "She's projecting, theorizing. We'll find the shield and disable it. I can help the planet resume her natural course. I'll make sure the waters return if I have to drag Glacial kicking and screaming to the planet surface."

Actually, she'd take great delight in dragging her water sister to the fire planet. Harassing any one of her sister Goddesses would be a fun bonus.

She saw the confusion cross his face. She'd thrown too much at an already tired, over worked man.

"You need to rest, warrior."

"I can't. I have too many things to fix."

"You can't fix them if you're dead."

"I'm not dying."

"Not yet, but you do need to rest."

He snorted and stood to his full height. She actually had to look up at him. Damn, the man was tall.

"I need to get information to my lieutenants. I need to find this shielding device you're worried about. And I need to get my teams ready for battle."

"Battle?" She perked up. A battle, something to take the edge off? Not that she didn't have enough to do already.

❧ SIX ❧

"You're not invited."

Phyxe stuck her tongue out at him. She couldn't resist. Something about his irksome denial of her abilities made her want her to behave like the child she'd never been. It invigorated her. "You still need to rest."

"Sleeping quarters are upstairs to the right. Shall I prepare rooms?" Zen's efficiency made her smile as his frown deepened.

"Yes, Zen," Phyxe said.

"No," Tru swayed on his feet.

There was that word again. It seemed to be the one he favored. "Keep scowling, it's going to be permanently etched there. Come, show me where I can sleep. Then, you can come back here and plot with your AI."

He stood to his full height, confusion laced with fatigue in his gaze. She knew he was a little off put by her sudden shift in tactics, but he was also too tired to keep up. He needed rest. One way or another he was going to get it.

"You were asleep before I left the Haven. Yet, you're here."

She nodded and reached out to loop her arm through his. She bit back a wince as her ribs reminded her of how she'd gotten there. He walked with her through the brass doors. "Yes. It happens."

"It took me hours to get here."

"I have friends."

"You are Other."

"Yes." She couldn't argue his point. To his people, hell to the majority of the galaxy, she was Other. She was always going to be Other, except among her sisters. A slight pang ripped through her before she stepped on it. She would find no equal in a male.

She'd been made, not born. Her destiny etched out to

protect and guide. To find someone to care for her, she would have to give up her position and return to a planet human, without the ability to help. A finite lifespan, the idea repulsed her.

"That hurt you." His fingers stroked her skin where her hand came in contact with his arm.

"No. It is a fact of my life, warrior."

He trailed a finger down to her hand. "Your long life."

"Yes."

"How long have you been alive?"

She cut him a glance, matching him step for step up the wide, curved staircase. "You're sure you want to know?"

"Yes."

"I stopped counting around 5,000." In truth, she'd stopped counting long before. It grew tedious. Every so often, Wystin reminded them all of their MadeDay. She took great delight in celebrating when Phyxe and Gaian would rather forget the passing annuls.

"You stopped counting?"

"Wouldn't you?" she asked.

He grunted. "I stopped at two hundred."

She laughed. She couldn't help it. Her smile infectious as she glanced at him and saw a half smile start on the edges of his mouth.

"In all honestly, I did as well, but I have a few sisters who take great delight in celebrating."

"Sisters?" he asked.

She tugged him along the hallway as she caught sight of the series of doors leading off the large, opaque hallway. "Yes, I have four: Gaian, Glacial, Wystin, and Zhanne. We live ... between the worlds."

He shook his head at her and followed along as she peeked in doors here and there. She sought something in particular and hadn't quite found it, yet.

"Lady Phyxe. The door you want is at the end of the hall."

"Thank you, Zen." She didn't bat an eyelash as the voice materialized out of nowhere. However, his dazed look deepened. She wondered when he'd last rested.

"How many days have you been awake?" she asked.

"I stopped counting." He grinned at her again.

She dipped her head. "Probably not a bad idea considering all you've been trying to get done, but your body is going to fail you if you don't rest."

She found the door she wanted and tugged him through the master suites of the palace. Nothing less would do for the leader. He would have been happy with a palette on the floor anywhere at this point, but he needed comfort. True rest would let him focus better. She was surprised he was absorbing as much as he had. On the other hand, perhaps the lack of sleep was why he was absorbing everything in such a stoic fashion.

Deep blue and emerald colors dripped from every imaginable point of the room. Soft fabrics clung from the ceiling to the walls and then cascaded down to pool in swirls of colors above the plush carpet. Phyxe sighed at the sheer heaven of it. She'd seen and done a lot in her lifetime, but luxurious, hell, sinful, trappings never ceased to stir her. She wanted to kick off her boots and sink her toes into the lush carpet.

"You like?" His breath tickled the back of her neck. He halted mere inches behind her.

"I love," she whispered. "It is suited for a Goddess."

Textures. She was all about the textures. She wanted to touch everything. The front room beckoned one to sit and reveal in sight and color. Overstuffed couches littered among chairs of glistening silvers and velvet covers.

"Keep going," he said.

She stepped forward and pulled him with her. She was far too easy to please. Lavish her with textures, gems, and, hell, she was easy. Her footsteps melted into the carpet. The front room led to a single back room, the bedroom. A large bed sunk into the middle of the floor. A small pool, fit for two sat off to one side its blue waters glistened as if untouched through the years. A fireplace loomed in the other, flames sparked at their entrance.

She sighed. She was going to have to replicate this for a while in her home. Someone had taken a lot of time and effort to build this treasure. She loved the bed sinking into the floor. This, from the tall woman who preferred to be able to roll out of bed and have her feet hit the floor at a comfortable angle.

His stare weighed down on the back of her neck.

"It's gorgeous."

67

"Thank you," he said.

She cocked her head at him. The tone of his voice...

Tru frowned as he looked around the room. He shook his head as if to clear it. "I'm not sure, but I think this is mine, my attempt at artistry. It feels … like it's mine."

Her eyes widened, and she glanced around again. "Warrior?"

His fingers rubbed his temples, "It feels like a dream. I'm confused, shhh, don't tell anyone." He voice slurred as needed relaxation began to overtake him.

"That's because you won't let me near anyone." She tugged him further into the room. He didn't resist. "Come. You need to rest. The pool will refresh you. Zen stoked the fire. You bathe. I'll see if there are foods about."

She ushered him forward to the pool. He hesitated in letting her hand go.

"Go on," she urged.

He stepped past her. Fatigue laced every movement. His hands rose to unlace the shirt.

Phyxe retreated. As much as she wanted to stand there and watch him strip and reveal every inch of his masculine body, he needed to relax and rest. And food wouldn't be bad either. She was certain she could do with some sustenance, too. Her stomach growled in agreement. Cutoff from her abilities to maintain herself, she now needed food like any humanoid.

"I'm having something brought to you, Lady Phyxe." The AI's voice broke through the main room

She almost jumped out of her skin. "Thank you, saves me having to hunt something down."

"You're welcome." The AI's tone softened from earlier. "I have begun searches for the logical places Lord Marius would have placed a shielding device."

"Lord Marius didn't place the shielding device, his father did."

"Yes, the previous Lord Marius, Riske Marius, also called Lord Riske, enabled the shield 242 years ago. Lord Truant Marius was 42 at the time."

Lord who? Phyxe stopped dead center in the main room.

"Lord Truant Marius?"

"Yes."

"Is how old?"

"242."

"Zen, what is the average lifespan of your inhabitants?"

"512 standard years."

Well, hell. Phyxe sat down on one of the couches. He hadn't been joking at stopping at 200. The average lifespan of most humanoids she'd encountered was 82.5 years. He had several lifetimes on them. No wonder she liked him.

"Lady Phyxe?"

"Yes."

"Do you need aid?"

She smothered a laugh. The AI was growing a heart. "No. I'm absorbing the facts."

"Which facts are those?"

"Oh, I'm very attracted to a 242-year-old warrior when I'm about 5,252."

"You've only got 5,010 years on him."

Phyxe laughed. She couldn't help herself. "Yes, you're right." Leave it to the computer to break it down to the numbers.

"He needs a woman."

"I'm not a woman." She sobered. She was Other. She was Goddess. She was above. She was also beyond. She would never be wife, mother, helpmate, or hearth mate. She traveled where the fates decreed.

The AI clicked at her. The Ancient One flared to life in her mind. Both indicated anger at her statement.

"I am not human," she reiterated to them both.

You are more than human, Mistress.

"All of your biological instances indicate you are human," Zen stated.

"Hmm, check them when these damn bracers aren't confining me," Phyxe said.

"Those are not of this plane," the AI responded.

She refrained from the "well, duh" comment on the tip of her tongue. She should spend less time on Old Earth. Those damn volcanoes there. She loved them.

You are bound, Mistress?

Yes, I am stuck and can't use my full abilities. Otherwise, the one who got me stuck here would be molten lava.

"They show signs of metals from three different

systems across the galaxy," the AI said.

Phyxe sat up. "What?"

"Yes, Lady Phyxe. Initial analysis indicates those bracers are crafted of materials from Phalon II, Xiansus, and Theriran."

"Those planets aren't even in this solar system," Phyxe said.

"Correct."

"Well, then how the hell did they get here?" she asked.

"I could give you a statistical answer, but I don't think you want one," Zen commented.

"No, I want to know how the hell they GOT here. The damn demon has more power than he should."

"Demon?" Both the AI and the planet chimed.

"Rais. He fled before I could decapitate him."

"Wise," the AI stated wryly.

"Yeah, who asked you?" Fury echoed through her all over again. Items from three planets not in this solar system meant there was a hole in the shield or someone had been waiting a long time to call her.

"Analyze crafting techniques. And figure out how to get them OFF of me. And while you're at it, start searching for the children from the Haven. Rais' men took off with them heading west from the Haven," Phyxe ordered.

"Yes, ma'am," the AI snapped back. "Your food is in the compartment to the left of the door."

She nodded and strode over to open the door. She pulled the tray from the compartment. Scents of long forgotten smells assaulted her nose. She should be out searching for the children even though she still needed to find answers leading to the demon's whereabouts. She glared at the bracers as she stared down at the food. It would have been better if she could splinter her consciousness and search her normal way. Instead, she had to rely on what the planet and the people could provide. She re-focused realizing that worrying would get her no closer to any of her goals.

"I included his favorites, and then added a few I thought might appeal to you," Zen commented.

"Thank you, Zen. Very thoughtful of you." Phyxe's mouth watered at the mixture of tantalizing aromas:

smoked beef, dried fruit, the scent of aged cheeses. She hadn't been this entranced with food in … well … forever.

"Regardless of how you got here, I know you want to fix things," the AI stated.

Phyxe gave a half smile to the room. "It is what I do." Well, that and destruction and revenge, but who counted that. In her younger days, she wasn't looking out to make things better. She sighed at herself. Look who was growing up.

Silence greeted her as she crossed the room back to the bedroom door. With her luck, Tru would be sound asleep in the bed and the food would go to waste. She should be scouring the planet for the children. She'd set Zen and Firon to the task since her reach was limited. And Rais, that damn demon knew more than he should. His entire being should have bowed down in fear at her arrival, or at least some tremors. Something aided him … someone. A powerful being. She wasn't stupid or blind. She could only rely on the tools on hand while she was so limited. She had no problem delegating to the planet and the AI. Well, maybe, a slight problem, but she refused to add fuel to that fire.

Tru waited for the door to close behind Phyxe before he stripped of his clothes. He didn't want her to see how his body, tired as it was, was reacting to her in ways he found distracting, yet tantalizing. He wanted to tackle her to the sheets, but he needed rest if he were to lead his warriors into battle with these off-worlders. A longing pooled inside him at the sight of the clean waters. It had been eons since he'd allowed himself a bath. Water was too precious of late. He hadn't been surprised when she'd told him their supply had dwindled. He'd known it for a fact. A fact he'd kept hidden from his people. He didn't want to acknowledge they were dying. He'd suspected, but hadn't wanted to name it. Naming it meant he had to acknowledge it. At least, it was something he could fix once he rid the planet of the invaders. He would see to it his people had water even if he had to re-open the trade routes for Firon.

His clothes dropped to the floor. His weapons, he set to the side of the pool, still within easy reach. With trepidation and reverence, he stepped into the waters and sighed at the feel of the warm liquid lapping around his body. They'd fled this place so long ago, how were the waters clear and tepid?

Hell, it had been centuries since he'd allowed himself this pleasure. He'd been alive for a little over two. He gave up caring how it was all still ready and waiting for him and just enjoyed the calming sensation the waters brought to him.

He sunk deeper into the pool and let the water buoy his body to the surface. He'd built the pool for two of his size. Phyxe would easily fit in here with him. He wondered if she'd even been enticed. She'd shown a distinct focus on getting him rest and helping him save his planet, since he'd found her in the computer hub. No hint at what transpired in their shared dream. His fault. He'd rebuffed her. She had every right to ignore him now.

He should be more worried about his duties than the woman who threatened him at every turn. She was his salvation or his downfall. If he let her out among his people ... gods, who was he kidding? The women would love her. The Matrons hadn't even blinked when he'd brought her to them. It wasn't as if they could emulate her. Sheer physicality was against them. The warriors? They needed to remain focused on providing for and protecting the women and children, not lusting after a goddess. Hell, he needed to remain focused on providing for his people, the planet, and not lusting after said Goddess.

He sunk under the waters. Damn, she was hard not to want.

Fire. Pure fire. When he'd seen her naked in the flames of his dream, he hadn't been sure whether to dive in to her to keep her from the flames or let her burn in naked glory. His body hardened. She was perfection incarnate. Brains. Body. Attitude. She met him temper for temper and showed no fear.

He wished he knew what the demon, as she called him, had done to bind her so effectively. Mostly, so he could undo it and she could use her powers to their fullest potential. He could only imagine how her abilities could aid his cause. She even seemed more annoyed than ticked off and ready to fry everything in sight. Although, he knew her threats of roasting the demon were more than idle.

There'd been times he'd like to do the same to the invaders.

She focused on finding out more about his planet, his people and sparred verbally with him to get her task accomplished. She cared and wanted to know more to help him.

Honestly, wouldn't a Goddess already know?

Firon was his to rule, but he rarely remembered names for every person in each Haven. Some days, his own name sounded off to his ears. It was hell when the spelling of your own name looked odd when you saw or heard it. She showed more passion than some of his lieutenants did about the fate of their people—and she'd been here less than a full cycle. He wished half of them showed her drive to fix their planet. The Matrons appreciated his efforts, but the upper level dwellers were still irritated his father closed their borders.

Slavery. It wasn't something the House of Marius could stand idly by and let happen. Selling their people upset the natural balance. To ensure it never happened again, his father decreed no one set foot off planet and no alien set foot on their surface. He enacted many precautions of which Tru had no idea or had been made to forget.

Then, enter the off-worlders ... and then, one Fire Goddess.

One bound and stuck Fire Goddess.

He wasn't sure where the new images flowed from, but since finding her in the desert sands, images started to dance in his mind's eye, whether he was awake or asleep. He alternated between thinking the demon had done him a favor or cursed him. Instead, something deep inside flared to happiness over the fact he now had someone to share things with. This Fire Goddess understood what it meant to rule, what it meant to have people look to you for food, shelter, and protection. She knew what it meant to give up everything and take care of others.

He dipped below the surface of the water and submerged his entire body. Below water, he hovered and let it buoy him in silence. Being a man of the desert, his home was with fire and sands ripping across his body, the sun beating down on him, the sands flowing over his body. This wastefulness was a luxury, a sin.

For the moment, he enjoyed the sheer feeling of otherness.

Phyxe strode into the room and about dropped the plate of food when she saw Tru below the surface of the water. She set down the plate near the edge and ventured closer. She hunched to her feet and hovered as close as she dared. The naked man drifted below the surface. He stared up through the water shallows.

He bolted up and showered droplets of water everywhere. Phyxe reared back.

"Careful," she growled.

Tru grinned at her. The boyish smile transformed the hard lines of his face.

Phyxe glared at him and brushed the few droplets clinging to her skin. If she'd been able to, they'd have vanished in an instant.

"Come into the pool, Lady Fire."

"No." She shook her head. "You're crazy."

He smiled.

Something in him changed while she'd been gone. His eyes looked less tired, fewer lines etched around them. His body looked more relaxed.

She shrieked as he grasped her arm and pulled her forward, fully clothed. Phyxe landed in the water with an unladylike splash.

And sunk like a stone.

She struggled, her feet kicked as she pushed her head to the surface. Water clung to her, wrapped around her.

No!

She finally broke the surface.

"Get me out of here," she sputtered.

The taxed fires in her body retreated and shriveled.

Tru stared at her in confusion.

Her teeth chattered. She turned unsteadily and reached out for the edge. Her vision grew hazy. Hints of blue swept across her outstretched fingers.

"Holy," he cursed. The blue and purple colors crept over her skin. Her body turned ashen. Her wet hair clung to her head.

"Cold. I'm cold. Get me ..." Her teeth snapped together. She found the edge of the pool. His arms locked around her, and she didn't protest. He pushed out of the pool and his naked body followed.

"I didn't realize." He rubbed her arms.

She sat on the edge and shivered in her wet leathers. Her wet hair hung in burnt sienna ringlets down around her face. The fiery edges dulled as they curled against her breasts. He swallowed. If he'd thought the leathers had shown off her form before, now, wet, they tightened against her skin. Her nipples pearled beneath the vest. Her skin, where it showed, turned various shades of blue and purple. Her teeth chattered in eloquent cacophony.

"Warm. I can't warm myself. These. Damn. Bracers." She wrapped her arms around herself and tried to draw within, to find a way to make a spark.

"Zen!" he shouted.

The AI flared to life. A fire roared in a corner fireplace. The temperature dramatically climbed in the room as high as possible for both occupants.

"Get her into the bed. Get the wet clothes off her. You'll have to warm her. I can't change the temperature high enough to warm her and not harm you." The AI's voice resonated around the room.

Tru pulled her to the bed and began to fight the wet silks off her body. Phyxe didn't ever struggle. Hell, she'd have helped if she could feel anything in her body other than the severe shivers wracking it as her muscles tried to generate enough action to promote warmth.

"I am so sorry," He tugged the clothes from her body. "I'll get you warm."

"Water ..." She chattered. "Sucks."

"I should have known." He stripped the boots off her feet and tossed them across the room. "You are fire. The Goddess of Fire. Water won't help. Hell, in my dream I saw you bathe in open flame. That should've been my first clue."

"Thought. You. Didn't. Believe. Me."

He growled and wrestled her pants down her shivering legs. "I'm an idiot."

She refrained from agreeing with him and instead tried to breathe deeply and generate some semblance of warmth from inside. The last time she'd suffered such horrible shivers was when Glacial encased her in ice to prove a point. Of course, then, she'd been able to spark an internal flame and burn her way out— and warm herself up. She'd never been this cold.

"Under the covers. Zen, I need more covers," he commanded.

"On their way, m'lord. Please don't kill the delivery bot."

"At this point, I don't care if they simply appear in front of me. Look for a place to get her warm enough and a way to get her there."

Mistress, come to the lava pits. I can warm you.

Phyxe shivered, all her energy focused on trying to warm herself. She couldn't even acknowledge the Ancient One's offer of help. A violent wave of shudders hit her before her body stilled. She tried to curl her knees to her chest.

She couldn't feel her toes. Gods, this sucked.

"I can't get her warm enough, Zen. Do something," Tru begged.

"M'lord, if I do anything more, it'll kill you."

"So?" he shot back.

"I'm sorry m'lord. My programming will not allow me to do any direct harm to you."

He cursed.

Phyxe tried to smile. She didn't have the energy or the will to tell him she couldn't die. At least, she didn't think she could. But, this was as close to hell as she would ever define it. She wished she could get her teeth to stop chattering. It disrupted her focus. Her heart rate dropped.

Tru crawled under the covers with her. His hard masculine form warm to the touch as it came into contact with the cold flesh of hers.

Mistress, if he can't warm you up, I will open a crevice and bring you to me. Your life is more necessary than his.

No! Phyxe screamed mentally. Her body arched in its fetal position as she protested the Ancient One's decree. *I will warm. Let him help me.*

If your heart rate drops too low, I will remove you, as

much as it would pain me to do so. You have the power to restore the balance. He does not.

No. Focus on finding the demon, and the children.

Phyxe shut down all mental chatter and forced herself to focus on re-warming herself from the inside out. She knew if she fostered the idea of fire inside, it would extend far faster than the heat outside.

Tru ran his hands up and down her body and nestled her as close to him as he could. His legs trapped her between them. His arms wrapped around her and pulled her into his hard chest. Between shivering convulsions, Phyxe alternated between cursing the cold and admiring the strong striations in the chest pressed against her nose.

"Come on, fiery one. You've got to get your spark back. You can do it. Think warm thoughts."

Yeah, where was he when she'd thought warm thoughts in the Haven? She shivered again and then stilled.

She took shallow breaths. She forced a focused breath and took another one, deeper. Action would warm her. She needed her body to move to generate enough heat to force the cold out.

"Come on, Sparky." He ran his hands down her body.

Phyxe managed to bare her teeth at him and not in a smile.

"Hell, you can only manage a spark in your hand. What kind of Goddess are you? A real Fire Goddess would have roasted me the minute she saw me."

She forced her eyes open, and glared at him, but was put off by the smile on his face. Damn man was goading her. He wanted her anger to flare.

"Come on, Sparky. It'll warm you up. Get mad at me." He dropped a light kiss on her neck.

He trailed the kiss down her throat. His body still trapped hers.

Phyxe bit down on her back teeth. If she could force her mouth to work, she'd tell him what she thought of his humor and his methods. Sparky? What kind of endearment was that? Hell, if she could force any part of her powers to work, she'd roast them both and damned with the consequences.

Gods, she hated water. Right now, she included Glacial, too.

Tru trailed a tongue down her chest and leaned in to taunt her cold nipple. Her eyes flared wide as her body responded, heat awakened from her core at his touch. She fed it, focused on it.

The fire spread.

"That's it, Red. Warm. Think warm thoughts. Don't flame us both." He murmured as his tongue danced an erotic dance across her nipple and caused it to harden in pleasure rather than cold. Phyxe ignored his words. The man talked too much. Besides, she wanted more of his tongue across her body. It spread liquid heat through her body making her want and ache for more.

Her hands moved and reached out from around herself to get closer to the warmth of his flesh. She began to feel her fingertips, ever so slightly.

"Come on, Red." Tru's hands ran down the arc of her back. His strong fingers played rhythmically across her cold, taut skin. Everywhere he touched, heat followed.

Phyxe groaned in pleasure as warmth began to seep across her chest and abdomen. The man had power in his hands. The rough calluses on his palms generated a friction against the texture of her soft skin. With infinite care, she relaxed from her fetal position. Her muscles released the tension. Shivers still overcame her moment to moment, but the warmth he spread with his hands and his kisses soon put those to rest. As her arms relaxed, she tangled her fingers in his hair, buried them in the baby fine hairs at the nape of his neck. Her legs muscles unwound, and she leaned into him. Damn if he hadn't spread the heat.

"There you go, Red."

She shivered, but no longer from the cold and pulled him closer, fire swept to her core. Now, she was warm. This, she revealed in. Her body moved under his, hip met hip. He'd ignited a spark, one she wanted to follow to the end.

"You talk too much, warrior."

She smiled as he grinned against her skin.

"It's Truant, Red."

"It's Phyxe, Warrior."

She locked her hands around his head and pulled him back up her body. She loved the sensations his kisses created as he trailed them across her stomach, but she wanted his lips against hers.

"Something in mind?" He settled between her thighs, his cock rested hard against the outside of her core.

"Your lips on mine," she said.

He leaned in. "Agreed."

He tilted his head. His lips slanted across hers. She wasn't sure whose body sparked in pleasure first or if it was even separate from them. Fire flared in her chest and struggled to reach out. She wanted to encase them both in sheer sensual heat.

Her lips parted as his tongue demanded entrance. She met him motion for motion and reveled in the feel of his kiss that demanded heat and produced it. His hand swept up and pulled her harder into his chest. Her back arched. His lips left hers and proceeded to press hard kisses down her neck. Her head tilted to the side. Her hands dropped to his shoulders. Her fingers dug into the muscles in his back.

"Inside, I want you inside, now." She shifted her hips and moved his body to the entry of her own.

"I want to taste you first," he said.

"Later. Heat. I want you inside."

Tru shifted, teased her tight entry. Phyxe relaxed and opened her hips to give him free rein to thrust into her body. Her eyes swept open in shock and pleasure feeling him bury himself in her inch by inch.

"Gods, you're tight and warm," he said.

She grinned. "You're hard and warm."

He smiled a wicked smile and pulled out to thrust back into her. She tangled her fingers in his shaggy hair and tugged his head to hers again, demanded he kiss her while she met him thrust for thrust. She wanted all of him buried in her, lips locked against lips. Fire rolled over them. Trembles started deep within where his body met hers. The spasms of orgasm rippled across her hips. The heat liquefied and stole up to her chest. Tru's body reacted in kind when the fiery spasms reached from her to wrap him in their control. Phyxe's body arched up off the bed into the hard planes of his body. He stilled and reached the height of his own pleasure. Their cries of release echoed around the room.

Phyxe collapsed back on the bed and pulled Tru with her. He protested about remaining on top of her, but she kept her legs locked around him for a moment.

"I'm too heavy."

"You feel good. Deal with me a moment," she murmured.

He released a tired laugh. "I'll fall asleep on top of you."

"I can always move you, warrior. Right now, I like where you are."

He nipped her on the shoulder. "I need to move."

She pouted when he pulled himself out of her and rolled to his side. He trailed his arm across her body and let it rest around her waist. A smile replaced her pout. A sigh of contentment escaped him. His body relaxed and fell into a deep slumber.

She should be annoyed he'd fallen asleep. Instead, she turned to watch him for a moment. When was the last time he'd slept? Or even relaxed? A warm, unusual feeling welled up from deep within. He looked so innocent in sleep. The muscles in his face relaxed. The hard lines of his cheeks and jaw still stood out, but the stress lines around his eyes smoothed out. The care and worries of leading his people retreated as his body let go. She reached up and trailed a hand down the harsh angles of his face.

She needed to help change those worries but in the morning. For now, she'd take the slumber offered and the sheer satisfaction of exceptional sex and the rejuvenating energy it provided. Phyxe rolled to her side and snuggled backwards into his body. Contentment welled up when he reached out in his sleep and pulled her closer. His strong arms tightened around her. Tomorrow, she would take him to task over the water incident. Right now, she would enjoy sleeping with a man for the first time in her long, long life.

She would have to make sure it didn't become a habit.

❧SEVEN ❧

Tru rolled over in confusion. For a moment, his surroundings were hazy and unfocused. Sunlight teased the edges of the dark curtains blocking the oversized windows in the room. He blinked and realized he was alone in a bed, rumpled sheets and the hint of embers the only indication of his companion. He fell back into the pillows and stared up at the ceiling.

How long had it been?

Decades. He'd given up sharing his bed decades ago. If he'd wanted release, he sought out a willing widow. Those women of his age, unmarried, brought too much drama to his life and high expectations whenever he showed any signs of interest. He had a planet to take care of and didn't need the demands of a household added to the pile of responsibilities.

But, Phyxe? He'd brought her to bed and then fallen asleep on her. He'd never been relaxed enough after sex to curl up with a woman and sleep.

"Zen?" He tested the request aloud.

"Yes, m'lord?"

"Where is the Lady?" Relief washed through him. He hadn't imagined the AI.

"Downstairs researching, m'lord."

Of course. He groaned. He'd met his match in stubbornness and workaholic ethics. "What time is it?"

"You've been asleep for a full day and a half, m'lord."

"What?" He bolted upright and struggled to get the covers off him. Hell, a day and a half? He didn't have time. His feet hit the floor.

"Lady Phyxe demanded I let you rest. Her logic seemed reasonable."

Her logic? He laughed. He couldn't get the lost hours back. Clothes, where the hell were his clothes?

"I've replicated you new ones, m'lord. They're at the

foot of the bed. Your weapons have been cleaned and sharpened." The AI sounded put out. "Lady Phyxe took care of your weapons and refused to allow me to have a bot prepare them for you."

He glanced at them while pulling his clothes on. He'd have had a problem with a bot as well. He finished putting the new leathers on and admired the softness.

"These are perfect, Zen."

He'd have sworn if an AI could preen, she did. "Thank you, m'lord. I will replicate more and place them in the closet along with other dress garments for formal occasions. The bots your father made before his passing have been set to cleaning the palace now that you've returned. You will need to put a call out for the staff to resume their duties as well."

He nodded and picked up his weapons. They gleamed with well-polished care.

"She cleansed them in fire, m'lord," the AI said.

Of course, she had.

"They're in better condition than I could have gotten them," he commented aloud.

The AI remained silent.

"She is in the command room?" he asked.

"Yes, m'lord. I'll have breakfast sent in."

"Thank you."

He strode through the doors into the upper halls of the palace. Home. At one time, long ago, another lifetime, this had been his home. So long ago, yet in the drop of time, it factored to nothing. The rooms he'd come from had been his own. He remembered some of it. Mostly though, when he tried to remember, he saw nothing but hazy images dancing in his mind's eye, followed quickly by a piercing headache. The room, those he remembered now. They'd changed some to account for his current age.

His parent's suite resided across the hall, but he wasn't ready to investigate or test his memories. Instead, he made his way to the central staircase and down to the main level. He should have been annoyed about being left to sleep, but his body hummed with newfound energy. And, somehow, with Phyxe working and looking out for him while he slept, he'd slept deeper than he had in ages. He wondered if he could say the same if any of his lieutenants had been about.

"Good morning, warrior." Her voice swept over him with sensual warmth when he strode through the door; she hadn't even turned to look at him.

Thoughts of sex and tangling her up in the sheets again flowed through him as he caught sight of her when she turned in the command chair to face him. His eyes trailed over her body. Long red hair with blond highlights cascaded to her slender waist. Her outfit changed some from the cycle before. Zen must have done the same and crafted her new clothing. She sported dark brown, form-fitting leathers in the same style she'd worn when she'd been pulled to the sands, but these held hints of gold and red, and gave her the illusion of sparks when she turned. Her breasts strained against the deep V in the top. Her arms were bare from sculpted shoulders to the golden bracers. Her abdomen bare, lean and muscled showed off her core strength. Pants dipped low on her hips. Damn the AI for not crafting something more suiting to the women of their planet, and bless her for it.

He fought back the immediate desire to repeat their performance from the previous night. What the hell was wrong with him? He never responded this hard and fast to a woman.

"Good morning, I think." He smiled and forced the thoughts of sex to the side. It was going to be a long day if he couldn't get himself under control.

He marched across the room to her and halted when he realized two command chairs now sat side by side. She'd taken the one nearer to the door, so he hadn't seen the other when she turned.

"Zen replicated another one. She figured we'd argue less." She grinned at him then kicked herself back to face the main screen.

She'd rearranged some and made the center easier for two people to access everything from the central chairs.

"That'll happen." He cocked a smile at her when her eyes darted back up to his. He stepped around her and dropped in the other chair. He set his sword to the side in the new resting place for it.

"You're going to have to explain most of this to me," he said. "It's hauntingly familiar, but it's also as if I'm seeing it for the first time."

She nodded.

He stared at the keyboards, glittering lights and images flashed too fast for human consumption across the large screen in front of him. None of this had been here before, or had it? His memory faded in and out, hazy images beckoned. He forced himself to focus. He would track down those memories later.

She hit a few buttons. "Here, I'll slow it all down some. She is running scenarios. There have been a few topside disturbances while you slept. They were minor, so I refrained from acting on them."

A map flipped up on screen. Beacons began to flash in three separate areas on the map.

"I was going to investigate the skirmishes, but Zen sent bots to record your warriors since they occurred when the sun was down, and we thought we could do so undetected," she said.

He nodded and sunk back into the chair, amazed. All this she'd done from a remote position? She'd even honored his request and refrained from contacting any of his people. She was better than ten of his lieutenants' put together.

"Here are the vids from the incidents. Timed and executed with precision." She hit a few more buttons and sat back to watch them stream by.

Tru leaned forward, his arms rested on his legs, his hands curled under his jaw as he watched the events unfold before him. Three separate attacks.

"Tell me what you see." Phyxe's voice flowed over him.

His eyes remained glued to the screen. "They're not my people. They've never done battle with my warriors. It is a test. A game. They're slighter in build, but faster. Yet, their endurance lacks the quality of a true warrior."

He pointed to one of the aliens who, like all the others, was covered from head to toe in black, only his eyes showing. "His chest rises and falls too fast, he can't catch his breath."

She nodded. "What else?"

"They're faster, but it costs them. They're looking for our weaknesses and attempting to build up their endurance. They're not used to our atmosphere."

"And?" she prodded.

"What don't I see, you mean?" He couldn't help the

84

half smile from crossing his face. She was testing him. "The attacks are all timed. They have a technological advantage. They're in constant communication with each other. They know when to attack and when to retreat. This time there is no objective in their attack. They're not taking anything or anyone. These skirmishes are practice."

She nodded again. Her fingers tapped an unsteady rhythm on the arm of her chair.

"The question is how?" He frowned at the screen trying to focus on the minute details of the battles as they flowed across the flat panel.

"Well, and why?" she murmured. "What do you have here of value to off-worlders?"

He shook his head.

"You have something of value; otherwise, they wouldn't be here."

He shook his head again. "This is a desert planet. We don't harvest. We don't sell. We're warriors and artisans."

"Your women are uncommonly beautiful."

He turned his head. "What?"

She flipped a few images across the screen. Various pictures of the women of Firon flashed past them, some dancing, some crafting, and some caring for children.

"Not a single ugly one in the bunch. Your people have gemstone-colored eyes, tanned skin and, while petite, there is not an ounce of fat on anyone on this planet. From the physical genetics standpoint, your race is genetically perfect."

"You're telling me these people invaded us because they like the way we look?" His eyes widened and his jaw clenched.

"People have been invaded for less."

"Yes, but that's absurd."

"I didn't say it wasn't. I was giving you one of the reasons behind the invaders. Slavery. You're the one telling me the planet has no value on the interstellar market. No harvests, no mining." She shook her head, pulled up statistics from the past, when they'd been one of the most notable vacation spots. "People came here for a reason, what was the reason?"

"Visual stimulation," he admitted.

"Yes. The planet looks good. People love observing

beautiful people. It's a fascination with the human aspect of the race. They want to own beautiful things."

He agreed. "It is a ridiculous reason to invade."

"You said you'd closed your borders because you couldn't deal with the politics and the total acceptance of slavery of the ruling body."

"Yes." He dropped back into the chair. " My father closes the borders because of slavery and selling his warriors to battle. And, now, they're sneaking in to steal the women and children anyway. This is absurd. "

"No, what's absurd is how are they are still getting here."

His teeth gnashed, and he sat up again, his eyes fixed on the screen.

"How are they getting in?" she questioned.

He turned his gaze on her. "You don't know?"

She shook her head. Her hair cascaded around her. "No. We've been through multiple scenarios. We've determined you have a traitor."

"Yeah, I figured that, Red."

She smirked at him. "Fine. We know the demon is a part of this all, but we've narrowed your traitor suspects down to three."

"What?" How the hell?

She flipped screens and pulled up three pictures for him. Two of his lieutenants stared back at him. His seconds, Devos and Eriaku, one with burning eyes, the other—the calm grey gaze of the moon. The third, far less likely in his estimation, one of the Matrons in the Havens.

"I trust them all." Hell, they'd saved his life on numerous occasions when they'd battled off planet. He'd stepped in the paths of numerous swords and had the favor returned. As for Sierriana? She'd helped Etheria put him back together more times than he could count.

"Your men's appearances at certain sites and times coincide with attacks. They're either a part of this, or unknowingly facilitated the acts." She pulled up the map again. "They're in the same spots at each attack. Either the off-worlders know them or they're tracking them."

"I don't like you suspecting a Matron any more than my men."

She tilted her head at him. "Never underestimate your women." She took a deep breath. She should tell him about the children ... no, he would run off and start hunting. She already had a head start on that particular issue. Thanks to Zen and Firon. He didn't need the added issue. A hint of unease flowed through her before she squashed it.

He frowned at her. "No, I'm starting to realize that." He stood up and began to pace. "How are the aliens getting to the planet?"

"I'm not sure." Phyxe flipped screens faster because his attention was elsewhere. "I've been through some scenarios. We've been trying to determine the placement of your satellites, which have to maintain the shield, but there are no electronic records. There are several dead spaces on the planet. Places Zen can't reach and places Firon feels off kilter, but we can't tell whether that's because of her being off her trajectory, the shields, or the demon."

She pulled up an old interstellar map, his family's last known map of the galaxies. "We've figured out the likely trajectory of the satellites, or at least as close as we can get based on some assumptions. The demon has to be a part in it all, some special ability or technology to allow passage through the shield. It's not like he's native to your planet."

He stopped pacing and turned to face the map. "No, him, I'm pretty sure I'd remember. How do we shut them down, if we don't know how they got there?"

She turned to him. "What?"

"You said we'd upset the natural balance of the planet because of the shields. Our water supplies are dwindling. Our home is being invaded. Someone miscalculated." He refrained from naming his father as the perpetrator of the miscalculation. He knew full well the man had his faults and couldn't be accused of functioning under sound mind when he'd shut the planet off from the rest of the Universe. He might have done the same.

"You're planning on fixing that."

"As if you were going to let me do anything less."

She smiled. Hell, she radiated warmth. A flush seeped up his body at her direct gaze.

"I need to check in with my warriors."

"You need to introduce them to the technologies again," she said.

He nodded.

"Your counterparts out there have an advantage," she commented.

"Not for long, not if I can help it."

"Good." She smiled.

He paused. "You will remain here?"

It was the first time he'd asked instead of demanding. She glanced at him and bit her lip as if she made a decision against her better judgment.

"I will make you a deal. You allow Zen to give you something, so we stay in constant contact. I am allowed to intervene if I deem it necessary, or you ask."

He scowled. "If you deem it necessary?"

"You asked for my aid. I could have left anytime while you slept and defeated many of your invaders with or without my true powers. I did not."

His jaw tightened. She was that good? Hell, he couldn't even catch an invader. A live one anyway.

"I have more resources here than you think, warrior, bound or not. Either you agree to this. Or, I follow you and keep you safe no matter what."

He frowned at her. Didn't seem like much of a choice.

"It is the best choice I can offer you. I am not one to sit on the sidelines, but you are determined I would upset the balance far more than I would help. Contrary to my nature, I am trying to adjust to the way your planet functions. I am war. I am battle. Right now, I'm trying to do a slow burn. I will remain here or within the Haven. I will not venture out unless you, or the world, is in imminent danger." Well, after she found the children. Then she'd remain in one spot. Maybe.

Slow burn? If this was a slow burn, he was a dead man. Tru released a pent up sigh. How could he ask for more? He knew her nature. He was witness to it first hand. She was Fire. He shouldn't be denying the Fire Goddess from her right and her calling. Gods, he knew if the situation were reversed, he'd ignore any of her requests and go about business the way he thought it should be handled. Hell, had he acknowledged her right to elemental flame?

"Deal." Damn it, he had. He bit back a growl at himself.

She looked startled. "Just like that?"

"Yes," he said.

"You are far too easy to bargain with."

"You're far too logical in your attack." He smothered a smile.

She laughed. "I have never been accused of being logical."

"Must be the after glow."

She shot him a look. Her eyelids dropped. "You lookin' for a repeat, warrior?"

He strode back over to her and hunched on his feet next to her, eye level since she was in the chair. "We'll do the next time without the water, Red. I am sorry. I should have realized what would happen."

Her hand reached out to stroke his face. "You didn't know. And, honestly, if it weren't for these damn things." She clinked the bracers together. "I wouldn't have a problem in the water."

He dropped his head.

"Hey, this is not your fault." She tiled his jaw up, so their eyes met. "You have a demon loose on your planet. It's not as if he was part of your close personal advisors."

He gritted his teeth. "You don't have any advisors. You might think a few of them are demons."

She laughed, her eyes sparked. "You haven't met my sisters."

"How many do you have, again?" he asked.

"Four. But, Zhanne is more like our mother since she combines all of us." She sighed. Her eyes took a faraway look.

"You miss them." He knew it was more. He could see it in her face.

"They are never far from me. But something here is blocking me from them. I cannot call them. I cannot talk. I'm sure they're frantic."

"They'll be searching the universe for you?" he asked.

"Or tearing it apart," she said.

"I'd prefer to think they're searching." He grinned.

"So would I." She laughed. "And three of the four will be searching. Gaian will be planet hopping trying to find me."

"She does what you would do," he noted.

She slanted him a glance. "Yes."

He nodded. He'd have left his advisors in charge while he ripped the galaxy apart to find the answers he sought. Hell, he'd have done the same for his own mother if his father hadn't trapped him home.

"We'll bring the shields down and get the bracers off." He reached up and stroked her jaw line.

"We'd better." She turned and wrapped her lips around his finger. Her tongue reached out to stroke.

Tru groaned. Gods, what she did to him with a sheer look was nothing like what she did when she touched him. Her tongue wrapped around his finger sending waves of molten lava through his body. If his cock could get any harder, it did.

"You're leaving me here, aren't you?" She nipped lightly enough, so she could talk without releasing him.

"I have to." He didn't want to. Hell, the entire planet could go up in smoke right now, and he wouldn't care. Well, not entirely true, but if he was to check out now, it better be in a ball of flame at this point.

"Play with me first." She sucked on his finger and turned the chair so she could drop to her knees next to him.

Tru reared back as she stood over him. Her body forced his to the floor.

"You had a specific idea in mind, m'lady?" He loved the fire spark in her eyes. He gave in and rolled to the floor pulling her with him.

"Oh, I have centuries worth of ideas to work on." She released his hand from her face.

Her hands quickly worked on the buckles to his pants. Her nails dug into the hard flesh as she found it. She edged his leather pants down his hips then trailed kisses across his hip bone.

"I love the male form. I glory in it." She licked and caressed her way across his skin nearing his straining cock.

She lapped at the strong member as it reared up. Her tongue darted out to taunt him.

"Yet, I have never revealed in it so much as I do with you." Her mouth dropped around him then elicited a loud groan.

Tru was beyond caring. He wanted her mouth wrapped around him. She taunted him, dropped down and then back again. He lost himself in the sheer feeling when her mouth cocooned him.

She growled around him. Her breasts rested under him, cradled his balls worshipping him with her mouth. Tru strained against her. He wrapped his hands in her hair and pulled it up to reveal the slender column of her neck.

He shivered as her lips caressed him with a smile.

Tru pulled himself upwards, pulled her into his lap, and reached out to grasp the edges of her top. She groaned at him and tried to force him back down.

"No, Red."

He tugged the top off over her head and cradled her hips letting her straddle him. He wanted to see her glorious body, every line, every curve, and every hard muscle. He met her line for line.

"I was harassing you." She pouted.

"So?" He grinned at her, his gaze heavy. He wanted to play. If he was going to leave her, he wanted her to remember every sigh, every ache, every pleasure he could bring her.

"Screw it." She kicked off her leathers with his help and then helped him out of his.

Her body cradled him. Tru growled in pleasure. Nothing equaled having her hips locked around him, her arms curled about his body; her core rested against him. Hell, he hadn't even buried himself in her, and he enjoyed her far more than he should.

"Yes, Red."

She wrapped her hand in the hair at the back of his neck and tugged. "You disrupted my intention."

"You'll enjoy yourself more this way." He urged her up, gave her a moment, and then pulled her down, plunged himself deep inside her.

He watched her eyes flare open in pleasure. Pleasure was what he wanted to see. Those amber eyes smoldered with heat—heat he caused, not some external anger or fire. He buried himself deep within her, helped her ride him. He held himself off, wanting her to release before he did. This time, it was her pleasure rather than the sheer heat of the moment. Her body shuddered around his. He held her when her back arched, buried himself as deeply within her as he could.

"You planned that," she said, breathless.

"You started this." He flipped her so her back pressed against the floor. Her hair pooled around her. Her eyes hazy with the relaxation of a recent orgasm. She smiled up at him and dug her hands into his shoulders.

"Unfair. I wanted you to come first."

"Tough." He swept forward and plunged into her. She lifted her hips and surged upwards to meet him, Gods, she was tight. A sound rumbled from deep in his throat. She tightened even more around him. She was fire and ice all at once.

She made him want to melt into her.

He slammed into her again, determined to take her, to fill her. This time, he wanted her to convulse with him. He wrapped a hand in her hair and pulled her up to meet him, so she could see him move deeply into her. She groaned in pleasure. Her nails dug into his back. Her head turned and she sunk her teeth into the flesh of the hand in her hair. Convulsions wracked his body as he tightened. He stilled and she flexed her hips and pulled him into her. Sheer pleasure made a smile on his face, his body releasing into her. Gods, what woman had made him ever respond like this? The fact she could sidetrack him from work was insane.

She was definitely a Goddess.

And the way she was smiling up at him. He'd have given into any of her demands.

"You look far too satisfied, warrior." She smiled up at him.

He dropped a hard kiss on her lips before he pulled his body from hers. "You are too good to me."

She stretched and turned her body watching him when he stood. "Yes, I like the way you play. You make me hum."

He laughed struggling to get back into his clothes. He'd turned into a sex driven machine. One look at her, and it was his undoing. Hell, he'd be in the middle of battle and those sex-sleepy eyes would stare up at him and disrupt his focus within seconds. He'd take her on the middle of the battlefield, warriors around them be damned.

"Besides, I want you to realize what you'll be missing without me by your side." She winked when he turned to look at her.

He sighed then worked his way into the rest of his clothes. He didn't want to feel guilty about asking her to stay hidden. This was his battle, and although he'd wanted help, he needed to fix it himself. He needed to be the one who brought resolution to the situation.

Hell, he needed her.

He gave it up. She was fire, pure and simple. She fueled the fire in his blood. She outranked, outthought, and probably out-fought his lieutenants. She looked out for his people within the restrictions he placed. None of which she had to do. She could take over at a moment's notice, but she kept the balance. She wanted life to function the way it should on his planet, for his people. She cared. Far more than he could say about most of the population he protected and provided for. She was their essence.

And still, he turned, and he left her there.

❧EIGHT ❧

Gaian glared at Zhanne across the conference room table. The Goddess of Energy was being unreasonable, as usual. Zhanne's blue eyes stared back at her, unblinking, unnerving in their full blue gaze. No matter how long they all lived, the zero whites in her eyes would still unnerve her.

"No," Zhanne stated.

"That wasn't a request." Gaian stood her ground. They'd been discussing the status of her search for the last hour. She'd visited seven planets with no results. She'd marked one to return to—the one with the Voice—but that was entirely for herself. Her body warmed at the thought. A humming feeling vibrated through her. No, she had four more left. She'd be damned if she wasn't going to visit the rest. "And I'm not taking commands. As I see it, we're all equals, sister."

"And I'm telling you." Zhanne stood to her full height, energy snapped along the blue highlights in her otherwise snow white hair. "The odds she is still in existence are ..." She nodded to the screen on the wall. "Not good."

"Eat them," Gaian snapped.

Zhanne lifted a fine blue eyebrow at her.

"Oh, don't get all holy on me, sister, simply because you claim a portion of all our powers. Deal with it. She is one of us. She is alive. We'd feel it if she were gone. There is no void where she should be. There is a curtain, a shield. I'm not about to do a ceremony to call a new Goddess into being until I've seen evidence for myself that one has been destroyed." And she meant a body or ash or something real and tangible, like Phyxe's head on a pike or something equally as dramatic. She wasn't taking anyone's word for it.

Zhanne heaved a sigh, her tall form shivered in her

cloak. "Fine. Four more planets."

"Careful, sister. We'll start thinking you have a heart." Gaian darted out of the command center before Zhanne could blast her, verbally or otherwise. She'd be damned if she'd let her sister whither away wherever she was. She knew she was still alive.

She was a Goddess after all.

Phyxe paced.

"Lady, you are wearing a hole in the floor."

She rolled her eyes at the AI even though she knew full well the machine couldn't see her. Tru left her hours ago with a hint of regret in his eyes. At least, she'd hope it was regret. With a mere touch of a button, she'd be able to talk to him, but doing so would indicate she missed him.

She never missed anyone.

Instead, she paced. She needed something to do with her pent up energy. Pacing was the best she had for the moment. It wasn't as if she could hurl a good fireball at the nearest incendiary target. She should go investigate the planetary anomalies on the surface and see if they gave any clues to either the invaders entry points or the satellite placements around the globe. She should check in with the Haven and see how the fires fared, as well as see if she couldn't do something with the Matrons and work some fire magic on their planet. She should be out following the trail to the children.

Do you require a pathway, Mistress? Firon's voice echoed in Phyxe's head.

I'm thinking about it.

The computer will not like you disappearing.

She can contact me at any time now. She stretches across your surface again. When I awoke her, all her data banks came alive. Plus, she seems to be attached to me now.

Damn it all. She didn't need an electronic baby sitter. She would have to undo that tracking ability, at least for herself.

A good thing, yes? The planet asked.

Maybe. Well, yes. She's trying to find a way to take the shield down so we can restore your path. And running scenarios, while searching out heat patterns. Phyxe wished she could stretch her senses across the planet; it would speed up their results.

It can't come too soon. I am holding as much of the heat at bay as I can. "Since we're not detecting any heat patterns, I'm going to have to hit the sands. I've delayed too long. The demon must have some shielding technology for his men as well. We know the general direction the children were taken in, yes?" She'd waited too long. She'd allowed the planet and Tru to sidetrack her. The demon had stolen them for a reason and there hadn't been any anomalies to the west of the Haven, only the northwest and north.

"Yes," Zen answered.

"Give me the last known coordinates." She'd be damned if the children were hurt on her watch. Tru's demands or not.

Phyxe sunk down into the sands, reveling in the slight heat that still emanated up from the fine grains. She hadn't questioned Firon's and Zen's ability to get her where she needed to be. She could see the tracks in the sands, and that was all she cared about. The children would be returned to the Haven, no worse for wear.

And heads would roll in the process.

She didn't sense anyone else nearby other than the two men who'd each taken a child. They'd darted across the sands of Firon, believing they were safe on the planet. She could sense their calm. *Aikares.* Idiots. They believed the Ubilin could keep them safe no matter where they were.

She was going to enjoy proving them very, very wrong.

She inched close to their fire on the outer limits. Both children, Sethen and Narissa, sat with hands bound and mouths gagged at the edge of the fire. The two human men laughed and toasted themselves on a job well done.

Phyxe gauged her options. She could kill both of them in a heartbeat. As much as they were drinking and so sure of themselves ... or she could simply remove the children, freak the demon's followers out and cause havoc.

She toyed with both ideas and then realized Sethen saw her. His eyes lit up. His body remained still, but his head lifted. As if he sensed her. She knew the child was too young, no way he could have sensed her. Unless ... she frowned and cast a hard glance over his form. His aura flowed red and brown. Perhaps ...

She shook herself. No time to dwell on the possibilities. She needed to move the children to safety.

Her sword slid in effortless silence from its scabbard on her back. Her other arm flowed up, and she plucked a throwing dart from its sheath.

The dart hummed through the darkness with glaring accuracy. The first man died on the spot. She hesitated, waiting for the second to realize what had happened. She waited longer than she should have.

He leaped and grabbed for the boy. But the young one kicked his legs out and flipped his sister over into the sands, sending them both into the darkness.

Phyxe smiled in approval as she flowed up and out of the sands.

"You took something of mine. I would like them returned," she said.

The man's eyes widened with fear. He reached for a weapon, but Phyxe's sword was already there. Her blade sliced into his wrist, just enough to make a point.

"As I was saying. You took something. I want them returned." She drove the sword deeper.

The man cried out, dropping to his knees. "They're yours. We were only sent to hide and move them. We weren't going to hurt them."

Phyxe tilted her head. "You hurt them by removing them from my presence." She nudged the sword and severed the man's hand at the wrist. "You will never cross the Goddess of Fire again—for any demon or human will. Do we have an understanding?"

The man cried out in pain. He dropped to his knees with his head bowed. "Yes, Mistress. I understand."

"If you don't, I will not be so kind the next time. Be glad all you lost was a hand. Now, get away from me," she commanded.

She knew the story would flow back to the other invaders. She would add fuel to that fire anyway she could.

Demon 1. Goddess 1.

Phyxe glanced around at the faces in the room. Older women remained seated in various positions on the floor; their hands clasped before them as if they'd been in silent prayer. Here and there, girls and young women of various ages littered around them on the floor or stood near. That explained why no one greeted her at the Haven's entry. Did these women think nothing of their safety?

As one, they all stared at her in expectation.

Phyxe grinned. She loved making an entrance. This one, Tru would have a fit over.

"I do believe you were looking for the return of these two?" When Sethen and his sister stepped from behind her, none the worse for wear over their desert trek home, several of the women rushed forward to check over them.

Etheria looked up at her after having made sure both children were fine. "M'lady. We were praying for you and the children." She motioned with her hands to two of the women who quickly disappeared with both children into the depths of the Haven.

Phyxe staggered when two small bodies came racing back in the room to tackle her around each leg. Warmth raced along her body, and she knelt down so she was level with them both.

"You're home safe now," she whispered. "The sisters love you and wish you no harm." Except, she thought, the one who'd started the fire. She was pretty sure she knew how to flush her out. "Go on, get cleaned up and I'll tuck you in when I'm done here."

She stood to her full height as Sethen and Narissa released her. She watched him grab his sister's hand, and together they walked out on their own. Those two were going to do her proud one-day. Not that they hadn't already. They'd never offered up a complaint during their trek back through the desert. She could already see the fire flowing through their auras.

She turned back to Etheria whose wise eyes filled with something she couldn't quite name. "Praying to whom?"

She couldn't keep her smile at bay. She'd find this

even more amusing if her sisters were here.

The matron cocked her head in confusion. "M'lady?"

"Whom were you praying to?" Phyxe asked again.

"Our Fire God, so he would return you and the children safely."

She smiled at the Matron. "Etheria, there is no Fire God."

She might work to balance Tru; however, these women didn't need her to balance. They needed the truth. Dead silence. Phyxe tilted her head and noticed Etheria's face was calm. She glanced around the room, searching each face. All calmly gazed back at her.

"And somehow you already know this don't you? Your planet and your 'god' are both feminine."

Grins swept across the room. Eyes lit up.

"Oh, the men aren't going to like that one." One girl giggled.

"No, I'm sure they won't. Your Lord Marius isn't too thrilled with the fact either."

Etheria gazed back at her, her old eyes unfaltering. "M'lady, how would you know this?"

"You're an off-worlder, here to help them." *Seirreana.* She lifted the name from the other woman's consciousness. The bitchy one who'd been "helping" Etheria heal her earlier.

Phyxe shot a look at Firiea. She cast a sideways glance at the wall behind her. The fissure had not entirely closed from when she'd exited earlier.

"These invaders are sneaking to the planet, somehow getting past the shields."

"And how does this affect us?" Seirreana asked.

She lifted an eyebrow at the one who questioned her. "Well, let's see ... they set fire to the Haven, flushed you out and stole the children. How's that for a start?" The other woman had the grace to bow her head as a dull flush rose up over her cheeks. Phyxe continued, "Right now, they toy with your warriors."

She strode further into the room. The women moved back to allow her access. She pivoted slowly, standing at her full height in the middle of the room well aware she stood taller than any female on the planet. "I am the Goddess of Fire. It is by my right and nature that I respond to all requests made of Fire. I was pulled here by a demon who haunts your planet. He did not pull me here to help, but that is what I'm going to do."

Silence.

"No questions?"

Etheria smiled at her. "No, m'lady. We know you." Her hands unfolded. "Our history goes back further than we share with the men. We know our origins and our roots, but we rarely speak of it outside our group here."

Phyxe swept a look around the room. Smiles flowed back at her. Except for Seirreana, who glared at her from lowered lids. Phyxe tilted her head and studied her for a moment. Heavier set, not as slight and graceful as the others, but then her attention was drawn elsewhere.

"We've been waiting a long time for you to visit. It has been centuries," Etheria said.

"I would think so. The universe has been too quiet for the Elementals for a long, long time," Phyxe agreed.

"Come. You can explain more of what happens topside. Let us show you the alcoves. Firiea started a fire basin for you and has kept it going for you in the chambers below since your disappearance, hoping it would draw you back."

Phyxe allowed herself to be pulled along in happy shock. They hadn't forgotten about her. Hell, they KNEW about her. They expected a female goddess, not a god. A wellspring of emotion threatened to overcome her. She wanted to cry, but such an action would honor Glacial, and she'd be damned if she'd honor the water goddess on her planet. She matched Etheria step for step through the caverns.

Mistress, shall I close the pathway?

No, you've sealed it so it cannot harm them. We'll figure a way to hide the entryway into the palace.

I will craft a hidden pathway to the control center. We will need to figure a way for the AI and I to communicate.

Wise idea, Ancient One.

They traveled down several levels, close to the lava pits below, but far enough away to avoid the heat. Phyxe bit back a gasp of pleasure as Etheria opened the chamber doors. The Matrons stood back and allowed her to enter first. Her eyes darted everywhere at once. Her heart rate accelerated to keep pace. Amber walls blended with obsidian and created the illusion of black fire. Small alcoves of flames glimmered in the walls, recessed to case and reflect the light and the flecks of gold, which danced in hidden glory in the walls. Hard floors of cooled lava stretched before her feet. The hardness suited her, yet the gemstone quality appealed to the diva in her.

"This is stunning, Etheria."

The older woman bowed and stepped forward. "Our woman are great artisans. We work with what the planet supplies us."

"You are beyond great."

And once she gifted them with the proper thanks, they would be universal renowned artisans. The Haven would become her new Primary Reflectory and the palace in Tian, her home. This would be her Home, not Sanctuary. Zhanne would have to deal.

The woman twittered in appreciation.

Etheria pushed forward and urged Phyxe further into the caverns. "We have several rooms here for you. A sleeping chamber. A fire pool with a sealed door will lead you to the lava pits. This is this receiving chamber and a prayer chamber allowing almost all of us to join you."

Phyxe stopped in the middle of the room gazed around it. "Is there anything you haven't thought of?" They'd done all this? Without her knowing? Without an actual confirmation of her powers. She was honored to her core.

"Well, if you wanted to be above ground?" She looked thoughtful for a moment.

Phyxe cast a quick look at the obsidian ceiling and shook her head. "No, this is perfectly acceptable. Firon will provide us a way to access the night and the stars, if we should feel these caverns need access above and below."

"M'lady?" Firiea stepped forward, her hands hidden deep in the sleeves of her robes, her hooded head bowed.

"Yes?" Phyxe's heart melted at the sight of the young girl. Glacial had been so much like that in her younger years, but this child was one of hers to watch over. She sensed the elemental flame at the core of her being.

"She is alive, isn't she?" the young priestess asked.

Silence descended around the room.

"If you mean is the planet sentient, or alive? Yes."

"She knows we work for her? And not against her?" Firiea looked up at her, hazel eyes wide with concern.

"Yes." Phyxe could have stumbled on the weight of her worry. It had been eons since anyone had cared so much about their planet as the people here did. First, Tru, now the Matrons, and more importantly, this one young girl. The child's worry alone would stay Phyxe's hand from destroying the realm. Her resolve hardened. She would get to the bottom of the issues here.

"And she knows we're trying our hardest to take care of her?"

"Yes."

The girl hesitated.

"Ask, Firiea." Phyxe bit back a smile. The gentleness of her tone would have shocked all who thought they knew her well.

"Then why is our water disappearing? We are not like you. We cannot exist on fire alone."

"She knows. She maintains the balance as much as she can. But the House of Marius, when they recalled everyone home, placed a shield around her, while protecting you from interstellar travel it also put her off her natural course." Phyxe wished she had a holographic map to show them, some of the women, those who'd been alive when the planet was open, they might understand. The young ones were at a loss. "Zen, please see about installing some technology down here so this can be a training area as well."

"Yes, m'lady." The voice rippled across the room from the band on her wrist. She had more items wrapped around her wrist than she ever cared to, but for now, it all worked. She'd keep the transmitter once she killed the bracers.

Those nearest her peered in curiosity at her arm. Was there nothing she could do to startle them?

"Zen is the computer intelligence running Lord Marius' domain above ground. Firon is the planet. Make sense?"

Nods greeted her question. She couldn't be sure if they were nods of understanding, or simple acceptance of whatever she had to say.

"She is going to help me install some technology to make it easier for me to train you."

"Train, m'lady?"

"Yes." She nodded. "Tru is going to train the warriors how to protect and defend you with sheer strength. I'm going to show you how to use your minds. Since strength is not your, well, strength."

Etheria frowned at her, lines marring the forehead of an otherwise smooth face. "M'lady, that seems familiar, why is there a hazy memory of something?" The old one placed her fingertips to her forehead as if it pained her.

Phyxe bit back a curse at herself. The women continued to surprise her, but now she had an uneasy feeling … first Tru, now the Matrons. Someone had tampered with memories, but how and more importantly why?

Phyxe laid a hand on the woman's temple attempting to draw the pain away. "Tru seems to be having the same issue. When you have time, you will have to tell me what you do remember of the planet being shut down. For now, if the memories do return then the learning curve won't be steep at all."

Etheria smiled, her forehead smoothing out. Her slender yet curved body quivered in delight at the fact they could work again. "We'll focus on what we do know and let the memories come as they may. Perhaps these things will help trigger their return. Let us bring your fire. We'll set your rooms up here. Your previous chambers above can serve as the gateway from the palace I'm guessing?"

Phyxe nodded, listening but lost in thought. Had Tru's father tampered with his people's memories? How would one person have that much ability unless he'd been blessed as an avatar? Even then, one of the Goddesses would have known about it. Truth be told, since it was her planet, she would have been the one to allow that kind of power to spread. She hadn't.

"Makes it easier for us to repopulate the planet's home base. The younger girls will need to be trained."

Phyxe nodded again, refocusing on Etheria. She would set Zen to researching, better to keep the AI occupied anyway.

"Only one question remains, what else would you demand of us?"

Phyxe bit the inside of her cheek. "Who would have

access to the demon's spells?"

"Demon? Spells, m'lady?"

"Yes." They never even questioned whom she meant ... Tru would be wiser to seek the counsel of his Matrons. He hadn't understood the term.

Etheria glanced around. "None of us m'lady. In my known years, we've never had a demon on Firon. We've only read about them in our studies. You rid our sands from them long before I was born."

True, so very strange there was one here now. But then, Phyxe encountered those far odder in her lifetime. "I need to know the ritual he used to bring me here."

Etheria scowled. "He used a Goddess ritual to pull you here?"

"He used something. I want to know what it was."

She nodded and spoke in whispers to a few of the girls who darted out quickly. "We will find it, one way or another."

"Thank you." Although, she still wanted to decapitate him. Painfully. Several times, over and over again once she figured out how to repeal this spell.

Tru was going to have a fit. Oh well, she hadn't revealed herself on the surface, and she'd promised she wouldn't unless he needed her. He'd never asked how she'd gotten to the palace, and she wasn't one to volunteer information. At this rate, the Ancient One was going to be riddled with pathways. If push came to shove, the Matrons in the Haven had already known she was a Goddess. So, she hadn't upset the balance of anything, but restored it. Technicalities. She could find a loophole anywhere.

"M'lady. Let me get you something to eat and drink." Firiea stepped forward as many of the others retreated to begin doing some work.

"No, I want to see the entire Haven."

Etheria smiled. "Firiea will be happy to show you every nook and cranny we have hidden. I'll return with the others to getting our work done and your research. We will all return here for meditation at sunrise."

Women bowed and retreated from the chambers. Each offered a blessing as they stepped over the threshold. Although, Phyxe noted that Seirreana's blessing was forced from her.

She would do well to watch that one. She made note of it and then moved on.

Phyxe re-situated her weapons even though she knew she wouldn't need them. After her last impromptu trip through dimensions, the one resulting in her body being flayed with a whip, she'd be damned if she'd be caught without them ever again.

"Lead on, Firiea. Let's see what else your Haven reveals."

Firiea offered a brilliant smile back at her.

Some days, it was good to be a Goddess.

❧NINE ❧

He'd only left her hours ago, with that satisfied look, but it was too long to be apart from her. His body hardened at the thought of her lips parting for his kiss, her bare skin wrapped in leather. Instead of falling back under the covers with her, he'd retreated into the dark of the desert sands. He headed to the caves where his men waited in the small underground city they'd been building, a space from which to hunt. The desert heat camouflaged their body heat. Homes left, abandoned. Their way of life had been totally uprooted and shifted. He'd had to adapt to keep them safe. Damn it all, he should have been better prepared. Hell, they'd apparently had the technology. Instead, his father had remained secretive, telling them it had been destroyed and hiding everything, and then, doing something to their memories, while making upgrades and enhancements. His head pounded every time he tried to think about it.

Enter one Fire Goddess. Suddenly, the memories were coming back to him, albeit painfully.

Her fiery eyes and porcelain skin flared to life in his mind's eye. He could feel the heat of her skin against his again. No. He forced himself to focus. He had a job to do. Gods above, he wanted a vacation. He was tired of the caves. He wanted to be back in his home in Tian. He wanted his people back in their homes.

He sat in the chair, tilting it back further on two legs, balancing on the floor of the cavern office. No, he hadn't ever uttered the fact out loud, but hell, the sheer incompetence, which greeted him upon his return, sometimes he wanted to beat his warriors senseless. Few could command. Few used their brains. So many of them wanted to fight and fight well. To see what they could pit their brawn against.

He was ready to beat them all.

He let his head drop and closed his eyes. No, gods, not true. Most, he adored and called brother. It was the few who made him want to bash heads. He would have done it too, in his younger years, when his passions ruled him more than his responsibilities. He'd gone from one extreme to the other, perhaps he needed to rethink his balance.

Hell, he could be tired. Again. Still.

"Tru?"

He opened his eyes at the familiar voice. Devos stared back at him from the doorway, tall, lanky, wiry, with dark eyes in tanned features.

"Yeah?" He dropped the chair back to the ground and rested his arms on the desk before him.

"You're far too serious about something, man." Devos ducked through the door and strode into the room, ignoring the usual protocol of requesting entry first. He'd known the man since birth. Hell, he'd been practically raised with him and Eriaku. He wouldn't ask for any others next to him in battle or planning strategy. And Devos cared less about protocol and image.

"Life sucks."

Devos laughed, his dark eyes seemed to flare red for a moment. "Yeah, pretty much sums it up."

Tru thrust his chin toward one of the chairs on the other side of the desk. "Sit. We'll plan."

"You plan far too much." Devos dropped his tall body into the chair opposite his, long legs stretching out.

"Yeah, you jump first and ask questions later." Not entirely true. Devos always had his back. He mentally shook himself wondering where the anger stemmed from.

"Gotta get it started somewhere."

Tru shook his head. "No, tell me what happened in the skirmish."

"We battled. It ended. They ran off." The warrior leaned over and pulled a knife from his boot. Sitting back, he began to clean his nails with it.

Tru glared at him.

"What?" Devos held open his hands in mock innocence, knife still firmly in place in one.

Typical, Devos. He should have known better.

Devos laughed and went back to entertaining himself with the blade. "You are too serious lately. It was five on five. Battle swords, no off-world weapons."

"But these are off-worlders."

"Yes." Devos eyebrows lifted and then forked. "They fight with grace rather than force. Our warriors are more force, but you know that."

"How the hell are they getting to our planet? Much less moving around?"

"Some come on gliders of some sort. Crude devices, no elegance to them at all." Devos kicked his feet up on the edge of Tru's desk, ignoring the raised eyebrow that hiked up at his action. "Others, well, they seem to appear and disappear. If I didn't know better, I'd say magic, but those are Matron tales. They're testing us."

"I'll refrain from the obvious comment. And get your feet off my desk." Tru rolled his eyes and sat back in his chair. He both loved and hated his best friend. Some days he wanted to kill him; others, he wanted to kick back and share a good drink. Neither ever got him far. "I still can't fathom how they're getting onto the planet."

Devos shrugged, his feet still on the desk, a lazy smile on his face. "I'm laying odds on the idea of magic. Seems more entertaining in telling of the tales."

Tru snorted. "I've been hearing stories of demons."

His second in command lifted his chin. "A demon? What the hell is that?"

"Not human. Not like us or the off-worlders. Something capable of great evil." Tru mulled over what Phyxe told him. "We're supposed to avoid his poison tipped claws."

"And you put stock in such complete and utter nonsense? Who fed you this crap?" Devos stopped cleaning his nails with his blade and stared at him.

Tru shrugged. "It doesn't matter where I got the knowledge. When you're leader, you take into account all sources."

"Yeah, my opinion used to matter." Devos put the dagger away and crossed his arms over his chest, the leather tightened, his eyebrows forked.

Tru snorted at him. "Your opinion still matters, but you and I are battle hardened. We're not scientists. We're not in tune with the magic of the planet like the histories tell us we used to be."

"No, I believe in what I can see and feel," Devos

muttered. "Well, and fire."

Tru ran his hand over his eyes before placing it flat on his desk. What he could see and feel was embodied right now in one package called Phyxe. So was the fire. But, he wasn't sure his best friend would believe there was a Goddess incarnate much less that he'd had her in his bed. Well, scratch that. He'd believe the bed part. He was Devos, after all.

Devos shot him a look. "Something up?"

"You could say," he said.

"What?" Devos asked.

"I keep seeing things, dreaming things. I went back to Tian. I have memories coming back of those days before father closed the planet off." He admitted.

"Memories? Of what?" Devos sat up a little bit straighter, his feet still on the desk.

"Technology that we used to have. There is an entire computer room behind that painting in the lower hall, the painting of my father commission after my Trials." The old man had to have done something to them. The flashes he'd been seeing were real. He knew it. If he could just remember, maybe he'd figure out a way to solve the issues for his people and the planet.

"You sure the desert heat hasn't been getting to you." Devos grinned, but it was a pained grin.

Tru cut him a look. "Right, and that sudden headache you now have randomly appeared after I'd told you."

"We wouldn't have forgotten something as important as that." Devos argued. "How did you find it anyway? The room."

"You wouldn't believe me if I tried."

Devos shrugged. "Whatever, Lord Marius."

The hand on his desk clenched. "Unfair."

"Oh, hell, you're telling me our memories have been fucked with and you're keeping something from me. So, whatever. Play lord of the manor. You want to tell me shit then tell me. You want me to function on seek and destroy, I'll do that too, but don't bullshit me."

And there was one of the reasons he'd made him his second. No questions with his friend. Of all the suspects Phyxe could have named, Devos was the furthest from a suspect as one could get.

"You wouldn't believe me," he said.

Devos dropped his feet from the desk and rolled his eyes. "You met this woman. She flies and can cook."

Tru bit back the laugh. Hell, he didn't know if she could cook or fly. She was hell in bed. And she was fire, through and through.

His friend cut him a lazy glance from his chair tilting it back on two legs. He let out a low whistle. "Oh, hell, you did meet a woman."

"Yeah, and … ?" Tru asked.

"She has nothing to do with battle."

"She has everything to do with this battle."

Devos' eyes flared and his muscles tensed—ready to leap at his best friend. "You let a *woman* help you decide strategy?"

Truant remained relaxed. He knew better. Gods love Devos, but the man had a definite idea of where a woman fell in the chain of command. He'd been burnt long ago and hadn't let it ride. She'd been gorgeous, too, but a little too calculating. Since then, the lieutenant was more the love-them-and-leave-them kind. Hell, all his warriors were. None of them needed the distraction. Let his friend come at him. He could use the brawl. He rolled his shoulders, letting himself relax even more. They hadn't fought in a long time.

"I let those with reason and knowledge help me decide on the best course of action. You know that," he said.

Devos snorted. "And apparently, getting laid helps."

Heat raced through him. How dare he belittle what had happened between them. Tru sneered back at him, a deep guttural growl. "You know nothing of this situation."

"And you're infatuated. Who's the desert dweller? She's certainly not one of our ilk? In all these years, not one of the houses could turn your head towards their daughters."

"Watch it, brother." His hands curled into the desk in front of him. Wood splintered upon contact.

"Watch what? You've been taken by some skin? By the whim of your cock?" Devos shook his head at him and leaned so his elbows rested on his thighs, clearly at peace with his harassment. "You've berated me for less."

"She is a warrior. Long in battle before us," he snapped.

"Right." Dark eyes rolled at him.

"You trespass where you shouldn't."

"As if that's stopped me before. You need a level head now, not to be ruled by some cunt," Devos sneered.

Tru launched himself out of his chair and over the desk. He hit Devos square on and toppled him from the chair landing them both on the hard cavern floor. How dare he? He knew nothing about the situation. He knew nothing about the attacks other than what he'd experienced first-hand. He took it all as play.

Devos threw both arms up to block him. He rolled them both out of the way of the furniture. Tru's arm arched up, attempted to get a hold of him and force him back. Devos shoved him and rolled to remove himself from immediate harm.

"Coward." Tru came to his feet, arms out and ready to attack again.

Devos grinned at him from his crouched position, balancing on the balls of his feet, one hand down, the other resting on his thigh. "Bring it, brother."

Tru snarled and circled him. Fire leapt inside of him. "You speak without thought."

"No, I was pretty clear with what I said." Devos nodded with a wry grin.

Tru noted how Devos' eyes tracked him. The flame seeped along his bones and spread into his muscles; it fueled him. He bent to its will. He watched Devos, could feel his pulse beat, saw it ticking on the edge of his neck. His gaze took in the slight movements betraying which way he'd move next. When his friend moved, he was a half step ahead of him.

Devos drew back in surprise as Tru met one of his attacks. "You've been practicing."

"You betray yourself."

He watched, calculated, and sidestepped Devos as he lunged. He'd sensed his movement before he'd acted. Usually, they met motion for motion. This time, Tru got ahead of himself. The air behind him shifted as Devos rushed him. He whirled and stepped to the side. Devos tumbled past him.

Tru moved back and rose to his full height and shook his head. He looked down at his hands, his body. "There is something off."

"You're telling me. I haven't been able to touch you, yet." Devos stood to his full height, casually readjusting his leathers as if they hadn't been at each other's throats.

"By now, we'd both be bruised." Tru took a deep breath, checking his body once more. Nothing different.

"Agreed. What the hell have you been doing the last few days?"

Tru cut him a half smile. "Consorting with a Fire Goddess."

"Well, hell." He shrugged and grinned. "Would rather you fuck her than a Fire God."

"Yeah, me, too." He broke into laughter.

Leave it to Devos.

Phyxe strode on as fire danced along her skin, teasing her, and tempting her through the obsidian halls as Firiea trailed behind her. The poor girl struggled to keep pace with her for the entire day taking notes and running to fetch items she needed here and there. She'd been itching for something to do, no, needed something to do. No matter how much Tru wanted her to sit still that wasn't her style.

At least she'd managed to make time to tuck Sethen and Narissa in. They'd been so happy to see her, overwhelming in their hugs, their pleas for her to stay and fall asleep with them. They needed to catch up on their sleep after their ordeal. She hadn't stayed long, although she'd wanted to. She'd tucked them in, whispered wards over them and then left. She would have set stronger safeholds in place, but she did the best she could while bound. The fire taunted her, slightly out of reach and yet under her skin. She couldn't stay and keep them safe. At least, if someone tripped the ward she'd set, she'd feel it.

She'd started out topside, where Tru had entered the caverns through the sands, and worked her way down. As she walked, she took inventory, strategized, and learned what she could to help keep the caverns safe and protected. She was certain Tru had done everything in his power to reinforce the caverns. However, it would be nothing compared to the things she could implement, and she'd be damned if she didn't add some value while she was here. Above her, corridors crossed the interiors of the volcanic mountain.

The women had made a network of homes in the underground island labyrinth and crafted areas and healing spaces for the sick. Right now, no men could be found anywhere within the Haven. Etheria informed her this was not the norm since Tru had them out training and hunting for the off-worlders. Men usually roamed freely about the caverns, leaving a few levels off limits, sacred spaces for the women. No man entered those chambers, not even Lord Marius she was told.

"Firiea." She turned her head slightly to comment over her shoulder.

"Yes, m'lady?" the eager voice piped up.

"Do you know the status of the hardware being installed in the prayer chambers?" She asked.

"I was told they'd be done within the hour."

Efficient. The women here were not only intuitive but also efficient. She liked that, respected that. Phyxe nodded and continued down the hall. She'd moved from the spaces the Matrons shared with the rest of their people to the levels where only the women were allowed. These levels housed more technology, more honors to their beliefs. Fire signs greeted her at every turn.

Her search led her to the good stuff. Phyxe smiled to herself as she sensed what lie hidden on the other side of the wall. The gliders. She palmed the door open, confident Zen controlled the technological domain no matter where it resided on the planet.

"Greetings, m'lady." The AI's voice chirped to life when she stepped through the door into the hanger.

Firiea gasped.

Phyxe cast a look at her young protégée. "The gliders or the voice?"

"Both." The girl looked around with the wide eyes of a curious cat.

"Zen, key on Firiea's voice."

"Her pattern is locked in my databanks," the AI droned.

"Thank you. Status report and inventory please." Phyxe walked across the hangar and took a visual inventory. The gliders were lightweight, elegant in their design, varied in size and littered the floor as if their riders had haphazardly landed them and left in a hurry. She glanced up around the cavern walls. There, at the top, the hint of a fissure. There was a way to reach the surface with them, and rather quickly at that.

"Fifty gliders. All in working order. All with onboard AI systems tied directly to me."

She nodded. Wise. The AI could run them with or without passengers, effectively a force doubled in battle.

"Weapons cabinets line the west walls. Devices range from bladed weapons to more advanced laser rifles and pistols," Zen continued her inventory report.

Firiea shadowed her stepping closer to a glider. The machine lit and came to life when she stepped within range.

"Good evening, m'lady." The masculine machine voice drew another gasp from the girl.

"Good evening. I did not mean to wake you." Phyxe glanced over the console as it lit, taking a quick check on the controls. Her eyes took mental pictures of the console, memorizing and theorizing how best to use the gliders if need be.

"I am never asleep," he said.

"No. I would assume not."

Firiea laughed a nervous laugh. "M'lady, you talk to it as if it were alive."

Phyxe glanced down at the petite form hovering next to her, yet a little behind her. The wide eyes were curious, yet cautious. "It is, in a sense. The AIs can reason. Depending on their programming, some can be downright human in their attitudes and responses."

"We do not have attitudes, m'lady," Zen's voice rippled across the room.

She lifted an eyebrow at Firiea.

The girl grinned back.

"Zen, I want warrior leathers for every woman in the Haven. Get rid of the desert robes. Make them form fitting and serviceable. Inventory and ration out the weapons based on height and build. There are 47 women of varying ages in the Haven, correct?"

"Yes, correct."

"Get the gliders in order and not littering the floors. This will be our training ground. We need space."

"M'lady?" Firiea's shock showed in her face.

"Yes?" Phyxe turned toward her.

"You want us to become warriors?" Shock had tightened the girl's muscles. Phyxe could see the stress beginning to radiate.

"No." She turned and took stock of the room again. "I'm going to give you the weapons to become the protectors you can be. You have smaller builds. You could not battle as I do. We will prepare a better way to fight. You will be smarter, faster, and stealthier."

Firiea bit her lip. Phyxe knew the girl was dying to say something.

"Is there a problem?" she prodded, since Firiea obviously needed it.

The girl hesitated a moment longer and then burst forth, "It is not our way."

"Exactly." Phyxe smiled.

"M'lady?" Firiea shook her head.

"First rule of fire, little one, do the unexpected."

Knowledge lit across her face and eyes as she made the connection, and Firiea nodded, rushing to catch back up with Phyxe's longer stride as she turned to make her way out of the hangar.

"You have an hour, Zen." Phyxe strode out of the hanger.

"Of course," the AI responded dryly.

Behind her gliders rose and reconfigured themselves into straight lines and created a more ordered, open space on the hangar floor. Zen's lights blinked furiously about the room.

Phyxe glanced down at the petite priestess struggling to keep up at her side. "Pass the word. The ladies have an hour to meet here. I'm going below to test the fires and will meet you back up here."

Firiea nodded and sprinted off ahead of her, her robes kicked up as her legs carried her down the hall.

Phyxe smiled. He'd told her to stay hidden. He was going to be surprised how well hidden she stayed.

❧TEN❧

"What are you doing?" The deep baritone voice whispered across her inner ear.

Phyxe stood encased in flames and her body lit higher when he spoke. He'd been so quiet. She'd begun to wonder if he'd remembered the transmitter. She slid fiery hands up her naked form, gliding over her hips and across her abs ... reaching up and trailing over her breasts, lifting and flowing thru her hair before dropping back to her sides. Her head tilted back, and she let the flow of fire roll down over her body. Texture, skin, warmth. The fire pit the Matrons crafted her in the new rooms was far more sturdy than the basin she'd bathed in earlier.

"Bathing," she whispered back.

Silence.

"Cat got your tongue, warrior?"

"Naked in the flames again, are you?" His voice sounded rough in her ear.

She bit one side of her lip, the corner lifted in a smile. "Is there any other way to be?"

"For you, no?" The heat in his words ripped over her, causing cracks and fissures, sparking.

"Come back and join me." Flames slid over her skin, but the thought of Tru joining her sent the fire higher and hotter. She trailed a hand over her abdomen wishing it were his strong hand instead. She wanted the texture of his skin closer to hers. Skin on skin would be divine.

"Trying to kill me, aren't you?" he rebuked her.

She sensed his laughter under the growl, but she shivered in the flames nonetheless. Goosebumps broke out across her body.

"I'll protect you."

Fire licked up her backside and teased her sensitive skin as visions of sex on the control center floor seeped into her mind. She lit higher, flames trembled around her, taunting her, elevating and moving closer to the ceiling.

"I'll keep that in mind for the future, Red. Are you staying out of trouble?" He sounded as though he were forcing himself under control, even across the transmitter. His breathing was heavy.

"I'm bathing, how much trouble can I be?" She licked her lip and arched her body, letting the flames flow along her skin, soothing the goose bumps.

"Loaded question."

"Hey, you left me on my own." The fire caressed her, as she reacted more to the images. Her body flared. Gods, she wanted him. "Come play with me."

She wished she had full control of her powers. She'd have pulled him to her. She floundered as though she were in her first century and learning all she could do. Her body was practically humming at her. She never hummed. Maybe a purr or two.

"I can whisper in your ear, Red," he murmured. She could feel the fire in his tone ... it was reaching him, too, but then she hit the wall. "There is too much going on here for me to leave."

"More battles?" She lifted a hand and allowed the flicker of flame to dance along her fingertips. She watched it, entranced by the way the light moved across her hand.

"No, we hunt them now."

A smile of satisfaction crossed her face as the flame snaked down her arm. "Good, better to be the hunter than the hunted."

"You sound as if you speak from experience."

She flipped the fire from one arm to the other as it lifted, relishing this ability to play since she could when she was outside the flame. "You don't want to hear the tales of my being the one hunted, warrior. They are not pretty stories."

The anger in him blazed causing the fire around her to surge.

"They dared to hurt you?" he snarled in her ear.

She pushed the flames back and imagined them encasing him with her. She could do so much more in full power, but now, she would do what she could. She was untouchable, unless she allowed it. Even with these damn bracers. She was Fire. "Many have tried. None have succeeded."

"I'm surprised if you let any of them live to tell about it." As quick as that, his mood changed and his laughter flowed into her ear.

"Some did. Many didn't. I wasn't patient in my youth." She frowned as the images of her past flashed through the flames. Fire, wrath, pain, destruction, she shook them off. He was quicksilver tonight. Fire must be spreading along his body as well hers.

"Were any of us?" His pain wrapped around her through the link.

"You didn't want to talk, warrior, did you?" she purred. She refused to think about what had hurt him, her. Now was not the time. She could do nothing outside of the now. And for now, the flames stoked her inner heat. She wanted to play.

"Talk is all we have. I need to leave for the next hunt. We've covered a quarter of the quadrant," he muttered. She sensed him picking up on her energies, yet fighting them. Voices grew closer to him, whispers coming over the link. She knew he was no longer alone.

"All work and no play." She sensed his grin.

"Makes us one step closer to getting rid of the off-worlders."

She stuck her tongue out at him knowing full well he couldn't see her. He needed to lighten up some. She wanted him with her, in the fire. Damn it, she wanted another release ... something that sent them both over the edge rather than focusing on this alien invasion. If she'd been in her full power, she'd have ejected them all and set up sanctuary.

But she couldn't. She let the fire lick her. "Go then, hunt with the warriors. I'll go back to behaving."

His sigh stretched across the link. "That's what I'm afraid of."

"Night, night, warrior." She clicked off his pathway. If he didn't want to play with her and wouldn't let her play, let him stew. She had women to train. This heat was distracting her, and if he didn't want to fix that, then he had other things to get done. And once she was done, she was conducting a hunt of her own.

Fire style.

Tru groaned and took a deep breath of desert air. He tried to let the cool, crisp night soothe the heat that had built during their conversation. His hands clenched when she shut off communications. He'd come out to be alone on the dunes. He should have known better than contact her, but he hadn't been able to stop himself.

He lifted his hand and toyed with the idea of crushing the communicator. Then he could be sure he wouldn't fall into temptation. He knew full well she hadn't stayed out of trouble. Dropping his hand, he refrained from destroying his only link with her. Damn it, he knew she was going to cause a ruckus and then not be around to deal with the results. When things were back under control here, she'd leave. He knew it.

He shook his head. All these years of fighting must be getting to him. How could he expect less from her? She was used to being in the middle of things, fixing things. As far as she was concerned, this was her planet as Fire Goddess. He may still be struggling with the idea, but when he'd asked her to remain hidden and stay quiet, he'd known he was asking a lot. Regardless of how the women in his world were viewed or behaved ... she was a doer.

Like he was.

"Gods," he muttered to himself.

He'd have ignored the request, no, the demand he'd made, and he knew it. He had to respect she worked within the confines of his decree. It was how she worked within them that had his internal radar going off.

He closed his eyes for a few moments, allowing his body to relax into the sands.

"You look sad, my son." Gisele Marius' voice was soft and modulated, flowing over him as she stepped out on the palace balcony next to him. "You should be enjoying the party your father put on for your graduation."

Tru cast a glance over his shoulder at the streaming masses of people on the dance floor of the grand ballroom behind and below them. "They're getting along fine without me, probably more so, Mother."

She tsked at him and stepped closer, resting her white gloved hands on the cool marble barrier that kept them both from stepping over the edge and tumbling down into the pool or the stone patio beneath them. Couples milled about in the warm night. His father had outdone himself, or his assistant had. Tiny lights glimmered in the pool, floating about the water, creating an ambiance of softness that normally wasn't there. Matching strands of lights dangled from each of the trees creating a mini-wonderland in the dark night of the desert.

He glanced over at her. Three hundred years into her life and the woman was still a vision. Long dark hair, upswept tonight when she usually wore it down, but this way allowed her ladies to lay gemstones in her hair so she sparkled whenever she turned. She had no need for a crown tonight. The way they'd laid out her hair, it looked as though the crown glittered iridescently in her dark hair. Smooth skin, flawless even without makeup, but, again, tonight, her lids and cheeks sparkled with a multitude of colors and shimmers.

"I'm surprised Father let you from his side with as beautiful as you look tonight." Tru smiled at her. Truth be told, she was a gorgeous woman, makeup and gemstones or not. His mother had always moved as if the world was a dance and she merely a dancer in it. And, his father rarely left her side ... he knew it wasn't due to overprotectiveness as so many claimed, the man loved his wife.

She laughed. "Oh, he didn't. He never does, but the guards were kind enough to wait at the edge of the balcony." She winked at him. "I believe they think you can take well enough care of me."

He laughed with her. If he couldn't protect her, then he had no right being next in line to the throne. The desert only allowed the strongest to survive and rule. He'd braved the Blood Hills Trials and the Fire Pits, and made his way to the other side of the Energy Fields in the last week. It was required by all in his line to tackle the harshest area of their planet once their academic studies were done. So while the party his Father hosted below was for his academics, most came to recognize him as their next leader and celebrate his victory in surviving the

Trials.

Truth, he'd rather be holed up in his rooms relaxing after it all rather than being ushered directly into the baths and ceremonial clothes. After the week he'd had, he wasn't as fond of the ceremonial clothes as he'd once been.

"You're not enjoying your party, Tru," his mother scolded.

He glanced up at the stars in the night sky. "I wasn't expecting to return home to this and have to fend off every eligible daughter, and some not so eligible, on the planet."

His mother turned to look back over the throng of people dancing. Her white silk dress swishing as she turned. "None catch your eye?"

Tru smirked. "They are all beautiful, mother. We don't breed ugly people."

One of the reasons they had so many off-worlders were planet-side lately. They flocked to see the women perform their elaborate plays and dances. He laid his hand on the sword strapped to his side. "The daughter from Creeyal clearly the epitome of their blond locks and lean lines." He nodded to the far left. "Therill's daughter, her olive complexion is of the finest shade. While Ipisilon's family has produced a line of dark-haired, doe-eyed beauties."

"And, yet, not a one calls to you?" She asked pulled him forward with her back into the palace. "Any one of them would bring grace and beauty and intelligence into our home."

"I'm sure they would, Mother." He sighed. His trip through his Trial had changed something in him. No longer the carefree prince thirsting for knowledge, for fun, for power. Firon had shown him a different path than the one he'd been set on before, things to add to his being and that of his people. As for a wife, whom he had to protect and shelter? He wasn't ready for that, yet. He felt there was something more he needed to focus on, something more he needed to be doing.

She laid a hand on his arm. "Good for you. Don't let him force you into a match you don't want. You know he'll try it. I've worked to keep him at bay with it, giving you time to grow, pass your Trial, let Firon reveal your path on her planet, not his. You're different than he is Tru, and as much as I love your Father, that is a good thing."

"Mother?" Tru couldn't keep the shock from his voice. His mother never spoke out against his father, instead kept to the shadows and quiet. He knew they talked about planetary issues, but never out in the open and always one on one. It was her way of participating in their planet's rule, but allowing his father the semblance of sole power. Tru might not agree with it, but that was the way it had always been. Sole rulership, male.

"You are your own man, Truant Dare Marius. Don't let him run over you. I love him. I always have. So, I have worked to make our lives balance for the best of his leadership, but don't think for one minute I let him walk all over me." She smiled and it radiated into her eyes. "We have our own battles. I have elected to never have them in public, for the better of the people. You may find your rule will flow differently." She tilted her head and looked at him, pursing her lips. Her gaze grew hazy for a moment. "Your match isn't here. She won't be for quite awhile, but you'll be ready for her. And Firon will need her."

Her gaze sharpened immediately as lights lit up the palace. Laser fire ripped across the floor. Screams echoed all around them, and Gisele's guards raced towards them. Tru moved his mother behind him, trying to draw them both closer to the wall nearest the balcony.

"M'lord!" a guard cried out, a firing arm angled in his hand. "Behind you!"

Tru turned, but it was too late. The shot fired over the balcony, ripping through his mother and into his side. He turned in time to catch her before they crashed onto the floor. Somewhere, in slow motion, he registered the blood red stain on her gown, the shocked look in her eyes and the fire racing through his body where the laser tore a hole in his side.

"Mother!" he cried out.

"We have her m'lord. Let us get her to safety so the Matrons can help heal her. They're waiting below. Your team is right behind us," the Captain of his mother's guard spoke as he gently pulled the woman up into his arms. The other guard kept them covered.

"She's so still." He hesitated.

The guard nodded. "She breathes. She dropped herself into a healing state as she's been trained to do, as all our women are. Let us get her to safety."

"I see you couldn't just have a quiet party like normal noblemen," Devos drawled from the shadows of the balcony. Aiming his gun, he offered his own blend of fire power back at the invaders. Six men, half of his personal warrior guard, appeared silently around him. They bore down on Tru, determined to offer their aid and protection.

Tru unholstered his laser and nodded at his mother's guard. "Get her to safety and get word to my father. My team and I will be taking care of this issue."

Tru ripped off his jacket, dropping the white coat to the corner of the floor and re-holstered his sword and scabbard across his back. His chest was bare except for the slight laser graze to his side. He ignored the graze of the laser threatening his side. It wasn't a mortal wound, barely a nick. He didn't need the white giving him away in the night. Many of his warriors followed suit.

"We should probably invest in laser-proof suits." Devos cut a glance at his wound. "Looks like you'll live though."

Tru snorted. "Lived through a lot worse. Let's get these guys and explain what we do to uninvited guests."

As one they nodded and slinked out into the shadows. They hid in the desert night amongst the sand dunes where no body should be able to hide, least of all men of their size. Each one pulled the power of the desert around them, blending and fading into the darkness. Other shadows moved in to join them.

Devos stuck to Tru's side. He knew it was only because he'd been injured. Otherwise, his brother in arms would have made a flying leap over the balcony rather than sticking to the shadows. Devos always had a death wish which never seemed to acknowledge him.

Tru signaled the men, hand signals that only those born of the desert could see and interpret. His men flowed out and around the courtyard. His father's guards would take care of those inside the palace. Tru and his elite team maintained a wild card status. They answered to none other than him. Their schedules and training set by him. He'd spent years researching training methods throughout the galaxy and the results crafted and honed in those with him.

He glanced around the courtyard walls. Seven, he counted. His gaze cut to Devos who nodded in return. Seven off-worlders for his twelve warriors. No match. Shadows moved across the walls, scaling heights most men would fear. Not his team. They'd trained for this. He'd set about making sure they could adapt to anything thrown at them. Each just as schooled in knowledge and training as he was. Each completely capable of stepping into his command, yet none wanting to do so.

Each ready to behead the one who'd harmed his mother.

A wicked grin crossed his face ... time to die, this desert held no mercy.

The fight faded from his sight, grew hazy and dim. His sight sharpened as he entered the palace, dirty, bloodied, torn.

"Sir?" The Captain of his father's guard greeted him as he and his team entered the doors. None lost on his part, invaders dead or gone.

"Report, sir," Tru lashed out. His body demanded rest and fuel—not necessarily in that order.

"Your father is in the war room waiting for you. Baths and clothes have been prepared for your team." The captain nodded at the rest of his men, who waited until Tru gave a hand signal.

Devos stayed by his side. The captain frowned at him. "Orders were just the Prince, Lord Devos."

"Suck it. Last time I left him alone, he ended up wounded. You'll do well to remember that I have no soul right now." Devos smiled at the Captain who seemed to back away without moving.

"I'll leave it to Lord Marius to explain your departure." The captain withdrew and allowed them both to pass.

Tru cast a glance over at his brother in arms. "Do you purposely make them not like you?"

"I don't like them," Devos drawled.

"And people wonder why you're my second," Tru commented.

"I am your second because I believe in you. As the eldest of Fintar, I have every right to challenge you if I feel you're unfit. But Firon knows, I don't like people, so setting me up to lead would be the worst idea possible." Devos grinned back at him.

"Far too true." Tru laughed as he pushed open the door to the war room. His smile died at the sight of his father, seated at the head of the table, tears in his eyes.

"Father?" He stopped, his hand outstretched to stop Devos from advancing before him. He needn't have bothered as the warrior hesitated, just out of sight.

"She's gone, my son," was all Riske Marius said. The man's hands clenched on the war table before him.

Tru growled and strode into the room. A part of him realized Devos stayed behind; his foot lodged into the door just enough to allow him listening privileges. If any other had tried it, Tru would have had his head.

"She was taken when her guards tried to get her to the Matrons. The two of them were descended upon in the upper east wing. Her guards report her breathing was labored after the shot to her lungs. In all likelihood, she's gone." His father scowled at the table before him. He took a deep breath. "This will not go unpunished."

"We'll find her, Father. If she was taken, it was for a specific reason. Ransom, negotiation. Yes, she was shot, but it wasn't a fatal shot. Her guards were wrong. It missed her lungs. I was there. I saw where she was shot but to the side of her heart and lungs," Tru said. It had hit him on his lower left side. To do so, it had to have gone through her chest, but the very edge the way he'd been hit.

He'd never seen his father cry and was thrown off balance ... was his mother really gone, or did his old man only think so?

"Wherever she is, she is no longer here. I can't sense her. That means, to me, she's gone." His father shuddered and took a deep breath.

"Father, no!" Tru bolted across the room, taking a seat by the old man's side. Out of the corner of his eye, he noted the door didn't fully shut. Devos. "She's not gone until we see her still."

"No son, you don't understand, but you will when you find the other half of your soul. You will sense it." Lord Riske Marius bowed his head, leaning down into the table before him ... another shudder raced through his body. Then, he took a deep breath, and lifted his head. "Call them all home. Every warrior. We will fix this."

"Yes, sir." Tru stood and turned to stride out of the room.

"You won't understand my reasoning, but eventually you might. Call them home, son." His father's voice resonated at his back. "We have a realm to fix."

His back tightened, but he didn't turn around. Instead, he marched forward, not even acknowledging when Devos kicked the door open for him.

He shook himself, coming back to reality.

"Talking to yourself?" Devos' voice swept out of the night as Tru stood up and trudged to the top of the dune.

He stepped up next to his second in command. Darkness yawned before them. The moon shimmered down on the night sands. The desert glistened under the light of the full moon. The stars shown brightly, sparkling gems in the black velvet sky.

"No."

"A man wandering in the darkness of the sands talking out loud is talking to himself."

"It could appear so." His gaze fixed on the gliders appearing below.

Only ten darted across the sounds now, sweeping in patterns over the rolling sands. Their training was going well. The older warriors picked up with their skills from where they'd left off before the gliders were hidden. Some even returned to the same AIs as they had before. Tru still only had vague and faint murmurings of his memory about all the technology. Had it been so long ago? Where had his memories gone? The younger warriors were delighted with the technology and sprinted across the sands racing each other and conducted mock battles as they could.

Devos snorted. "You're getting cryptic in your old age. One would think I was rubbing off on you."

Tru cut him a glance, a smile broke out across his face. "Scary."

"Or educational." Devos grinned back.

Tru turned serious. "Send them out on searches. I want the invaders found. If need be, have the AIs run the gliders and put the men on the ground."

Devos nodded and issued a series of whistles. The men turned from their practice and play and spread out across the desert, blended with the night.

"I'll be back at daybreak. Have the AI transmit any findings if you need me."

Tru sensed the dark eyes of his brother on him as he descended.

Some things, a man had to work out for himself.

Gaian cursed as she landed on the balls of her feet on solid earth. The last teleport had been an unpleasant one. A ripple had passed through her when she moved through the universal energies. She took a few moments to let her energies level out.

She remained in the crouched position and gathered her wits. For a moment, she allowed the tiger within her to stretch to the surface. She listened in the darkness for any sounds. Her head lifted, and she sniffed at the air.

Night time smells. Orchids. A smile crossed her face. She loved the scent of orchids.

In a fluid movement, she rose to her feet, her body weight balanced.

She should be used to the landing now. This was the fourth planet on her list. She'd even selected a remote place on purpose. She'd scared a few inhabitants on the last planet when she'd materialized out of nowhere. In lands where gods and goddesses had long been forgotten, where technology reigned supreme, she'd been hounded with questions.

It wasted too much time. This way suited her much better. Land, get a feel of the place, determine whether human or animal form would suit her search better, and then trek around the planet to see if she could find any hint of Phyxe.

Lather, rinse, repeat.

She should find a safe place to sleep and regenerate, but Zhanne grew restless with the sisters out of balance. The Goddess of Energy was maintaining the harmony by allowing the fire in her nature to flare to balance the rest of them while they hunted. And the repercussions of her doing so was something they could all do without. With the fire flaring through her, she was actually bitchier than Phyxe. At some point, they would all need to rebalance themselves.

So far with this scouting mission, she'd gotten nowhere. From the reports, her sisters were faring no better with the paths they used to search. Nothing in the galaxies. Zilch. No signs. No hint. No trail. Gaian allowed her gaze to narrow and determine a trail to the nearest town. From the outskirts, she would watch and wait, then she would hunt.

The long blade of her sword settled securely against her back, and she flipped her hooded cloak up over her head. Better to remain as hidden as she could for a while. She'd encountered too many varying responses on the other fire planets she'd landed.

At least they were habitable, so far. She wasn't looking forward to landing in anything hot.

❧ELEVEN ❧

Phyxe watched the women move through the drills as she'd shown them. Some balked at the leathers, far too used to their gowns and flowing clothes, but most came around when they realized the freedom of movement they had in the new clothes. A few were modest enough to want longer coverings for their torsos, and she'd conceded to allow them more comfort. Overall, the women's smaller desert forms barely had a spare ounce of fat on them. Lean desert living cured them of any issues.

"Again," she commanded.

They moved as one through the motions she'd shown them a few minutes before. She lifted a brow. "Either you ladies have done this before, or there is something you're not telling me."

Firiea smiled at her from her place in the front row. "We are trained dancers, m'lady. While we may not have the force you want, we do have the coordination."

She laughed. "Hell, most people can't get the coordination to save their lives. The focus and force will come."

"M'lady," the AI's voice washed over the room.

"Yes, Zen?" Phyxe asked.

"Lord Marius approaches. He'll be here within the hour."

So much for him surprising her. She grinned at herself. Still, he disrupted her training. She glanced over at Firiea.

"Young one, come here," she said.

The women ceased their exercises upon hearing the AI's comment about Lord Marius.

Firiea dropped from the troupe and approached. The others fell in around them.

Phyxe wasn't sure if what she wanted to try would work. She wasn't sure of the limits the bracers put on her.

But, she needed to try.

"Etheria, bring me a flame." She dipped her head to the eldest woman. The matron lowered her head and did as she was bid, bringing forward a torch from the basin they'd brought into the hangar.

"I am going to try something. It may or may not work," she cautioned.

"Yes, m'lady." Firiea gazed back at her, acceptance and trust radiating in her eyes.

"I don't think it will hurt. It never has in the past. But, in this instance, I am unsure."

"The bracers ..." The girl nodded to them.

"Yes. Do you still want me to try what I'd like to do?"

"I am your servant, m'lady." She bowed her head.

Phyxe hated the word, but she'd cope. She nodded and cast a glance at Etheria.

"You have the final say here. This is your Haven."

"We are yours, m'lady." The elder held the flame forth, her arm strong and sure.

She took a deep breath. The women around them stood in silent support. They trusted her. They honored her. She was touched and unusually nervous at the same time.

"Hold the flame steady then between us," she said.

Etheria did as she was bid. The torch lowered between them as they stood barely a foot from each other.

"Firiea, what I am about to do is going to elevate you beyond this space and time," Phyxe warned.

"Yes, m'lady." The girl's eyes were wide, but steady.

"Etheria will be your guide. She is your Matron."

"Yes, m'lady," she said.

"All here in presence will be affected in some manner, but not to the same intent as you. You will be the first. But, I will remind you, your elders are still your Elders."

"Yes, m'lady."

Phyxe was impressed. The girl's voice remained strong and sure. At Etheria's nod, she raised her hand and reached into the flame. The flames licked her skin and caressed her with their warmth.

"Let this fire cleanse and bless." Phyxe swept her hand through the flames.

Whispers echoed around the room, repeating her

phrase.

"Let this fire transmute and change." The flame danced in her palm.

Again, the whispers followed suit.

"Let this offering bring knowledge and power." The fire flared higher.

Whispers.

"With this fire, I offer the power of Fire. Let the elements of change pass the power of Fire from me to you." She cupped her hand, fire flaring, licking her skin, yet stopping at the bracer. She nodded as Firiea began to lift her hand. "Bring your hand into the flame with mine."

Quiet descended. With bated breath, the women watched as one.

Firiea's hand remained steady as she lifted it upwards. Her only hesitation was at the edge of the flame when the heat began to lick her skin.

"You cannot hesitate as the First Priestess of Fire." Phyxe locked eyes with Firiea.

Determination lit Firiea's gaze. The girl swallowed and her hand pushed forward into the flames. Gasps echoed around the room as the fire leapt forward to caress the girl, encasing her body, flame licking around her, through her, and over her but not burning her.

Phyxe breathed a sigh of relief as the flame accepted her. She'd been worried it would burn rather than birth.

Firiea stared in wonder at the flames caressing her skin. "It does not hurt."

"No, it never will." From this point forward, fire of any kind would accept the Firon child as one of her own.

"You have blessed me, m'lady," she whispered and turned her hand over to watch the flame dance along her skin.

"You have a good soul. You will lead well after Etheria. She will be your guide, your education when I'm gone."

"M'lady?" Her eyes lifted in worry.

"I gave you the Fire. I can tell you how I learned to control it. You are my ... avatar ... here. Not my full powers, but those which I can share." Phyxe gazed down at her, proud that the young one had been accepted so well. Others had not fared as well.

Firiea nodded and watched as the flames curled up

her arm and ever so slowly dissipated into her skin.

"The blessing can be passed on now as well. Each woman who wishes may step forward to share in the fire. Those that do not wish do not have to do so." Phyxe turned and offered the flame.

Etheria spoke up, "I have only a few years left, m'lady. But I, too, would accept this blessing." She handed the torch to Firiea, so she could take her place, next in line.

The others lined up behind Etheria all nodding as one. Tears welled in her eyes. It had been eons since she'd been so accepted, since she'd been able to share herself so well with people.

"Then step forward and reach into the flame."

One by one, each woman in the Haven stepped forward. The scene unchanging as the fire reached out and accepted each and every one of them when they offered themselves into her service. Only Seirreana hesitated, the fire pulled back before reaching out and finally accepting her, too. Phyxe frowned, but refrained from saying anything. The fire blessed her, but that could be both a blessing and a curse. She would keep a careful watch on that woman.

Mistress.

The women around her gasped as the voice of the planet echoed through them all.

Well, hell, there was an unexpected outcome. *Yes, Ancient One.*

Why can I now hear more of you?

Because I have brought your caretakers to you. You can communicate directly with them now. They are yours, and mine.

"M'lady?" Firiea stared at her.

Phyxe turned back to her First Priestess. "Yes?"

"She is alive?"

"Very much so. And very appreciative of all those here have done for her."

Murmurs swept through the group. They began to test their abilities with the flame. Etheria still held the fire in her hand.

"Your first lesson is to learn to spark a flame in your hand." She smiled at them. "For now, we'll let the Ancient One learn to communicate with each of you on her own."

"M'lady?"

Phyxe turned to Etheria.

"Thank you," the Matron whispered. "We'd lost her, so long ago."

She nodded at the elder's bow. "You are more than welcome. She'll welcome you back, but I'd be careful around the men."

"Of course." The Matron smiled back at her. "He draws nearer."

"Then I will leave you ladies here to practice while I sidetrack your resident leader." She winked at the laughter flowing around the room. She was impressed a few of them could already spark a flame with nothing more than their hands and sheer willpower.

They'd be a formidable bunch when the time came. She hoped they'd have time to learn a little more about what she'd gifted them with. Otherwise, she'd be racing around and putting out fires.

Tru strode through the strangely silent corridors of the Haven wondering where they'd all gone. It was rare he didn't encounter a single woman in his transit of the Haven. He hadn't arrived during the dinner hour. And, hell, the Haven wasn't that big. Were they all below in the women's only area? It wasn't a festival or prayer time. He frowned.

"Looking for something, warrior?" Phyxe leaned up against the corridor wall when he rounded the corner to her suites. Her fiery hair glinted in the dark light of the hall. Her body glistened with the faint shimmer of sweat from her workout.

"Someone. The halls are too quiet." He gazed at her. His body heated higher than it had already been.

"They're in prayer. Something they do quite frequently I'm told." She smiled at him.

He cocked his head at her; his entire body hardened. In prayer? Yes, it was part of their daily cycle, but at this hour of the night? He knew he'd made insane time across the sands, but still, it was late. Someone should be guarding the entryway into the Haven. Of course, that someone should be a warrior or two, but they'd all been detailed to the sands and the search. He shouldn't expect the Matrons to post a guard. He'd have to detail a few warriors to return and keep them safe.

"You do not join them?" he asked.

"They have no need of me." She continued to smile a soft smile at him.

That soft smile bothered him. Something in her tone hinted at fun and mischievousness, yet her eyes remained direct and fixed on him.

"You apparently were hunting tonight." She slid her hand up her side.

He couldn't have stayed away. Something in her called out to him, pulled him back to her. He'd grown antsy in the hours they'd been apart. He should be focused on the search, on finding the satellites. Instead, he wanted nothing more than the hard length of their bodies blended together, of matching wits and words with her. If he thought he could get away with it, he'd drag her across the sands with him.

"You were taunting me on purpose." He groaned, feeling the fire of attraction flare through him. Damn her. He couldn't control his body's response, every cell responded to her. He would cut off his arm before leaving her. This was beyond ridiculous. She was somehow becoming a part of him.

"Me?" Her amber eyes widened at him.

"Yes, you."

"Poor warrior. All pent up frustration and no one to take it out on." Phyxe teased him. She slowly moved backwards, down the hall behind her.

"You want to play in the hallway?" he asked her, thinking he was ready to pull her to him against the hard obsidian wall.

"No, I have something far warmer in mind," she whispered with a slight smile.

Warmer? He wasn't sure his body could tolerate being much warmer than he already was.

"Follow me, warrior." She turned and led him down the hall, deeper into the Haven.

Tru followed her steps, his eyes drawn to the subtle sway of her hips. She made walking erotic. Her long, lean legs moved confidently through the darkness. His body hardened as he pictured plunging into her soft core again, the heat of her body surrounding his. He glanced up, guiltily when her amused chuckle floated back to him. Her amber eyes glimmered in the darkness. He reached up and ran a hand through his hair.

"What?" He lifted an eyebrow at her.

Her eyelids dropped and then rose again slowly before she turned back to her lead down the hallway. "You give yourself away, warrior."

"Yes, but only to you." He reached out and snagged her around the waist. She squealed in mock horror and turned into him. Their bodies hit muscle for muscle. Tru spread his hand against the bare skin of her naked back. Her breasts crushed into him and threatened to spill from their tight top.

"You are addictive," she murmured as he stared into her upturned face.

"I think I could grow accustomed to being your addiction. I'm certainly thinking of you with every spare second I have."

His chest swelled with the revelation. He'd cared about no one on an emotional level for so long. This fascination and attraction startled him. Something about her pulled at him, physically and mentally. She was power. She was tough. She was a sounding board. She was caring and kindness. She was nothing of his world, yet all of it. And he had no idea where it was all going. Long ago, he'd learned to accept things as they came. This should be no different. He hadn't planned on her, hadn't factored her into his realm.

"You're thinking too much, warrior." She lifted a hand to trace the worry lines in his brow.

"Part of my nature." He pulled her tighter into him, wanting to feel every inch of her body, needing it.

"Ah, let it go. Come play with me. Relax. Feel." She stepped back and pulled him through the doors. He didn't even glance around the room, trapped instead in the fire in her eyes. Her gaze was hypnotic. He knew it, yet still he let himself be trapped. Power swelled up. She allowed nothing into her gaze but him. He was honored. Her gaze never strayed.

"I can do nothing with you but feel. My body can't help itself and my mind ... follows where you lead."

"Ah, then let me lead for the moment, warrior. Learn

to relax in the moment," she whispered, pulling him closer.

He allowed her to tug him further into the chamber. From the corner of his eye, he saw soft couches and floor pillows littering the room. The temperature hiked from the elegantly appointed fire pit cast in the center of the room. Flames flickered from the center, neither flaring too high or too low.

"First, the clothes must go." She smiled as she kicked off her boots and shoved them to the side. Her hands lifted to her hips and settled on the edge of the leather pants. She shimmied and tugged them down over lean legs.

Tru swallowed, hard, as her soft pale skin appeared inch by inch. She was glorious naked or clothed. He wanted to reach out and caress the leg where she'd tugged the leather from, but she lead.

"Like what you see, warrior?" She lifted an eyebrow at him.

"Never a question." His eyes never strayed from her.

Her smile softened, her hands reached up and unclasped her top. The leather spilled from her body. Her breasts burst forth from their constraint. She stood at ease in her naked beauty.

"Physical perfection," he breathed. His body begged to be released from the confines of his clothes.

"In your eyes." She smiled and stepped closer. Her hand fluttered around his body to work his clothes from his tired, dusty body. He wrapped his larger hands around hers.

"In all eyes." With a few quick flips, his shirt dropped from his body and pooled at his feet.

Phyxe ran her hands over his naked chest as he stepped out of his boots and struggled to undo his pants. Her nearness made it difficult for him to maneuver around him. She seemed to want to be everywhere at once. She bit her lip and stared up at him through half lowered lashes when he was as naked as she was.

"What?" He saw the question in her eyes.

"I like your form, warrior," she murmured.

He grinned and crushed her to him again. "A good thing."

She purred as his lips crashed onto hers. He wasn't

going to be denied this first kiss. He'd wanted to pull her into his arms when he first saw her in the hallway. He needed to feel her in reality and not as a figment of his imagination. Phyxe met him kiss for kiss. Her soft lips soft yielded under the harshness of his need. Her arms wrapped around his neck and pulled herself into him.

"With me, warrior." She broke the kiss and backed up across the room.

Tru warmed as she neared them both to the fire. His body reveled under the heat. Liquid desire wrapped around him and stole across his conscious.

❧TWELVE ❧

Phyxe stepped back. One more foot and she'd be on the hot rocks of her flame, which continually burned in the Sanctuary. She had no idea if he'd be able to tolerate the flame. She'd never even thought to bring someone into the full flame with her, to share herself in such a manner, but desire moved within her. She needed him to feel the heat as she did. She took the last step. Her gaze locked on his. Her fingers trailed soft circles along the bare skin of his arms. He was warm, but not unduly so.

She watched as he hesitated. His hazy gaze sharpened when the flames flared up to welcome her.

"Come with me, warrior. Feel." Fire licked across her skin and moved out and flowed along his forearm. His arm tightened in amazement as the flames caressed him rather than burned. Wanton warmth curled within her and leapt through the flames. Tru's eyes flared open, and he sucked in a deep breath before his eyes dilated. The flames welcomed him.

"It does not burn." She watched him watch the fire caress his skin. He turned his hand over. The flames flowed over his palm and around his fingers.

"Not in the way you're used to it burning, but it will burn." She crooked her index finger at him and urged him forward. He needed to be in the flames with her. She wanted them to burn together. He could play with the fire later. Right now, she wanted him playing with her.

Amazement and wonder deep in his eyes, he looked away from his hand and back at her. Desire flared as his gaze landed on her. The heat elevated another notch as his body lit. He stepped forward, confident in his nakedness. Confident in the fire. When he stepped into the flames, her arms curled around him pulling her to him again. Her breasts crushed into his chest. Her body liquefied when they met inch for glorious naked inch. His cock was thick

138

and hard against her stomach. Her nipples pearled and hardened where they crushed into him.

"You could have warned a person." His tone harsh, but still lit with wonder.

"I've never tried it before," she whispered up at him. Her body nestled against his.

He dwarfed her, making her feel slight next to him in the flames, an unusual yet heady feeling. A warrior strong enough to handle the flame and met her skill for skill. Her heartbeat accelerated watching his eyes trail over her face. His mouth hit hers in a hard kiss as he demanded and yielded nothing. She matched him strength for strength, groaning when his lips commanded. Hers stepped up to the challenge. A growl of satisfaction passed between them, their lips parted under the onslaught, and their tongues taunted and caressed each other.

Phyxe ran her hands down the hard planes of his back. She enjoyed the texture of the fire warming his skin. Awareness ripped up her body when his hand splayed across the small of her back and locked her against him even tighter. The flames danced around them in a fiery veil. She gasped when his hand tangled in her hair and pulled her head back, neck exposed. Satisfaction ricocheted through her as his lips trailed fiery kisses down her neck. Her fingernails dug deep into his back. Her hips slid even tighter against him.

Fire swirled around them, between them, shielded them from the world.

His hand dropped from the small of her back and reached down to cup the cheek of her ass. He lodged her against his hard length. Phyxe groaned again and reached one hand down to caress him, her fingers trailed the length of him with exquisite slowness. She kept her touch light at first, testing, teasing. She loved the feel of hard and soft. Her hand curled around him. His hand stroked the curve of her hip and slid between her thighs.

"If you're going to play ..." he murmured and dipped his head to a breast. His tongue swirled around an already hard nipple.

She arched up into him as his finger slid slowly inside of her. Her breast filled his mouth. Liquid shivers swept up from her core. She'd thought the fire made her hot. He caused the heat to sweep over her in waves. Her hand tightened around him.

"If this is play," she panted. "I'd hate to see us get serious."

He drew his hand out, a smile against her breast as his teeth grazed her. His finger began slow circles around her clit. She panted harder. The flames around them surged higher.

Phyxe release her hold on him and wrapped her arms around his neck. She slid up his body. Her body slickened, moist and ready for him. She wanted nothing more than the feel of him planted deep within her while the flames flickered around them.

Tru released her as she used her hold to pull herself up and wrap her legs around his waist. One hand cradled her ass and the other still tangled in her hair. He helped glide her down his hard shaft. He filled her, brought her down to the very hilt of himself. Her body stretched and then clenched around him. This is where she wanted him. She dropped her head. Her lips sought his in a kiss as he used both hands to guide her up and down the length of him.

She used her legs to lock herself around him and help her catch the rhythm, meeting him with each motion. She broke from the kiss. Her head tilted back, focusing on the feel of him within her. Tru's fingers dug into her skin. His head tucked between her breasts. They both lost themselves in the sheer rhythm of movement and feel of skin against skin.

The wave began slowly. Slight trembles rippled across her abdomen. Her body clenched around Tru's and created a soft vise. He stilled inside her. His orgasm ripped through him as the trembles in her body shifted to full convulsions. Hers rushed through her and caused her to arch up and into him.

His arms caught her when she sagged against him, little shudders still whispering through her. He helped her release him, sliding her down his body. Their breath still panted in unison. They both tried to slow their heart rates down. She wrapped her arms around him and leaned into his chest. The fire flickered and the light began to retreat. She grinned a happy grin, snuggled against him. He dropped his head and rested his chin atop hers.

"You kill me." He tilted her chin up to lay a soft, light

kiss against her lips.

"I'd say we pretty well kill each other," she murmured through the kiss, a smile still on her face.

He laughed, breaking off the kiss and tightening his hold. "Agreed."

Awareness seeped into them both. He pulled back and glanced around. The fire hovered about knee height now, relaxed and warmed in its efforts.

"In a little while, I'll ask you to explain this. Right now, I want to know where the nearest bed is so I can hold your naked body against mine for a while."

Phyxe smiled and curled herself into him as he lifted her up and strode from the fire as if it were nothing more than a mere nuisance. From somewhere, deep inside, a wellspring of satisfaction swept forth inside Phyxe.

The fire had accepted him.

❧THIRTEEN ❧

He struggled in the blankets as though they trapped him in another realm. He thrashed. His arm landed hard across Phyxe's stomach.

She bolted upright, scanning the room, and then realized Tru was the one who'd startled her. She reached out to soothe him, thinking he was caught in the throes of a nightmare, but when her hand reached his chest she gasped. He was so hot. Lovely, pure, radiant heath, but the heat emanating from his body meant one thing. Universe alive. He'd been caught in her ritual of transference for the women. What the hell had she been thinking? She should be banned from rituals for the next millennia. She'd darted out of the ritual without ending it. She must've lost a few brain cells over the millennia. How old was she? Where the hell was her common sense? Apparently, she was as cut off from it as from her sisters at the moment.

She darted out of the bed, blankets pooling on the floor in disarray as she scrambled. *Ancient One. I need water. I need lava.*

Yes, Mistress.

Stupid. Stupid. Stupid. She raced to gather her clothing and his. As fast as she could, she redressed herself, sword and daggers back in place. Hell, she wasn't sure what she was going to be able to do with the bracers on. She hadn't thought she could affect any of them with them on to begin with. The fact any of the transferences worked could be claimed as a minor miracle.

She bit her lip as he shouted and thrashed again. She knelt by his side and laid a soothing hand on his head. He quieted some, the thrashing stopped but his breathing remained fast. She wondered how much and what she'd transferred to him. The women hadn't reacted this way, but they hadn't stepped fully into the flames. She'd never

142

had sex in the flames before either. Damn it all. There was a first time for everything.

Hell. Zhanne was going to kill her. When she found her.

"M'lady?" Firiea stepped into the room. Her eyes glowed with an inner fire. In her hands, she held a small basin of water. Behind her, the elder matron, Etheria followed with a basin of lava between her hands.

"Etheria." Shock and horror ripped through her, and she began to rise.

"Yes, m'lady?" Etheria lifted her chin, her eyes wide in question.

Phyxe halted in mid-motion. A frown wrinkled her forehead. "You should not be handling that."

"It does not burn m'lady. Nor, is it melting the basin." The elder tsked at her and smiled as she drew closer.

Phyxe nodded and then returned to her spot next to Tru who started to thrash about on the bed again. He quieted when her hand touched him again.

"Set them down over here." She tossed her head in the direction near the bed.

Neither woman looked surprised to see him there. Their wide, caring eyes indicated they were more concerned about helping them both. She covered his body with her own as his thrashed and became more violent. His brow beaded with sweat. Firiea leapt to action with her basin and pulled a small cloth from her repertoire to kneel next to the bed to wipe it across his brow.

Phyxe smiled at her First Priestess. "Thank you, not too much. He's going to change and water could harm more than help at a certain point."

"Yes, m'lady." She dabbed at his forehead.

Etheria knelt at his other side, the basin of lava next to her. She watched every motion.

"Etheria?"

"Yes, m'lady?"

"Bring the lava to me; I don't want you attempting what you think you're going to try with it."

Etheria cut her a glance. "How do you think it got in to the basin?"

Phyxe stared back at her as she kept Tru pinned beneath her on the bed as well as she could. How much power had she transferred? Lord, Zhanne was going to kill her. She left all thoughts of her sister goddess behind as the fire in shifted in his body, it flamed out of control, and she was powerless to help him control it. Any other time, she would lay her hands on him and pull the power into her body rather than let it consume him.

He was going to have to survive this on his own.

Damn these bracers. He shouldn't have to do this. She wished he didn't have to. If the sweat beading his brow and the tension in his muscles were any indication, he had quite a battle raging in his body and mind. Normally, she'd be able to share both.

Tears threatened to well up in her eyes. Damn it. She would not honor Glacial when this was her doing. She flipped her eyelashes several times to pull the tears back.

"M'lady?" Firiea's voice caused the stress to retreat.

"Yes?" Thankfully, Tru's legs were tangled in the sheets. She restrained his upper body and arms. In his haze, he cursed at her in ancient tongues. Etheria's wide eyes gave away her knowledge of the ancient words. The elder shook her head at him.

"What happens here stays here," Phyxe murmured.

"Yes, m'lady." The other two women shared a look and agreed in unison.

"Not even if questioned by the Goddess of Energy." Cause, Zhanne was going to be hunting her over this one.

"Of course, m'lady." They both smiled back at her.

Etheria answered, "We are women of Fire, m'lady. Unless you command otherwise, we will always err on the side of the House of Fire."

She smiled and then struggled when Tru strained against her again. He fought in the inner battle of fire raged across the planes of his subconscious. She strained, the forces flowing through his body arched him up off the bed.

"Fire, now," she commanded.

Etheria reached her naked hand into the lava and warmed it before she touched it to his forehead.

"Water."

Firiea wiped his brow.

Steam whispered off his head. His dark hair plastered to his scalp.

For a brief moment, she wondered if he would ever enjoy the pool in his room again, or if she was going to have to ask the Ancient One to supplement it with lava. There's something he was going to love explaining to his people. She groaned at the thought of what this was going to result in when the dawn came.

He was going to kill her.

And, if she was correct, he might be the only one with the power to do so, especially if she couldn't rid herself of the damn bracers.

Fuck.

It was the only suitable Old Earth term she had for this situation. She could think of a million other terms, in a million other languages, past, present and future. But that one ... hell, it suited the moment. Even if the only one in the room who understood it was her.

Mistress?

Yes, Ancient One?

Do you require my aid? The planet asked.

Not yet. He is on fire inside. The external is a repercussion. He will have to make this transition on his own.

This bothers you.

Yes, Phyxe answered. It bothered her far more than it should. It bothered her that she could have done it at all.

Why?

Because he is a good man. He cares about his people and you. She'd met very few rulers who could claim the same.

And by inference, you.

I could be so lucky. But, I am a Goddess. People only care about what power I can bring them, what aid. She'd learned that lesson early on in her youth.

He asks you for nothing. Firon reasoned.

Yes.

He asks you to remain hidden.

Yes.

Perhaps he cares more for you as a woman than a Goddess? The planet asked.

I won't know unless he survives. I've never had a man love me for me, only what I could give him. Phyxe could count on one hand the men she'd allowed into her life. The first two, she'd had hopes and dreams. The last two, she'd selected for shear fun, knowing they'd part ways.

He could provide a sanctuary for you. Children. A

145

place of belonging.
    No.
    No?
    No.
    What do you mean?

Phyxe withdrew as Tru strained against her once again demanding her full attention. Firiea and Etheria both followed the same pattern as before as she continued to struggle with him.

I will never have a mate or children.
    Why should you not?
    I am barren. All Goddess are unable to procreate. We enjoy sex for sex, not because it will continue our line. We are never-ending. Children? The stray thought ran rampant through her mind. Little ones like Narissa and Sethen. No, she mentally shook herself, forcing her mind to stay away from that track.

You are women.
    In form.
    You are women in feeling and healing as am I.
    We are sentient which does not mean we are as other sentient beings. Can you procreate?
    I do each spring. Such is the nature of my being.
    Then my being procreates through transference. I create those in my image.
    But not. They have a limited set of your powers.
    Correct.
    They emulate you.
    Correct.

Her arms strained as Tru struggled against her, cursing in ancient tongues unknown to his planet. Wonderful. Now, he reached into her memories. This was going to be a long process, one she only hoped she could figure out how to undo.

A child of yours would allow you to step back and enjoy what the Universe offers.
    And what would a sentient planet know of childbirth?
    I have watched and participated in many, offering haven and solitude for the mothers as they require.

Phyxe nodded and ignored the looks from both women in the room. She had not been sharing the conversation. *Then you know the beauty of bonding and procreation. The closest I will ever come is through my transference ceremonies.*

As it will be, Mistress.

The Ancient One withdrew from her mind. She had not meant to insult the old one, but somehow she had. Procreation, while she understood it, was not part of her energetic makeup. Goddesses had been created, not born. She remembered her own becoming. Her sister goddesses could do the same. She remembered the years of learning. Of trial. Of error. She remembered Zhanne being the balance of it all as they learned as the beings on their planets learned.

In her younger years, she'd reacted with her base fire nature and responded in kind to any threat. She learned more balance from her sisters, tempering her immediate response. Some beings, some days, got the better of her, but she still prided herself on being a warrior with a heart. Then again some days, passion overruled reason. Passion fueled the fire. As such, she deemed it good. But she'd ask herself again, if Tru survived his transformation.

Hell, she might go hide a few weeks until he grew accustomed to whatever powers she'd shared. Perhaps, part of her next quiet cycle in the Universe, she'd spend time to learn more about her transference abilities and how to limit them. One would think, in five-thousand-plus years she'd thought of that before, but no one had pulled to her so much.

She snarled at him as she struggled against her. "Deal with it, warrior. You played with Fire. Accept it."

He growled back at her as if he'd heard her.

"Oh," she muttered at him. She wanted to rest. She wanted the damn bracers off, so she could think and feel as she normally did. She hated this limiting factor. She'd never been constrained. Yes, she'd had to deal with her learning curve. She'd had to deal with whatever dimension she'd landed in. She'd always been in full control of herself. Well, at least she'd always known what she was doing, even if her sisters hadn't understood or approved.

Fire lit up the room.

"Shield," Phyxe lashed out the command to the two women, unsure if their transference would even allow them such a protection.

Two small fire shields wrapped around the

priestesses. They glittered in amber and firelight.

Phyxe sucked in a deep breath. The fire soothed her lungs and her body. It refueled her in a way no food ever could. The heat swept through her, touching her very core. She locked her hands around Tru's wrists expecting the worst was yet to come. The fact he'd lit up the entire room worried her, but she wasn't going to admit it to anyone but herself at the moment. While she admired her two new priestesses, she wasn't ready to admit this to the closest of sisters.

Maybe Gaian. She'd give her too much grief though. She thanked the fires her two new priestesses followed her commands. She'd hate to see them burn because of her.

"M'lady?" Firiea's voice broke through her thoughts again.

"Yes?" She focused on the girl's face.

"How long will this go on?"

Phyxe detected no fear in her tone, only curiosity. "Until he can get it under control."

Firiea nodded.

"When he shies away from the water, give him lava."

Both women nodded this time.

Every muscle in her body tensed as he pushed against her again. This time though, his struggles lessened. He grew tired, and the transference neared its end, perhaps a good sign. She wasn't sure any of them would have lasted all night.

He quieted with a sudden still. Phyxe double-checked to make sure his chest still rose and fell with each breath. He'd accepted the fire far faster than she'd thought he would be able to. She withdrew her body carefully, making sure not to jostle him, but he stayed still, his breathing even.

"I think that went far better than it could have," she whispered as she stood. The priestesses murmured soft agreements. Either he'd mastered the powers or she hadn't transferred as much as she'd thought. Whichever, she was glad it was over. If she'd been able to, she'd have taken the pain of transference back.

He is stable, Mistress.

Yes. It seems to be.

He dreams of you.

I'm not sure that's a good thing.
In his mind it is. He will sleep soon.
Good, I think I'm going to need to as well.
Yes, Mistress.

Firiea and Etheria withdrew from the room, both gathered the basins they'd come with. Phyxe could only assume they'd overheard the Ancient One's comments this time. She hadn't been shielding the conversation. Fatigued, she took her weapons off her body and curled up next to him atop the covers. She needed all the energy she could get when he woke up. He'd been determined there was a Fire God. She wasn't sure how close she'd come to making one. She wasn't too sure she wanted to be here to find out. She sighed to herself and relaxed into the blankets. She'd never run from a challenge before. And, damned if she'd start now.

Tru panted. His breath coming too fast for him to catch it. Fire flowed over and through him. It burned. He tried to outrun the heat as it cascaded over him, but it consumed him. Flames licked at his bare heels as he ran. He had no idea to where he ran. He knew he had to keep going or he would be overtaken. He leapt over the volcanic hills the best he could in his forward flight. The ground beneath him smoldered. Pockets of flames nestled here and there. Cracks opened to the lava below. He swore he was on his own planet, but this didn't look like the Blood Hills. The energy seemed familiar yet new. A fire geyser lit up before him. He stopped, turned and continued in a different direction as the flames behind him subsided and then retreated. The terrain remained uneven. His steps unsteady. The heat encompassed all. He sweated but still he ran. Rivulets of fiery rain ripped open from the blood red sky above him. His body tensed, the pellets hitting his exposed skin. He expected pain. His steps faltered when they touched him as if they were soft drops of a rainstorm.

He stopped running. His breath came in hard gasps. He fought to get it under control. His hands dropped to his knees as he doubled over. Pain ripped through his body in a wave. Yet the fire rain still cascaded over him and brought warmth and energy. The pain tore through his insides. He forced himself to take a deep, calm breath. And then another. He fought for control over his body and worked through the waves of pain. When fire lit under his feet and swirled around him, Tru ignored it and focused on the control of his body.

The fire couldn't harm him.

He knew it. He knew it from before, when Phyxe had pulled him in it. He knew it now as it taunted and teased him. As his breathing eased, the pain subsided. He forced himself to stand in the flames. The flames surged up and wrapped him in a fire lit cocoon. He tilted his head back and let everything around him burn. For a few minutes, he stood and let the world around him rage. As his breathing evened out, the flames retreated. He opened his eyes and stared out across the dark, dried lava road. With a wave of his hand, the fire beneath his feet extinguished.

Tru flipped over his hand and started at it for a moment. If this was a dream, it was one hell of a dream.

With a sigh, the realm of fire fell away, and he crossed over. His eyes opened. The bare obsidian ceiling hovered overhead. He eased himself up in the bed, slowly, gingerly taking stock of his body. His eyes lit on the woman asleep next to him. In rest, she looked angelic. Her face relaxed, her breathing even, her red gold hair fanned out across the pillow. In rest, she didn't look as though the weight of a thousand worlds and millions of people rested on her shoulders.

He wondered how often she rested?

"I've slept more by your side than I have in the last couple hundred years, warrior."

Amber eyes opened to stare up at him.

He remained on his elbow to watch her. "And you accuse me of needing rest."

"I rest in different ways."

"I gathered that."

"How are you feeling?" She looked worried. If something could worry a Fire Goddess.

"Like I've spent more than a few days in the sands and the sands won." He ran a hand through his hair, his jaw sliding back and forth as if he were testing everything.

She nodded.

He wasn't sure what happened. Some of it was dream like. Some of it real. He remembered the sex in the fire. Reality. He remembered curling up in the bed and wrapping his body around Phyxe's. The next thing he could claim as real was staring down at her moments before.

Everything else remained suspect.

And she lay there looking up at him with watchful eyes. Something in the unreality began to crystallize in his mind. She was watching him too closely.

He stared at his hand and flexed it. Nothing was as easy as he wanted it to be. Want to play with a woman, get a Goddess. Try to lead his people, get nothing but havoc and grief. He'd almost prefer to go back to the days when his father led. But then, he could do no right in the old one's eyes. This way, he had no one to answer to him but himself and the multitudes of people who relied on him.

He stood up and reached for his clothes. His muscles protested each movement. His body ached as if he'd gone a few rounds with Devos and lost, badly.

"What exactly happened?" The fire curled and burned in his belly.

Anger threatened to surge forth as the heat licked over his skin. Damn it all. He'd been reasonable, responsible for so long, before that trying and never succeeding at acceptance. At least, not after his mother's disappearance. The heat unleashed something inside him.

"A Ritual of Transference." She stood across from him, not even attempting to sway his attention in another direction.

He couldn't help but sweep an admiring glance over her body. He would never fail in the desire to look at her every chance he got. But he needed to remove himself from the room, from the Haven, from everyone for a while. He needed to step away and think and deal. And figure out a way to control this anger welling up inside him. He'd been too well trained to let that anger out near a woman.

"Tru?"

He tensed and glanced over at her.

"I am sorry. I did not realize what the fire would do. I ..." She looked concerned. Not contrite, but worried.

"I need time." He pulled on his boots and strode out the door without another word.

Sirens shrieked through the palace sending Tru tumbling from his bed and reaching for his sword and laser before his brain engaged. Thankfully, he'd fallen asleep in the wee hours of the morning with his clothes still on. Hell, he hadn't even removed his damn boots. He dropped his sword over his shoulder and strode out of his rooms. Two of his guard flanked him as he exited the door.

"Report," he snapped at Devos.

His second shook his head. "Don't know, yet. Radio silence across the board." Anger flicked through his eyes before he tramped down on it.

Tru scowled at him. "Radio silence? As in that's what was ordered or that's what happened?"

Devos tapped on the earpiece snugly resting in his right ear. "Nothing there."

"I don't like the sound of that." He stepped up their pace through the upper halls. Since the last raid, they'd increased security tenfold. Apparently, it wasn't working.

He stormed into the command room; chaos greeted him. Voices surged over one another with orders being shouted out across the room. No one noticed the Crown Prince had even entered the madhouse.

"Enough." He didn't raise his voice or bother to shout, but every moving body in the room stopped as if he had. "Jerell. Report."

The nervous man stepped forward. "We're not sure, sir. Our systems all shut down at once. The alarm system kicked in. No raids are being detected, but we can't verify that except by sight."

"And who's scouting out the problem?"

"There is no problem, son." Riske Marius marched into the command center with his guards trailing him. He turned his gaze on the contingent of people in front of him. "Out, go on, you'll need to find other tasks to keep you engaged. The ones you have here will no longer be needed."

Around the room, eyes widened in shock, hurt, anger

and fear, but not a soul protested Lord Marius' decree.

"Check in with my assistant. You'll find other jobs already waiting for you," he said.

"Father?" Tru laid a hand on the holster at his hip.

Tru's father turned to look at him once the last of the workers left the room. "Have your men return all lasers and gliders to inventory. All technology is to be turned in immediately."

He heard Devos' low snarl behind him. He held up a hand to belay his second. "You need to explain yourself, Father. I can't just command them to hand over weapons they have every right to carry."

His father's eyes flared in anger. "I am still in charge, son. I don't need to explain myself. All guards will do as I command. All technology will be returned to the palace for inventory. I have shut our planet's borders to the Guild. There will be no more visitors joining us. The spaceports have been shut down and all visitors expelled." He placed heavy emphasis on the expelled.

"You shut our borders? Is that even possible?" Tru glanced around the now empty room, hoping against hoping that someone would be able to explain the insanity behind that idea.

"It is already done." The older man straightened to his full height, impressive even at his age, although Tru still towered over him and overshadowed his father in height and width. "Every warrior is to report in for detailed debriefs. I expect your team in first."

Tru debated about continuing to argue. He'd already called him out in front of two sets of warriors, not something that went over well with his father. He would be more reasonable in a one-on-one discussion. Maybe. Since his mother's disappearance, things had shifted radically on their world. It was as if someone else inhabited his father's body, his shell of a body. The man had dark circles under his eyes, and his cheeks had a hallow look to them.

"Yes, sir." Tru bowed and strode back out of the room. Devos and Eriaku followed behind him, both silent, for the moment.

When they reached a bend in the corridor, Devos exploded, "What the hell was that?"

"I wish I knew. It looks like he shut it all down." Tru

frowned watching people dart about the palace floor. "But how?"

Tru had detailed knowledge about every aspect of their defenses. Unfortunately, his father had built them all, so he had an even better understanding. He was the engineer while Tru was the strategist.

"And why? He's taking away our ability to defend ourselves and move quickly about the planet." Devos' fist hit the wall next to him. "He's hampering us."

Tru didn't even flinch at the sound of Devos' impact with the wall, nor did he scold him. "You know as well as I do that we are quite capable of defending ourselves with nothing more than our bare hands if need be. Maybe he thinks they can track the technology? He hasn't shared any of it with me. He's shut down since my mother was taken."

"That might explain it, sir," Eriaku's raspy voice finally chimed in.

"Fine, you recall the others. We'll do what he asks, and then, we'll do what needs to be done," Tru decided. "And I am going to go have a chat with dear dad and see if I can figure out what's going through his mind. And then figure out if I have to retire him before he puts us in even more danger."

There was one thing he refused to do, allow his people harm. While he worried about his mother, he knew she had the strength of the desert flowing through her. Until he saw her lifeless body, he would hold out hope she still breathed. She had taught him to survive and to fend for their people. To do less, would be a dishonor to her teachings and desires.

"Move it. We have little time." He strode back into the depths of the palace. Dear Dad had trained him well. He wished it wasn't coming down to this, but he was in react mode rather than defend mode.

It wasn't going to be a pretty sight. He took a deep breath. Was there ever a good time to tell your Father he'd stepped off the deep end?

❧FOURTEEN ❧

Phyxe cursed. Well, that went well.

Not.

She couldn't even be sure any transference occurred. He hadn't given her a window to discuss, explain or even test. He was going to go out there, hit the sands and something was going to strike at him. He'd torch the nearest settlement before he realized he could. Damn it all. She wasn't sure what he could do.

Halja. Hell.

"M'lady?" Firiea's voice called out from the outer room. Phyxe shook her head at herself. She'd swear the girl had the uncanny knack for knowing when she was going to go look for her. Or, she was telepathic.

"Get me some of the desert leathers your men wear. And something to cover my head so they can't tell I'm female." She took a deep breath and stood to her full height. Time to start blurring the edges of behaving.

"M'lady, they'll know you're a female."

"Not if I can help it," she muttered under her breath.

People would see what she wanted them to see. She would insinuate herself, become one of the men. She might be a slighter form, but she had to match at least a few of them in height. She would keep a close eye on Tru and his newly born powers, and find a way to keep training the women.

She was a woman. She could multi-task.

She hoped.

She walked into the outer rooms only to halt when she found Firiea laying out various items for her to choose from. She tilted her head in question at the young priestess.

"Precog, m'lady," she answered when Phyxe cast her a glance.

Ahh, great. Plus, her natural abilities were now

enhanced. She should have been paying more attention. She'd been too sidetracked by her warrior and his dark good looks and 'I don't need you' attitude.

She glanced over the clothes, touched a few here and there, and selected a few items. "Which group will accept me the quickest and get me the closest to Tru?"

Firiea bit the corner of her lip. "If you can come up with a plausible story, and not reveal your face, you could go directly to his main camp and contact Devos."

Phyxe nodded.

"But, he's a hard one. He's suspicious of every one. Especially those who try to draw too near Lord Marius."

"I should hope so. Isn't that his job?"

"Well, yes. He's ..."

Phyxe cut a look at her as she reached out to pick up one of the shirts. Oh, the girl had a crush on the man who claimed status as Tru's second in command. She would have to keep an eye on that. She stripped out of her leathers without a second thought. She folded the clothes and stacked them in a neat pile before pulling on the baggier clothes. She would look slight compared to the other men. Perhaps she could play on the youth.

"You will want to tell him you're from Tyren. It is an outskirt province. The men are built a little lighter there."

She nodded and slid the desert shirt over her shoulders. The soft linen caressed her breasts. Damn, she was going to have to bind herself down. She glanced over the pile of clothes and then smiled as Firiea handed her a soft strip of cloth. The girl was quick. The shirt and pants followed with the desert robes. Lightweight but tight in weave, the sand colored garments would allow her to blend with the environment. She was used to wearing a lot less. She rolled her shoulders to test her moving capabilities. Loose, but fine, she would work with it.

"Here is a cloth to wind about your face for protection. If the others question why you don't remove it, tell them you were severely scarred by the off-worlders."

Phyxe nodded again, amazed by her First Priestess of Fire. The girl picked up on her thoughts. The story was a feasible one.

"Keep your hood up. The robe and hood stay bound as tight as you can get away with." Firiea darted around her as she finished pulling the clothes on and began to tuck her together in place.

Phyxe glanced over herself when she was finished. The girl was good. She'd wrapped the robes well enough to give Phyxe's lean body a bit of upper body bulk. She tested her ability to move and found herself still able to move as if she wore nothing at all.

"I think I'm keeping these."

"Thank you, m'lady." Firiea beamed at her.

The fabric was soft and breathable and while she was wrapped rather tightly into it, she was certain her freedom of movement was unhindered as if she wore her own clothing. The women's craft abilities on this planet were beyond exceptional.

She stood to her full height and took a deep breath. "Firiea."

The girl stood tall before her.

"This is going to be a challenge. I need to be in two places at once. I cannot because my powers are limited at the moment." Firiea opened her mouth to protest, but Phyxe stopped her. "I am unlimited when I am not trapped. You and the others have a portion of those powers, each in your own unique way. Truant ..." She sighed. "I'm not sure what he transferred. I'm not even sure how he did it, or, how I did it." Painful as it was to admit. "I am going to need you to stay in constant contact with me. I don't want the women to go untrained for what I have planned."

Firiea nodded.

"If you go out into the desert, go out as I do now." She didn't want the off-worlders knowing about the force. She definitely didn't want them finding the Haven. "Use the channel with the Ancient One to find places of safety to test and taunt the off-worlders."

"Yes, m'lady."

"When you need to tap into my resources, get as close to the fire here as possible. It will help you channel my knowledge."

The girl's eyes lit up. Phyxe knew she'd been tempted to step into the flames, but hesitated.

"You will know when and if the full flame will accept you. Don't push it," she warned. The last thing she needed at the moment was a new priestess who thought jumping headlong into the flames would somehow accelerate her transformation. The ensuing explanations and healing would take eons.

"How will you get into the deep desert, m'lady?"

Phyxe grinned. "With a little help and then some walking."

Firiea tilted her head. "Be wary of Devos, m'lady. He is not bad, simply protective."

Phyxe nodded and picked up her sword and daggers to replace them in their sheaths. She would keep an eye on this Devos and hope Tru didn't accidentally flame his second lieutenant.

Now, if the demon were around, she might taunt him into losing his temper at the cretin.

That would be a fire worth watching.

Mistress, I have a path opened as close as I dare get you to his troops.

Perfect, she answered.

I have also picked up on several anomalies in the northernmost hemisphere.

What do you mean? Anomalies were never a good thing.

There are ... voids ... on the surface in the Northern areas. Since they are typically uninhabited, I had not done a more detailed check there.

Voids?

It is the best way I can describe them, Mistress. They are ... blank spaces.

Phyxe stared at the obsidian wall in front of her as the crevice began to split the wall of sheer lava rock open. Blank spaces. Several things occurred to her at once. Shields, off-worlders, and dimensional portals ... the list wasn't infinite, but there could be several explanations.

Can I send one of Zen's bots to investigate? She asked.

Yes, as I'm not detecting anything, and I would hate to see one of the priestesses put themselves at risk when I can't determine the reaction on my surface.

I will have Zen send a bot to inquire. I'll review its findings and then follow up with research on my own.

Yes, Mistress.

Stacia D. Kelly

Phyxe stepped through the crevice and clicked the communicator on. Better to get the AI moving on one thing before she stepped too deeply below the surface.

"Yes, M'lady," the AI's computerized voice washed over her.

"Can you send a bot to investigate the Northern Hemisphere and report back?" Phyxe asked.

"Yes. Consider it done. What should I have the bot look for?" Zen asked.

"Everything. I want a detailed recording of every nuance of the surface, the surrounding sky and atmosphere."

"Yes, m'lady." The AI clicked the communicator off with a definitive beep.

She was damned if she was going to act as if her powers were limited. Any other time and place, she'd have splintered her consciousness to affect her plans. Here, she would make do the best she was able. If it meant using the inhabitants of the planet to do some work, well, it was their home. They should have a part in getting it back on track.

She crossed the planes beneath the surface quickly as the Ancient One guided her along the different pathways she'd constructed. As fast as she could make them, Phyxe traveled down the paths. In only a matter of minutes the path arched upwards.

You're to the end of where I can safely transport you beneath the surface without coming up on top of them, Firon explained.

Thank you, Ancient One. You have been far more helpful than most of your kind.

You take good care of me when you're able to, Mistress. And when your powers are back to full force, you will reset my path to the correct one.

I'm certainly going to try.

I have never known you to fail.

Phyxe grinned. Failure wasn't part of her vocabulary. There was always a way to succeed. Maybe not win-win for all parties, but general success would happen.

Careful, Mistress. When I open this it will be all sand above you. You have to move fast.

I'll move the second you say to, Ancient.

The earth above her shivered. *Go.*

159

She leapt up and pulled herself through the sifting sand even as it threatened to overwhelm her. Phyxe managed to get a grasp on the earth above and pull her body through. Her legs inched through the sands as the earth closed behind her. She collapsed on the ground and stared up at the night sky and panted. She loved the physicality of this planet, but damned if she didn't miss some of her powers. She spit out some of the sand and forced herself to stand. Lifting her head, she let the cool air of the desert night caress what little of her face she'd left exposed. Her element. She'd rather run across the sands as she usually did, but that would cause more issues than it solved at the moment. Instead, she set off in the direction the energies indicated a gathering of people.

She hoped she'd arrived before Tru. Otherwise, she was going to have to explain herself twice. And she wasn't sure her disguise would allow her to get past Tru. Firiea passed on enough of the hand signals, so she could communicate without her voice giving her away.

The sands cooled with the sunset. She loved all aspects of the desert. The hot air under the full heat of the noon sun. The cool night air. The clear skies at dawn or dusk. The scent of heat and sands. All the things she lacked when she hovered between the dimensions. It had been far too long since she'd spent time planet side. The night-cooled sands sifted under her feet. She breathed in the dry air, so pure. She wished it were daytime with the full heat of the noon sun beating down on her, rejuvenating her. But the crisp night was still beautiful with a clear sky lit up with a multitude of stars. These were the things she lacked when she hovered between dimensions. The ability to experience nature, her nature. It had been far too long since she'd spent time planet side.

She wandered through the desert towards her target. She knew she should hasten her path, but, for the moment, she wanted to enjoy her quiet time. This was her time. Her element. Her realm of reality.

It would be better if Tru walked with her.

Krite. Since when had she wanted or needed someone with her in her element? Never. So what made this one different? She'd shared herself with men in the past, but leaving had never been an issue. Their time ended, she moved on. She'd known it when she'd started to play with them. Tru, he wasn't play. She'd pulled him into the fires, something she'd never done before. She'd never wanted to share the fire. Tru's energy was different. He didn't want her powers. Hell, even in the past, the men may not have wanted her powers, but they wanted her body. He'd fought the connection at first, too. He'd even turned her down.

He did take her advice, which honored her more than any of the others combined.

He listened.

She stopped in the sands. Silence descended. Even in the quiet desert night, something somewhere made some kind of noise, but all she could hear now was the sound of her own breathing echoing back at her. Others were near. Her senses picked up on the hints moments later than they should have. Tru preoccupied her thoughts. Only a fledging goddess made those mistakes.

Or one in love, Firon said.

Phyxe kept her comments to herself and ignored the Ancient. She focused on where the attack would come from first.

"State your purpose, desert walker."

The voice lashed out across the sands. Phyxe turned towards the sound. Not Tru's voice. A good sign as far as she cared. She lifted her hands and signed back as Firiea had shown her. She forced herself to keep the natural fluidity out of her movements and used more clipped, masculine ones.

A dark figured stepped out of the inky night and walked towards her, his movements those of feline grace, a hunter. "State your purpose."

She re-signed.

He stopped before her and watched. "Tribe?"

She signed again.

"Family?"

Again.

"Why would we take a cripple among the group of elite hunters?"

She almost laughed. He tried to goad her. Priceless. She signed again.

"I don't take those who can't fight, return home, pup. You're useless to me."

So, that was to be the way of it. Phyxe grinned

beneath her mask. She'd been itching for a fight. No, she couldn't kill him ... or even damage him. Tru would consider that unacceptable, but she sure as hell could give him a damn good fight and make it look good in the process.

She drew her sword from its sheath on her back.

Devos turned at the sound, his sword withdrew from behind his back in a single fluid movement. She watched his entire body pivot.

The others of his team drew around them in the dark, creating a shadowy circle. Eyes glittered in the darkness and stared back at them as they stood swords drawn a few feet apart. Twelve, the number of heartbeats she counted, a good number. She'd be sure it wasn't one less.

She waited, sword drawn. She watched his breath; his heart beat. Her gaze focused on his chest. His eyes would lie. His chest would not. He turned slightly and moved in her direction. Phyxe stepped to the side and countered him. He struck strong and clean, but underestimated her speed and agility. Besides, she had a couple of years of practice on him.

She grinned beneath her facemask when he stepped forward again, and she lunged. The third time, she countered and drove him to his knees. Satisfaction swelled up before she could stop it. When he could play with fire, then he'd be able to battle with her. Here, she played with swords.

He surged up, anger laced his movements, and she stepped to the side and swept past him. While she could have followed with a few more insidious strikes, she refrained. Tru would kill her if she damaged his lieutenant and friend. Honestly, she was proud Devos reacted the way he had. She'd known who he was the minute she'd laid eyes on him. Zen's vid screen hadn't done him justice, nor the hero worship memories she'd picked up from Firiea.

It helped to prove his innocence in her eyes.

"Why do I have the feeling you're toying with me?" He watched her.

She shrugged.

"You're good at sword play, desert walker."

She did the only thing she could do at that point. She shrugged again.

Devos dipped his sword to the ground and tilted his head back. His laughter echoed across the sands. His broad shoulders shook beneath his desert clothes. When he looked back at her, his eyes filled with laughter still.

"Your tribe is well known for your battle antics. You may be smaller than the rest, but you're fleeter of foot. Prove yourself and you can stay in the ranks. Screw up, I'll remove you myself."

She nodded and re-sheathed her sword. Slight disappointment laced her movements. She'd wanted more of a battle, something tangible.

"Devos, what the hell do you think you're doing?" Tru's voice growled out across the darkness.

The anger emanating from his body rolled across the sands, and she melted into the group. They moved in around her to welcome her with silent pats on the back. She let their more muscular forms block her from Tru's view. She watched with careful intent when Devos turned to face his leader. His mirth still laced his movements, which were a little freer and more fluid than they had been.

"Hunting, testing, recruiting." Devos shrugged, his sword returned to its resting place.

"You're supposed to be at the camp getting ready to move out." Tru's jaw set in a hard line. His eyes glittered in the dark.

Phyxe leaned around the warrior in front of her to watch Tru. His dark eyes lit with an unusual light. They'd not gone her amber color, yet, but the hints started. He held his shoulders rigid. His movements looked pained.

"We're getting there, Lord Master." Devos shot him an amused look.

Phyxe stepped more to the edge of the group. Tru didn't recognize what changes were happening in his body. Devos, she could tell, detected something off about his leader's personality, but wasn't sure what to do with it or about it. Tru snarled at him again and then turned to stalk back to the camp. Devos lifted a hand and signaled to the others to fall in. As one, the group set out across the sands and trotted a few hundred yards over and across a dune to return to their camp. Phyxe blended into the group as well as she could. Since most had their hoods from their cloaks up, she looked no different. She kept the hood so it shielded her eyes. The warriors all had dark, obsidian eyes. Her amber ones were going to cause a stir.

Unless, they noticed Tru's dark-eyed gaze going amber first.

He is starting to change, Mistress.

Yes, I know. I can see it.

I can feel it.

Be careful, Ancient. Soon, he's going to be able to hear you, too. Wonderful, more tricks, she hoped he adapted quickly.

He can now. He thinks he's hallucinating. It's making him grouchy, Firon answered.

I'd be surprised if he weren't. All that fire contained within.

He's going to need to release it.

I hope it isn't near his men.

Odds are not in the favor of that outcome.

Yeah, I know. I may have to sidetrack him.

"Move out," the command whispered through the men.

Phyxe dropped into line with the others. She nodded as one man, dark eyes with blond hair peeking out from his hood, indicated she keep step with him. She was thankful the hand signs remained universal among Tru's people. She knew her voice would be as much of a giveaway as her eyes. Better she remain hidden in plain view. Better she figure out a way to sidetrack Tru. It was only a matter of time before his powers flared.

And it was going to be a hell of a show.

❧ FIFTEEN ❧

Tru stalked across the desert sands. Devos kept a steady pace beside him. The men trailed behind in various stages across the sands in the dark. He itched to fight. He should have demanded Phyxe explain exactly what happened. He'd woken and thought it was all a dream, a hallucination, but his skin now twitched. He wanted to tussle, and he wasn't sure why. Anger ached to be released. He was mad and ready to hit something, anything, but he was equally as determined to keep himself from striking out when he couldn't pinpoint what the hell he was so ticked off about.

"You seem ready to fight tonight." Devos' tone was idle and slow.

Tru didn't even bother to glance at him. His eyes tracked every inch of desert as they wound their way through the dunes. He could see the sands shift before them. What was once dark and shadowy now danced with inner light almost as if it were dusk and the sun cast slow signs of diminishing light over the sands. He didn't even bother to try and reason that one away.

"Or not," his lieutenant droned dryly.

"Find our target."

"Of course." Devos trotted off at a brisk pace ahead of the group, scouting.

Tru watched his friend step further and further into the darkness. Unease swept across his shoulders. Shadows moved from the darkness and surrounding and descending on Devos. Tru's breath drew sharply in, but before he could even respond, a streak of light passed him and jumped into the fray to join Devos in battle.

What the hell?

His men swarmed past him, dark attacked dark. The world flowed in slow motion. All but one form moved as if time slowed. A slender, desert clad figure danced in the center of the fight, sword drawn, light arched with each thrust of steel. A turn, a parry, a hard knock back. The fire in Tru rose as a dark clad figure attempted to drive the slender form back. It flamed, pulled forth and threatened to overwhelm him. He held his body rigid and forced himself under control. Breathing, counting, forcing himself to remain still least he lose what little control he had. The darkness hid him for the moment. Neither his men nor the others realized he stood back and watched.

He needed the time.

The slender form danced among the fight. He flinched as slight red aura began to form around his vision. The one he refused to know glowed, and the glow began to seep out and encompass his warriors. Their actions became more fluid, more forceful. His warriors began to fight with renewed vigor, as if energized. It seemed new strength flowed through their arms. Their eyes lit with an eerie light as man after man turned on his counterpart and drove him back across the sands.

War cries of victory echoed when the intruders retreated in defeat. His men wanted to follow, but all halted at Devos' command. As one they turned to face him, the red aura began to retreat, it withdrew into the group.

Tru cast a glance at them all. Fire still burned in him, around them. He could see they still wanted to chase after the intruders. "You, new one. Follow me."

The slender form stepped from the group. Tru scowled when he could determine no features from the shadowy cloak. The aura surrounding the group dissipated and no longer emanated from any of his warriors.

He turned on a booted foot, his glare stopped Devos from following them. The warrior he'd commanded to join him set pace next to him as he led the men back to their camp. Step for step they tread through the dark.

"I told you to stay hidden," he said.

"I am hidden," she said.

He snapped at her. She had no right. Rage swept over his shoulders. No, he forced another breath through his body. He had no one to blame but himself. Somehow, Fate had it in for him. It wasn't his decade. Fire rippled across his back. He wanted to reach out and strangle something with his bare hands. He wanted to rip and tear and consume. No, he couldn't. He was a leader. This irrational need overwhelmed him and was ... something to control. He would control it, damn it. Rationally, he knew he couldn't blame the woman who kept pace with him now. She'd been pulled here and wanted nothing more than to help. She'd even done as he'd asked, for the most part. He forced another breath, willing himself to focus.

She'd never been required to help. Hell, she'd asked for nothing in return. She was a Goddess. She could have taken over at any point, with any decree. He'd hindered her.

He snarled low in his throat at the way his thoughts raced around his head. He wanted to retreat, to find someplace to let the anger consume him. He wanted to flame something. And, hell, he didn't know what he meant when he wanted to flame something. Action, he needed to do something.

"The fire rises," she whispered.

He glanced at her.

"You're in a tailspin. The fire rises within. It is not something you've had to deal with in the past. You had your youth, and the fires of youth. This, this is the essence of Fire. For that, I apologize."

His body shifted. He sensed the men trailing behind him at a good pace. Devos first, the men further behind. The smell of sagebrush and willow assaulted his nose as a faint breeze swept over them. A faint stirring of surprise washed over him. The plants still strived to survive even in the deepest part of the desolate sands.

"This is my doing. I will deal with it."

She hissed at him. "*Aikare*. Idiot. This is *my* doing. You will allow me to help you now."

"No," he snarled back, planting his feet, his arms crossed over his chest as he stared down at her.

He saw her cast a glance over her shoulder at Devos. He was far enough behind that he couldn't hear them talking, but close enough to know something was going on between them.

"You are an idiot." She matched his stance and lifted an eyebrow back at him.

His amber eyes glittered at her, more gold than green now. "I am in control at the moment, don't push it."

"If I don't push it now, you're going to lose control

with your men."

"I will not."

"You will."

"You sound certain I'm so weak."

She shook her head at him. "I know you're not. But I will not see you harm your warriors because of my miscalculation. They seem to be good men."

"You forget. A demon pulled you here."

"No," she hissed. "I am quite aware of how I got ripped through time and space without request, quite aware of the pain of reforming with such a calling. Of how I was bound to this place and plane. Of how I can do nothing ... but ... what ... you request because I DON'T HAVE FULL USE OF MY BODY AND POWERS."

She stopped suddenly in realization. Tru noticed movement out of the corner of his eye. Her livid whispers had reached Devos. So well in fact that he'd stepped back without comment and pulled the rest of the warriors to a halt far enough away to give them room.

Fire arched between them. A red haze seeped across their feet.

Mistress.

Not NOW, Ancient.

Tru shook his head, attempting to clear it. Now, he was hearing voices too? What in blazes was wrong with him?

"You want to whine and complain, Lord Warrior?" He cut a glance back to her when she stepped out and balanced the weight of her body on both feet. She crossed her arms over her chest. The hood still hid her face and eyes. She angled her body away from him, but the heat of her amber gaze from the shadows of the cloak rested on him.

Tru scowled at her and turned on her. Flames taunted the edge of his vision. His focus narrowed until he could see only her. "I do not whine. Nor do I ever complain. I am Lord here. It is my planet. My people. My responsibility."

"And, yet, here I am."

Red smoke rose up from the night sands. It curled around their legs and licked at their calves.

Tru balanced his feet on the shifting sands. His arms lifted to the side of his body. Every muscle tensed. His hands opened. He realized Phyxe stood her ground, watching him from the depths of her cloak. His body flamed, and he arched an arm out through the air, swiping at her. He never saw the fire start in the center of his palm. His arm lifted, but it never registered. The fiery flames tracked through the night, and the heat rushed forth. He missed her by mere inches.

She turned her head and allowed the fire to sweep over and past her when the fire ball flowed past her. Fire rolled across the desert after spilling from the palm of his hand. It swelled forth with no direction and intent and instead tumbled across the dunes and dissipated into the night.

Her head turned back to stare at him. "Done?"

His hand still curled against himself after he'd followed through with the swing. Silence descended across the sands. The fire wandered along the desert night and rolled without direction. He turned wide eyes on her. His breathing stopped and started again. What the hell had he done? He'd swung at her. He'd lost control. He hadn't done that since his learning years.

He'd tried to kill her with fire.

"You can't kill me, warrior." She stood balanced on her feet in the sands and stared back at him in the night. Now, her eyes glowed back at him. The fires he'd sparked started a flame deep within her as well.

"I hit you."

"No." She maintained her stance.

"I hit you with fire."

She corrected him, "You tried to hit me with fire. You missed."

"I shouldn't have done either." He stood and returned to his full height but brought his hand before him as if he'd never seen it before.

"You'll be surprised what you can do now."

He turned his hand over, staring at it as if it had somehow morphed into something new and unusual. "I hit you."

"No, you tried to hit me. You missed," she corrected him again.

He was having a hard time with the fact he'd lost his temper enough to actually swing at her. He'd never swung at a woman before. It was not part of his nature, his upbringing OR his beliefs.

"I am not one of your women, warrior. I am your *Goddess*." She dropped her hood and let her fiery hair cascade down her back and over the desert clothing. With one hand, she reached up and ripped the mask from her face.

"Do you need a reminder of who and what I am?" She dropped the mask in the sands at their feet.

"I hit you."

She snapped at him, "No. You missed. Try again, I'm game."

He looked up from staring at his hand. She stood before him in all her glory and watched him. Amber eyes glinted in fiery light through the darkness of the night. Her hair flowed in the fire haze, which refused to retreat from around them. They were cloaked in red.

"I hit you with fire."

"Yes, the fire hit me. You did not," she acknowledged.

He'd swung at her. Fire stretched out from his palm and swept across her face. He'd wanted to get her to stop talking, to stop long enough for him to gain control. He was not one who was ever out of control. She drove him past it as no other could.

It was maddening.

It was firing.

"I shouldn't have done either."

"Yeah, well, I goaded you to it. Try it again. I may hit you back." She smirked at him.

Devos' chuckle echoed across the sands.

Tru turned and broke the contact and the spell forming around them. His men hovered around Devos in a semi-circle. Some had swords drawn. Others stood with wide eyes watching them both. Fascination laced all faces staring back at them.

"You find this amusing." He lifted an eyebrow at Devos.

"Man, you hit her with a fire ball, and she barely flinched."

"Why is this not bothering people?" Tru lashed out.

Devos grinned. "I'm thinking it was better her than me. That was fire, man. As much as I am desert born, you hit me with a fireball, and I'm getting the hell out of your way."

The men around him nodded and laughed in unease, but no one stepped away from Devos or into the desert surrounding them.

"See, thus the reason I had him hit me with it instead," Phyxe interjected.

"M'lady, I'm thinking you knew you had it coming." Devos smirked at her.

Something eased in him as he watched Phyxe cast a glare Devos' smiling face. His people weren't freaked out. Well, at least the twelve men who milled about were watching them in curiosity rather than outright horror. Pride swelled up from within. He'd chosen his Elite Team well.

"Don't get too full of yourself, warrior." Phyxe's gaze cut from Devos back to him.

"Me?"

"Yes, the fire will fuel certain parts of your personality. You have to fight to control it."

"You've done this for years," he said.

"I've done this for many millennia. I've had a head start."

He laughed. His men drew back at the quick change in his demeanor. Hell, he couldn't help it. He kept forgetting she was far older than he gave her credit for.

"Devos, back to camp. We reset and strategize. Things have changed this night."

Devos nodded and signaled to the men.

Tru smiled to himself when Phyxe fell into place beside him with a fluid movement. She made no efforts to continue to hide. Instead, she kept pace with him across the sands as the team set out at a faster pace. Something seemed right about having her at his side. Perhaps her being pulled here hadn't been such a bad thing. He'd deal with having tried to strike her later. For now, he needed to figure out how he could control fire. He grinned to himself. He could play with Fire.

Hot damn.

❧SIXTEEN ❧

Phyxe stared up at the night sky, stars blinking in and out. She wondered about the shield around the planet. Wystin, her sister of Air, would want to know how it worked. She wanted it destroyed, so she could set the realm back on track. This imbalance was beginning to wear on her as well as the planet. Since they were linked, it wasn't surprising. It taxed her energy levels, and she was having a hard time keeping up, which was ridiculous.

Mistress?

Yes, Ancient?

Are you better now? Firon asked.

You should know. I'm sorry about earlier.

I should have known. You knew he was volatile.

Yes, but he cannot harm me.

You do not sound sure.

Well, no one has ever been able to throw flame at me before. My own flame is not only fire.

It was elemental fire.

Yes.

A problem.

Only if I can't control it.

Her gaze dropped from the stars above to stare at the bracers binding her forearms. If she could get the damn things off through sheer will, she would. Of course, she'd probably toast the demon who'd called her in the process, but as far as she was concerned, that was icing. They were wearing on her ability to control her nature and the energy around her. Even the Firon sensed the upheaval and responded to it.

He seemed contrite.

He was.

Will he be able to control it?

He will. He would do no less. It's not part of his nature to do otherwise. If she could have chosen a man to

172

share the fire with, she would have chosen him. He maintained such tight control and balanced it with a caring nature.

True. The men seemed to have accepted you.

I think they were in awe of Tru's actions. I did nothing, but stand there. They saw no value in that.

You underestimate them.

No, I know what they value on this planet. How goes the women's training?

They train as they did eons before.

And that means?

They were once warriors, too, simply more subtle than the men.

Phyxe dropped her entire body into the sand and stretched along the cooling grains, so she could continue her contact with the planet, yet still stare up at the universe beyond. The more time she spent here, the more she enjoyed the planet and its history. She could spend days reading and researching about their lines, their past. She would do so, once she had these bracers off and some down time.

They are good women. Powerful.

They were more powerful in the past. You've allowed them to reclaim their power. The shields have offset the balance in more ways than one.

So I gathered.

Ages ago, they hunted across my plains with the men.

Phyxe smiled at the image conjured by the Ancient's comment. The women's petite forms kept pace with the warrior's larger ones, small shadows next to larger ones as they crossed the deserts. They would be subtler in the hunt, as determined to provide for their families, and as dedicated.

"M'lady?" Zen's voice cut across the night as her communicator clicked on.

"Yes?" She folded her hands under her head.

"I have an initial report from the bot you asked me to send North."

"Report."

"The climate is colder than recorded history. Several species are near to extinction. The magnetic pole shifted 25 degrees to the West and caused shifts in the planetary alignment."

"Continue." Phyxe frowned and ran through the scenarios in her head.

Zen's voice droned on and reported on the flora and fauna and the lack thereof in the hemisphere. Phyxe's brain closed off her surroundings, and she let her mind start rapid calculations. The planet had been closed off for hundreds of years. The inhabitant's lives spanned several centennial. The elders knew of the time before, yet remained quiet, bowing to the request of House Marius. Missing the Lady of the land must have cut the people to the core. She didn't fault Tru's father, but he could have found another way, something less severe than sheltering them all.

Several scenarios played out at once across the darkness. With quick processes, she calculated out the probabilities of the current path as well. A few answers opened up to her. She would have to trek north to see for herself.

"Find me a glider and a pack of warmer clothes, Zen."

"Where do you think you're going now?" Tru's voice cut through the night.

Phyxe refused to move from the comfortable spot she'd made for herself in the sand. She opened her eyes to find him staring down at her. His eyes glittered in the dark of the night. She wondered if he realized his dark eyes, his beautiful coal black eyes, were now amber and gold. She took a deep breath. She'd come out to meditate and talk with the Ancient. He'd allowed her the privacy, but she should have known he'd hear her conversation with Zen. It wasn't as if he weren't wearing a communicator as well.

"North."

He stared at her. His eyes lit up in the dark light of the night.

"There are voids that need to be investigated. I don't like Zen's preliminary reports."

"I'll send some warriors to investigate," he said.

"No."

He lifted a dark eyebrow at her. She almost smiled at the severe expression as it crossed his angled face. He didn't like "no." She would remember that.

"Would you like to rephrase that?" he murmured.

174

" You heard me." She rolled herself up and out of the sand. When she stood to her full height, she took a moment and brushed herself off. "Your men have enough things to do and should prepare to hunt your off-worlders. I don't want any harm to come to your people since I don't know what to expect from the atmosphere up there."

He shook his head. "You're not traipsing off across my planet on your own."

She smiled at him. "Lord Warrior, I am never alone on your planet. She's in constant contact with me."

She stepped closer as a look of confusion crossed his face. When she drew near, he reached out and pulled her to him. She melted into the heat of his body.

"Explain." His arms wrapped around her.

She laid her cheek on his chest. She could hear the steady beat of his heart. "Your planet is alive. She thinks, she feels. She cares for your people as much as you do."

His eyes tracked the movement of her lips. "Figures."

The warmth flared up between them. Heat sparked. Her breath caught, her lips mere inches from his. She licked hers, watched his.

"Ah, you like women, warrior," she whispered.

"I like *you*," he corrected.

Pleasure seeped through her at his comment. It was the closest acknowledgement she'd had from him about the heat they generated. She wanted to preen. She wanted to know what the hell was wrong with her that she was acting like a fledgling in love.

In love? She drew back and startled both of them as she did so.

"What?" He frowned down at her, his arms tightened.

She shook her head and twisted to get out of his arms. "Nothing."

"Something went through that brain of yours." He released her with reluctance.

"Several things go through my brain at once, warrior. It depends on which dimensional plane I'm on."

He scowled. "You're still not going on your own."

"Yes, warrior, I am. You're needed here. I cannot ask you or your people to put themselves into unknown jeopardy due to a hunch on my part." She stood to her full height, surety and confidence radiating. "Let me do my job, Truant."

She watched as realization spread across his face. She hadn't meant for the pain to seep into her words, but he'd heard it and knew she needed to DO something. She wanted to hunt. Hell, she needed to hunt, but in her way. He needed to realize that. Hunting meant without the new priestesses shadowing her steps, without taking his men any further into her realm than they'd already seen. And it meant she needed time away from him to find out why the hell she was associating the word "love" with him.

She was a Goddess. Love didn't factor into the equation.

Love factors into it all, Mistress.

Hush.

He would to catch on to her communications with the Ancient sooner or later, and she'd rather it be later. She didn't need this now. Hell, she didn't need it ever. Goddesses didn't fall in love. They were bound to all people, to the Universe. Zhanne drilled that into them for centuries. She watched emotions chase themselves across his face. He didn't like letting her off on her own. She didn't need to be a telepath.

"You're going to go anyway." He sighed.

She nodded.

"Stay in contact. Stay hidden." His tone reeked of command, but his eyes shone with worry.

Phyxe smiled. "Of course."

No one worried about her, it was ... endearing. She turned before she let emotion sweep over her but glanced back over her shoulder. Her teeth caught her bottom lip between them. She drank in the sight of him, his tall form silhouetted against the black of the desert night. He was as much a part of the desert as she was now.

"Hey, warrior?"

"Yes?" His eyes glittered amber back at her.

"I like you, too." She smiled before she turned and disappeared into the night.

His laughter echoed across the desert behind her.

Phyxe traveled at a fast clip through the night. She'd started out at a jog and maintained the pace over the sands. She had no light but that of the full desert moon, and, even that, she didn't need. The shifting sands welcomed her. While she missed her ability to shift into another form and could travel faster that way, something about running through the night calmed her tumultuous emotions. The clean desert air, the soothing night sounds. It reminded her of all that she was and all that she could be, all that the people on this planet could be.

She'd asked Zen for warmer clothes and a glider. They'd eventually catch up to her, but for now, she maintained a steady pace on her own. She didn't force her speed, nor attempt to cloak herself. She knew full well neither would work until she could get rid of the bracers. They'd become part of her wardrobe now—not that she didn't want them off, desperately. She was learning to adapt. She'd survive no matter what, and the longer she had them on, the more nefarious ways she plotted to rid herself of the demon who trapped her. The demon knew what he was about. Phyxe suspected he knew a lot more than he let on. And right now, she'd bet anything he'd holed up somewhere in the North, one of the dead spaces they couldn't track.

One foot in front of the other, her heart rate never accelerated as she jogged. Had she wanted to, she could have kept up a full on run for a few days, but she didn't feel an urgency to speed up her pace. Firon had offered to open another pathway for her, but she'd wanted to run under the night sky. She needed the fresh desert air.

Love. The word rolled around her head. It wasn't part of her vocabulary, not when it related to one specific person. Yes, she loved her sisters. She loved her priestesses. But she'd never loved another soul for the all-consuming passion, which ignited every time she looked at Truant. He was kind. He was strong. He was determined not to need her. He was irritating in his determination not to allow her to help. All of which bothered and impressed her, and she wanted him with her longer than her time on the planet. Damn it. She never wanted someone with her all the time. Hell, half the time she couldn't even stand herself. She cursed as she ran. She didn't need this. She hadn't asked for this.

Fate loves to intervene.

Fate?

Yes, Mistress. None of us were meant to exist on our

own.

I was not born, Ancient. I was made.

Who's to say whether I was born or made?

Yet, you have a mate? Phyxe huffed.

There is a male planet with whom I've not spoken in decades.

Phyxe slowed for moment at Firon's admission. Her breathing skipped a breath, her heart jumped, and she had to re-sync to keep up her pace.

You have a partner?

I do, and while it is not the same as in human form. We are companions.

I'd never thought of that. I apologize, Ancient.

How were you to know?

I've met many sentient planets.

Yes, but you've never been in love, so you wouldn't have thought to ask.

I'm not in love.

Of course, Mistress.

Phyxe growled. Fire twisted through her, and she increased her speed. Energy raced along her skin. She tingled all over. She leapt through the sands determined to outpace her thoughts. Her legs strained against the dunes. The sands dragged her back as she forced her way over and across them.

Miles later—she hadn't bothered to count them—she stopped and bent over to catch her breath. With her hands resting on her knees, she doubled over and panted. Her lungs expanded as she fought to regain control of her body and her breathing. When she finally had herself under control, she stood and tilted her head back to stare up at the stars. Infinity. Beyond all the known universes she wanted no one else. Damn it all to hell, she was in love. It was a human experience, not suited to a Goddess at all.

Krite. Screw it. She was going to enjoy the emotion, the feeling, the attachment. She'd never had anyone to call her own, and—damn it—Tru was hers. He blended with her. He challenged her. He wanted nothing to do with her powers and everything to do with her as Phyxe, the human form.

Enjoying the feeling, Mistress?

Oh yes. It is exhilarating.

It is. It is also the most powerful forms of energy in the Universe.

Zhanne won't be happy to hear that.

She thought she heard the Ancient laugh, if planets could laugh. Damned if she wasn't right, it was a heady feeling. She'd have howled at the moon if she'd been in another form. Instead, she smiled up at the stars, happy, breathless and elated.

As she took another deep breath, the air closed in around her. She gasped, struggling to breathe. Pain danced through her chest. Her throat tightened.

Mistress?

Phyxe fought to focus, but the air collapsed around her. She tried to take a deep breath, but nothing. She turned, her body refusing to cooperate, and tried to find the source of her inability to breathe. As she turned, a luminescent shield around her turned with her. Through the opalescent film she saw a dark figure hovering at the edge of her vision.

Rais.

MISTRESS?

Phyxe gasped as her lungs strained for air. The figure drew closer. The fire tried to flare from within as a protective shield. No spark drew forth. Her heartbeat accelerated. She knew she couldn't die from this, yet her body responded in kind. Her heart beat triple time. She struggled for air, as a human would, because she was bound.

"It's hard to flame when you have no air, *goddess*," he sneered and stepped closer.

Phyxe flared for a moment in anger, but that flare drew the last of the air surrounding her. She fought to stay upright, to function without oxygen, but it was a futile fight. She collapsed to the ground with a growl on her lips. Tru couldn't kill her, but her own stupidity could. Blackness closed in around her as her senses shut off.

Krite. She was going to take the damn demon apart molecule by molecule, when she could breathe again, if her sisters didn't beat her to it.

❧SEVENTEEN ❧

Tru stared out across the desert. Unease laced his body as he watched the direction where Phyxe disappeared hours before. Sands sprawled in every direction, unending, unyielding. He couldn't pinpoint it, but something caused the hairs on his arms to stand on end. The muscles in the back of his neck twitched. If he'd been in battle, he'd have been watching his back. He should never have let her traipse across the sands on her own. His men could have gone with her until the atmosphere deterred them, or the weather.

"You're bothered." Devos stepped up beside him on the dune, the light of the morning sun starting to wash over them both.

He cast a side-glance at his friend before resuming his watch. He would stay here until the unease left or at least until he had to move. He was restraining himself from following her. Duty kept him here. They had plans to make and off-worlders to trap.

"If you are to be believed, she can't be harmed." Devos stared out over the sands.

"She can't."

Devos turned his head and snorted. "Then why are you standing here like a guardian angel pining for her return?"

"I'm not pining."

"Right."

Tru glared at him. "You know as well as I do, no one should set out across the desert alone."

"You do it all the time." Devos' tone dripped with sarcasm.

"It's *my* desert." Damn it all. His brother in arms was not helping. He barely maintained some semblance of control over the fire raging within him, and Devos, as was his nature, wanted to goad him.

Laughter echoed out. "Oh, I forgot. All bow to your will. Man, no wonder she doesn't want to put up with you."

Tru turned on his friend, the fire lit through his body. "What the hell are you talking about?"

Devos stood his ground, unflinching. "Truant, she's a *Goddess*. We all get it. We saw it. She jumped into battle full force and moved better and faster than all of us. You threw a fireball at her. She never even flinched. And you … you shouldn't be able to do half the things you suddenly can. She's used to nations, planets, universes bending to HER will. But from what you've said, she's bent to yours. As we all do. You've come to expect it. Now, she's said, no. And you're worried, because she's out of your control."

"She's never been IN my control." He shook his head, muscles tensed feeling ... wrong somehow.

"Bullshit."

"You cross the line." He clenched his jaw and forced himself to stay in his place. He would not strike out in anger, not while he couldn't control whatever was raging through his body. He may want to beat the living hell out of Devos, but he couldn't trust himself. Not until he learned to control it. And Devos always stood at his side, no matter what.

"No, there is no line between us. I support you because I believe in you. You're right, you're honest, and you want what's best for us. The minute you pass that I'll be your worst enemy." Devos' lanky form stood strong next to him, his arms crossed yet his body ready and willing to shift to battle or defend in a moment's notice. Tru recognized the stance even in his current state.

Shock swept through him. "What?"

"Don't get me wrong, brother. I love you. But when you cross the line, I'll be there to bring you back. Or, destroy you." Devos' eyes glittered back at him.

Tru was saved from having to answer as the earth rolled under their feet. They reached out to steady each other as the sands shifted and dunes moved.

"What the hell?" they muttered in unison.

HE TOOK HER.

Tru's hands swept up to his head pressing against his temples as a voice ricocheted through it. Gods, the knives of pain. It barely registered when Devos grabbed his shoulders to keep him from dropping to his knees on the sands as pain ripped across his brain. Damn it all, the pain. He howled and then groaned.

He took her. The voice repeated.

Tru tried to focus. He tried to maintain his sanity, one deep breath, followed by another. Devos' strong hands kept him from heading face first into the sand. His brother held him upright offering strength. Another deep breath. He bit down on his lip, drawing blood in his determination to defeat the pain.

Who took her? He forced the thought out without knowing how he did it, only knowing he had to.

The demon. He cut off her air. I cannot reach her. He's using the same technology as the shields.

His head pounded as if someone was ripping it apart, as if knives splintered across his skull. He shuddered. His fingers dug into his temples as if the physical pain would allow him to focus more.

Gods, this was—

Fire flared within, and he fought to keep the flames at bay. Devos was too near to him. He refused to harm his brother because he lost control. He forced himself to take a breath.

"Breathe, brother. Breathe," Devos chanted softly before turning to shout commands over his shoulder at the camp not far behind them.

Pain spiked through his head, behind his eyes. He growled. Demon. He focused on the word. He knew only one demon.

Focus. I cannot alleviate the pain of your first communication with me, Lord Warrior.

Tru's entire body went rigid as he tried to force himself into acceptance rather than denial. He'd heard things on the fringes, here and there and thought he'd been hallucinating. But the forceful entry of the voice ripped apart his beliefs. It was all so surreal since he'd woken in her bed.

I am a part of you. You were born to me as well as your parents, Truant Dare Marius. I promised your mother I would protect you. Now, I am calling you to me.

Tru snarled. Devos' hands dug into his shoulders as he steadied him. Pain, fire, anger ricocheted down his body. He splintered. His body shredded at the same time his mind did.

NO. You will not fall apart on me. Pull yourself together. She NEEDS you.

Tru took a deep breath and focused on Devos' hands, the strength and power radiating from him. The sand shifted beneath him. He focused on what he could feel rather than what he could hear. Solid earth beneath him. Strong muscles in his body. Firm hands on his shoulders. Reality. Focus.

Better.

The pain retreated. He took a deep, shuddering breath and then, another. The pain beat back further. His chest expanded and then collapsed.

Focus.

He refrained from cursing. He was trying to focus. Damn it. Voices intruded as his men drew a semi-circle around him. Devos hadn't yet let go of him. He issued soft commands so as to not disrupt Tru, yet provide him with a barrier, a physical barrier as if it would help shield him from the internal battle.

I am focusing.

Well, it's about time.

You know ...

Yes?

Forget it.

Are you ready to deal with the fact I'm real?

I'm kind of over it. You're real. I'm real. Where is Phyxe?

The demon has her.

And?

He captured her on her run to the North. She wasn't paying attention. Honestly, neither was I. We were having a deep discussion.

As she ran?

Yes. We can both multi-task.

Forgive me, I am getting used to this. He could barely stay on top of the conversation and ignore the pain that finally began to recede from his brain and body.

You'll learn.

He took her?

No, he killed her. Then he took her.

Tru couldn't keep the fire from flaring forth. Devos'

hands dropped from his shoulders as his entire body erupted in flame. His Lieutenant rolled out of the way and ushered the others back. Fire, the essence of it pooled around and through him.

Noooooooooooo. Echoed out across the sands and through his brain and body. His men fell further back as he gave into the pain.

FOCUS! The Ancient commanded. Her age and power ripped through him.

Tru turned, the fire flaming still. *She is gone.*

No. She is in between. She cannot leave. The shields will not allow it. She is neither here nor there. But, you have to get to her.

I will find her.

I will lead.

My men will follow.

Not where I lead. They can meet you there. As will the priestesses.

Priestesses?

Yes, those Mistress initiated before she did you.

With a deep breath, he pulled the fire within, forced it under his control and action. Flames flicked out around him and sucked within as if extinguished. He'd found his focus. He would kill the demon for this.

He turned to see his men standing a safe distance back from him with wide, wary eyes, swords drawn. There'd be stories about this, of that he was sure.

"You done?" Devos drawled.

He cast a hard glance at his friend, checking with a quick look to make sure he hadn't singed him. It wouldn't do to harm those he held near and dear. He'd never have forgiven himself. A half smile crossed his face as Devos shrugged and showed off he was unhurt.

"Suit up. Gliders and all. Trek North." He ripped the communicator from his wrist and tossed it to Devos. He wasn't going to need it anymore. "Stay in contact with the palace AI. The demon crossed the line. It's time for justice."

Devos grinned a wolfish grin back at him, "It's about time. We'll meet you north."

He turned and threw out commands. Men scattered into the night. Tru turned and started off.

Three hundred feet, m'lord, and the earth will drop.

Go with it.

Of course.

He gave into the power. Fire fueled him. Phyxe would be unharmed. He had no doubts. Either way, the demon was going to pay. And then he was going to bring him back to pay again. He'd figure out a way to make it happen. He finally understood Phyxe's need to roast the creature, over and over again.

Firiea's dark head swept up as pain echoed throughout the Haven. A hole ripped through her as if she'd been punched in the stomach. She bolted up and darted around the room gathering her clothes and weapons. Etheria met her at the door.

"You sense it, too?" The elder Matron looked worried.

She nodded as she drew her weapons into their holding places. "I think we all did."

"The others are gearing up. Zen has the gliders preparing."

"Good. I think we're going to get to put our new found skills and powers to use." She cursed to herself. She hadn't seen this. She should have seen this. Where were her precog abilities when she needed them?

"Bring the Fire," the Matron commanded as she turned and hurried down the hallway.

Firiea nodded and darted to the sanctuary. She hadn't quite figured out how to transport the Fire, but she needed to.

Without a second thought, she stepped into the flames willowing from the floor. It was either going to kill her or accept her. Whichever, she needed them now. Flames licked around her body, caressing her as they had her hand during her initiation. A sigh of relief escaped her before she could trap it. Fire flamed within now. She not only had control of what Phyxe had given her, now, she could call it to her. With a smile, she stepped from the flame and offered a blessing and a prayer of safety for her Goddess. Then she turned and darted back through the Haven to the hangar where the others waited for her. They'd been called. They'd been blessed. They could do no less than respond to her need.

A smile of sheer power burst forth. And she was looking forward to testing the elemental fire on the one who'd caused them all so much pain.

The demon was going to pay.

❧EIGHTEEN ৶

Phyxe hovered in the between spaces. She could see her physical form laying in repose on the bed on which he'd placed her. Her body peaceful on the covers, rested, quiet and calm. She liked her hair. She'd have to remember that style. She shook herself. Hair? No, she looked pale. She needed sun, too many years between dimensions. The thoughts all passed over her in a whirlwind. For now, she was ether. She was everything. She was nothing. So, this is what it felt like to be Zhanne.

She wondered if the Goddess of Energy was this splintered, disconnected and at odds with everything and nothing.

She could *hear* everything and nothing.

It was hard to make out distinctions. Every so often, she thought she detected a voice. However, if she tried to follow it, she became lost and disjointed. She glanced down, over her ether form and realized she wasn't trapped by the damn bracers.

Krite, but she wasn't in physical form either. The bracers meant nothing in ether, but her body was bound. The best she could do now was wreck a little havoc while she waited for the flame to return to her body. The demon encased her in a shield of no air ... she couldn't decompose either.

Ether form sucked.

Her sisters would be having a field day with this. She was going to rip him apart by the seams, if someone else didn't beat her to it. She wondered if she could take him apart cell by cell.

The air ripped through Gaian and then out of her in a brief moment. She gasped and stumbled as she stepped into the command room. Her sisters followed suit as their eyes darted around the room to each other in question.

Each paused a moment as the space-time continuum wrenched through them. Even Zhanne stopped momentarily, her thin blue hand resting on her chest as if she struggled to catch her breath.

"What the hell?" Gaian hissed. The hairs on the back of her neck stood on end. She'd been home for mere minutes and intended to report on her findings for 16 of the 17 planets she'd been. She had one more to go.

"Phyxe," Zhanne breathed out.

"Did you catch her coordinates?" Gaian recovered first and strode around the table. To hell with the rift. She was going to find her sister and this was the first indication they'd had in what seemed like weeks.

"I know the direction." Zhanne hastened to the terminal. Her fingers flew across the keyboard.

The holographic map lit up the room. A beacon resonated in one space on the map.

"There." Zhanne indicated with a nod of her head.

Gaian pivoted to stare at the map of the known universes as it shimmered into being behind her. The one place she hadn't been, yet. It figured. Where's the last place you find something ...

"I'm going." Gaian prepared herself for a fight as she rechecked the placement of the sword on her back.

"We're all going." Zhanne stated with a frightening calmness.

All eyes turned on her in shock. The Goddess of Pure Energy's blue-eyed gaze stared at the holographic map unblinking from the shadows of her blue skin.

"Unpleasant. And the person or thing who caused it will suffer the repercussions," she murmured.

Gaian smiled. Well, hell. One could anger the ever so calm one. Hot damn. It was about time. She may even step back and watch this time. She cast her elder sister a cocky grin.

"Then let's get moving, Blue. We've got some attitudes to realign."

Zhanne scowled at her but said nothing. She flipped her wrist at Wystin and Glacial as she strode of the chamber. Her long blue cloak flowed behind her. Gaian trailed along for once rather than taking the lead.

This was going to be entertaining.

Tru barely gave a second glance at the obsidian walls on either side of him as he jogged through the pathway the planet opened for him. When the earth dropped beneath his feet, he'd rolled with it. No questions. No comments. He hadn't even given a backwards glance at Devos and the men. He was sure Devos would have tried to stop him, so he'd given him no chance.

He was focused on action now. He'd wait to ask the questions later. Right now, all he wanted was justice. It was a fire in his blood, pure liquid heat. He wanted Phyxe, and then he wanted the demon's head on a pike. He had no idea where this path trailed beneath the planet's surface. He didn't care. He wanted to be that much closer to Phyxe.

Three hundred meters.

That's all? He picked up his pace. The heat from planet's core had warmed him, but it was warm rather than the fiery hot he'd thought it would be.

You run warmer and faster now, Lord Warrior. You won't feel heat the same way.

Of course. He was past the point of questioning anything. He gave up. The women knew more. He gathered that. Damn his history, his upbringing. When he had time, he was going to correct the stories. He would enlist the Matron's help and start to re-educate his people. They needed to know. All he could do now was accept and respond. He needed to respond. He needed to move. His body itched to do something. His mind demanded it.

Her body is dead.

You say that with certainty.

I am certain.

Yet, you state she is alive.

She is caught between. The shields bind her here. If you can get to her before we figure out how to bring the shields down, you can save her body.

Tru shook himself. This was beyond him, this esoteric crap. He left that to the Matrons. He was used to truths and reality, not mystic and surreal. He needed reality, hard, physical and in his face. He halted as the tunnel stopped. A black, dark wall greeted him. He glanced around, but obsidian walls greeted him at every angle.

Up. Quickly. I can open the chasm into his hideout, but I can't promise it will stay open long. He's using something beyond my control. It is unnatural.

Figures. The ceiling above him cracked open. He crouched, his body coiled, and then leapt up through the split. He left nothing to chance and surged forward in awe of his own speed. Behind him, the chasm closed as fast as it had opened. Had he been lesser than who he was, he'd have been caught between the rock. A good thing his men hadn't been with him. They'd have been cut off from him.

And dead. The heat from my core will not affect you or the priestesses now. Your men, I cannot protect too far beneath the surface.

He nodded as if she were next to him. He was growing used to the voice as part of him. Fire flared and spiraled. The cells in his body fired to life. He hovered in the shadow of the keep, Sian. He recognized it. Abandoned and left for the elements. Firon had managed to open a crevice close enough to the keep wall, on the inside, for him to stick to the shadows. His jaw clenched as he crouched there. Although night, his vision was as clear as it would be in daylight. These changes his body was going through took some getting used to. And, he'd thought his learning years were over.

Off-world warriors milled about in the snowy courtyard, hovering close to the random fire pits dug deep into the ground. Humans, some sharpening weapons, others working through drills. He started when the shadows next to some of them started to move as well. Wisps of darkness formed into the shapes of the humans they walked among. They stood next to the warriors rather than remaining as part of their shadows on the ground.

What dark magic was this?

His muscles locked. This planned invasion was going on under his rule. He stifled the anger flaring to life and causing the muscles in his body to tense, ready to spring to action. He took a deep breath and forced the air through his lungs. Now was not the time to take down these men. He needed to find Phyxe.

For some reason, I can communicate with you even though you are within the shields.

Promising. He watched as a few of the wisps began

training with the men.

Rather than weapons, they used themselves, their shadowy forms, to rip through the human bodies and send them to the ground quivering in shock ... or fear. He watched as the bodies convulsed in pain on the ground. The cries ripped though his head. Weapons fired, but didn't phase them. They simply passed through.

Gods, he would have to warn the warriors.

No, you don't understand. I lost my contact with her.

He pulled together his thoughts on how they could fight such dark magic. The constant contact with the planet might start to get on his nerves, if she continued to sidetrack him in the middle of strategizing.

You said she was dead. That might indicate a loss of connection.

You do yourself no service with such a tone, Lord Warrior. My Mistress is not gone. She hovers and waits, but the connection is weak.

I'm working on it. He wasn't sure how he was going to work on it.

There was no clear path for him to move from his hidden spot. He had warriors, dark magic and a dead goddess on his conscience at the moment. It was a little much. He needed to focus. Phyxe was far older than he.

She wasn't dead. She couldn't be.

He had to hold onto that thought. But this, twisted sense of reality before him, this was something he needed to deal with in the here and now. He groaned. No matter how much every cell in his body demanded he seek and find the other half of his being, he needed to deal with the reality in front of him. Honestly, she would do no less. He knew that, regardless of how much his conscience demanded he find her.

Yes, Lord Warrior.

He ignored the obvious sarcasm in Firon's tone. He didn't need the planet ganging up on him as well. He had enough with Phyxe and Devos. He needed to move here as if he were on the desert sands. He would not allow the demon a hint of awareness of a coming attack. And he would attack. He had a burning desire to rip the man's throat out. Even as much as Firon was harassing him, he was starting to like this planet's voice.

Ice cold fingers of energy wrapped around his right

bicep. Gut wrenching terror ripped through him followed by a numbing coldness as the shadows around him came to life and curled frigid fingers around his arms. Tru tried to protest but his body was held frozen. His muscles tensed, poised for flight. But he couldn't flee. He was lifted to his feet and carried forth into the heart of enemy territory. The fire in his body was trapped, contained. His breath caught and then he took a deep steadying inhalation.

"Now, Lord Marius, how is it you come to be so far North?" A deep voice washed over him and the heat flared momentarily.

Tru lifted his head. The heat gave him the hint of movement. Rais, it had to be the demon Phyxe was so hot about, stood in the heart of the courtyard, bare chested, tattoos glimmering in the night, iridescent. He seemed to be ignoring the cold. The demon stood tall and proud, muscles taut and toned. This man looked as if he'd battled hard and true. If Tru could have scowled, he would have.

"The last time I checked on you, you were battling nightmares in the Goddess' bed. I was sure she'd incinerate you even with those bracers on."

Heat coiled deep within. Spying, the wretch had been spying on them across the planet? His vocal cords warmed. "You are not what you seem, devil."

Rais tilted his head back and laughed. The men milling about them smiled and formed a loose circle. Tru was certain their dark hearts would radiate satisfaction if Rais killed him then and there.

"Close, but I am only demon and only half at that. The devil is much grander in scale than I." He stepped closer and the wraiths tightened their grip. "And you, you were so easy."

"How?" Tru let the fire continue to warm his body and quickly tried to keep it from his arms. He was learning, but he wanted—no, needed—to wait.

Rais leaned in close, his lips mere inches from Tru's ear. His breath was hot on his ear. "Darkness is tricky, my friend. Are you sure you know what's real? What isn't?"

The heat winged through Tru.

Your warriors come, m'lord. They are outside the gates.

NO. He hadn't figured out how to keep them from the

wraiths. He was certain the only reason he wasn't already dead from their touch was either by Rais' command, or the changes Phyxe had worked on him.

I will do what I can. Firon retreated.

"I know what's real, demon." Tru flexed, letting the fire spread throughout his body and flare. A red gold aura reached out and arced from his body. The wraiths holding on to him screeched and released him. But the fire he sparked engulfed them and burnt them down into the ground.

Surprise lit the demons dark eyes and a hint of something else. A half smile crossed the other man's face as he moved back a pace or two. His body was loose, and Tru could swear the other man was delighted with the turn of events.

"Ah, and I see she gifted you. I should have been paying closer attention. She found a way around the bracers. Good girl," he murmured. Tru could swear something akin to appreciation and victory flared to life in the other man's eyes before he tramped it down to focus on him again.

He let the flame continue to burn. "You are neither surprised nor in fear."

Rais shook his head. "I'd say we're better matched now, you and I."

The wraiths flaming bodies twisted in agony on the ground. The fire began to spread. Tru brushed through it with his mind, creating a circle around the two of them. It would keep the wraiths and the fighters out. This would be the two of them. Damn it all, the demon would die.

"Too bad you're fighting over a dead woman now." Rais titled his head. His body shivered, and Tru could hear a loud cracking. He bit back a start of surprise as dark wings unfolded and lifted out of Rais' back. His head reared back as he took into account the nine-foot span of black, feathery wings. What tricks were these?

"Surprise, surprise. I didn't think demons had wings." He drew his sword, rotated his hand to loosen the joints and pushed all thoughts of Phyxe from his mind. He didn't believe she was dead, but right now, he needed to focus on demon slaying.

The large wings stretched and flapped once. "You can thank my mother for that gift. Let's see how well you do with this battle, Lord Marius."

Tru let the fire build and when it reached a surge point, he lifted his hand and released. Maybe this time, he'd have better aim.

The fireball hit Rais dead on. The demon lit, his entire body on fire, but his laughter reached out and wrapped around Tru.

"Do you know why I was sent and not another, Lord Marius?" Rais strode forward, the fire licking along his wings. "I am of fire. You can't harm me."

Fuck. The old world curse tumbled through his mind as did a variety of different dialects. He couldn't be bothered with it now. He focused on the demon, balancing on his feet as the demon drew closer. Fine, all out brawl. He'd had years enough of practice for that one. He waited, and then launched himself at the demon. The fire retreated, hovered deep with in. He knew how to brawl.

Time to get the party started.

Gaian hovered and watched as Zhanne worked her magic with the shield surrounding the planet. It was an intricate tapestry of energy and ley lines, each blending and fading into the other. She could see them, but she couldn't fathom their connections, their dissonance. Each of the sister Goddesses hovered in energetic form as the Goddess of Ether manipulated her way through the shield. None dared breathe a word of encouragement or an offer of help. They let her do her thing.

Each fluttered in the background.

It took a while.

Firiea stood tall on the glider and allowed it and the main AI to guide them north. She wasn't sure what drew her in that direction. She only knew she had to follow the compulsion. The essence of Fire called her. Firon guided her, and she was not ready to question either power. The Goddess had chosen her as the First for a reason. She wasn't going to doubt, and she was going to do everything in her power to live up to the honor. If that meant listening with her heart more than her mind, so be it. The other would either follow or leave her to her peril.

Thankfully, every Matron and Maid stood behind her in consolidated response. Not a one a voiced a concern.

You need to hurry. Lord Marius battles dark magic. Firiea started as the planet's voice rippled through her.

And the warriors?

I am trying to slow them down some, but Zen keeps adjusting. She refuses to listen to me about the wraiths.

A murmuring began among the women of the Haven who trailed behind her in formation.

Wraiths?

Dark beings. I have not seen the like in many lifetimes. The Goddess removed them from the realms many millennia ago.

And they are back?

Yes. You cannot touch them. Only fire seems to destroy. Lord Marius lit two of them in flames.

Good. Delay the men.

"Sisters, we're going to have to be strong." Her voice was soft, yet carried to the women behind her.

"We heard. Elemental fire," Etheria commented.

Whispers of agreement swept through them all. Firiea smiled to herself as the resolution took root in each woman. The desert night opened and lit, guiding them north. The combined focus of the women empowered them all. She tramped down on the multitude of thoughts that emanated from them. Stepping into the fire had enhanced a few key abilities. She needed to learn to quiet the mental chatter. For now, she did her best to block it out.

A smile crossed her face. Later, it might prove helpful when dealing with one particular male. He'd never know what hit him.

❧NINETEEN ❧

Devos bit back a howl of frustration when he hit the wall. He slammed his open palm against the invisible shield. The solidness rippled through his core. His muscles tensed and then relaxed. Damn it all. This magic irked him. Warriors fanned out around the keep, staying to the shadows, cursing the snows as much as he cursed the invisible barrier. They could all hear the swords of battle from over the wall, the jeers and cheers, the taunts of men. They could feel the heat of fire, but an invisible shield kept him, them, from moving to the front gate. He'd hit a wall three feet out, and his mood darkened even more.

"Fire damn it, all," he muttered. Leave it to Truant to get himself into an impenetrable fortress, alone. The sounds of gliders moving in behind him had him turning and uttering his wolf call in a fluid motion. He had not called for reinforcements. He'd left word they were all to remain hidden as a last precaution. As one, the men with him turned, using the shield that was keeping them out as their defense.

Moonlight glinted off the silver gliders as they grew closer in the night. Figures, small and petite stood with casual elegance and determination on each one. They handled the machines with practiced ease. He detected no variances, no nuisances that indicted insecurity on the part of their navigators. Of course, the AIs could have been running them, but somehow, he sensed they weren't.

What the hell?

The lead glider touched down. The slender form stepped off, swishing her cape out of the way of technology and snow. Tiny booted feet landed in the snow. Devos gave a slight hand signal to the men. These were desert robes. And if he weren't mistaken, desert women.

"Having issues, Lord Devos?" Two delicate hands reached up and tugged at the hood, which shrouded her features. Firiea shook out her long dark hair and gazed back at him—a smile in her eyes when they lit on his.

"You do not belong here." He stood to his full height, relaxing from his battle posture. He should have known. The small one had shadowed their steps centuries ago. She had listened, absorbed whatever she could gather before she'd been run off. The fact she'd been regulated to the depths of a Haven, with the Matrons, should have warned him of her impulses.

Damn it all, if he didn't have enough to worry about with the men. Now he had the women to factor in, too?

The other women stepped from their gliders and came forward, flanking Firiea. Forty-three in all. He did the quick math. That meant every single one of them from the main Haven were standing there before him. Had the world gone mad? The women weren't to have left the Haven. They were protected there, deep beneath the surface, allowing Firon's core heat to cover their energetic pattern. It was the only way they'd learned to keep them safe.

"Oh, we have every right. And you're not going to survive this battle without us." Firiea flipped a hand up and gestured to the women, effectively dispatching them with hand signals. "One to every two warriors. Let them shield you."

"You cannot waltz into battle with us and then expect us to protect you at the same time, young one." Devos couldn't keep the incredulous tone from his voice. Out of the corner of his eye, he saw each woman step confidently between two men. Damn it all if his men didn't draw near, balancing them. "This is a battle, not a dance."

"It is a dance of death." Firiea stepped closer. Her wide eyes gaze looked up at him. He'd swear both innocence and cunning gleamed deep in the depths. "We can help you. Firon said there are wraiths in there. If your men touch them, they die. We are your best defense against them."

"What? You can't die?" he sneered. He wasn't about to let the women in there to battle. His warriors would be handicapped with protecting them. Tru would have his head if any one of them were harmed. Hell, he'd rake himself over the coals.

He watched as a shudder ripped through her body and then Firiea called out. "The shield drops."

The women all unclasped their cloaks, Firiea included. Devos bit back a snarl as the cloaks dropped into the snow with a whisper and a sizzle. Every last one of them was dressed in battle leathers. Some had small swords attached to their backs. A few palmed crossbows. Not a single one of them looked awkward in their handling of the weapons.

"When this is over, if you're not dead, I may kill you myself." Devos palmed his sword as he stepped in front of her. "You will stay with me. And, after this, you will explain it all. Now, stay behind me."

He called out to the others, "Keep them between you and the darkness. You let a female die, and I will have your head on a pike."

He turned his back on Firiea, but not fast enough that he didn't see the satisfied smile cross the minx's face. He'd have to deal with her later.

Damn it all, when had his world gone to hell?

Phyxe hovered in the room at a loss for what she could do. The room was small, big enough for the bed and space enough to fit a dresser. Her body lay trapped in a technological cocoon on the soft velvet comforter. At least the cretin had some sense of quality and style, or the previous owners had. She couldn't feel the velvet caressing her skin, but even in this form, she could see its texture. Good. She'd be damned if she died again in a hovel with rats eating at her body. That last incarnation had been hell.

And the shield, somehow, Rais had technology far beyond that which he should. Firon had a certain amount of technology, hidden beneath her surface. But this … this was alien for this planet. Her body was trapped, the one she was rather used to for the last few thousand years or so. She was partial to this form. The bracers still graced her arms. The shield around and within them was as unmovable as the one trapping the planet.

Double damn. She floated and hovered, feeling a

pang deep in her soul. She would have flamed it all, but the ties to Tru, to the Matrons, to Firon ... she wasn't ready to die in this incarnation, and she wasn't ready for any of them to die either. Bless it all, she was not ether, damn it. She was not ready to destroy and resurrect. There was no resurrection in this plan. And this was not her element. At best, her most similar form was smoke.

Smoke. Electric impulses sparked along her energetic lines as the thought ripped through her. Had she been in human form, her entire body would have lit with fire.

She focused, pushed it all aside, and began to realign her energies. Nothing died in the universe; it only changed form. Basic laws of energy—energy never died. She'd tried to train so many in that creed. And, so many had failed. But she was not the many, she was the one, the power of Fire. So, she wasn't in human form. She needed to get over it. She'd grown far too used to it.

She catapulted into etheric form, putting all her focus, all her beliefs, everything that she was and would be into it. She was energy. Full power. Divine right. Pure Fire.

She flamed. The bracers hadn't trapped her essence, only her physical manifestation of it. She could pull power to her. Dissolving her physical body meant pulling her powers into herself, not exploding outward. Why she hadn't thought of it that way before ...

If energetic forms could grin, she'd be grinning. Instead, molecules shifted and realigned. The tenuous hold she had on her physical form began to dissolve. The form on the bed in the physical realm followed suit. As energy, she had no need of her human form. She shaped and molded and pulled it from existence. It took a while, but she manipulated each cell, each molecule of energy until it bent to her will.

She wasn't a Goddess for nothing.

Positive protons rippled in excitement as the physical form within the shield began to dissipate. The form didn't die so much as dissipate. She realigned and took each molecule as it tried to disappear and reshaped it, reallocated it outside the shield. It took time. But then, she had nothing but time. It stood still as she was between realms.

Energy arched through the ether, separated her lines from those that crossed the universe to blend over and through the agony of separation, the sheer pain of otherness, disconnectedness. Her connections began to close off, shut down, limit her ability to reach out and touch everything in the Universe with a single thought. She screamed as only energy could as flesh and blood began to form around her energy lines--the limitation, the restriction, and the quiet.

Heaven licked across her skin. The pure heat of creative Fire swept over her, caressing, cajoling, promising.

Sensation after sensation tripped across the flesh and blood form that sheltered her energy. Cells, regeneration processes, a heartbeat. She would not be born into this plane as she had time and time again. She would be set down on her path, in the path of the others she was meant to help. Her all-seeing, all-watching gaze would be limited for few moments, until she learned to work with the shell she'd crafted. Her universal connections shivered in anticipation.

She flexed her extremities in the ether. Fingers and toes curled and uncurled. Movement. Naked, skin formed last. The body she'd created was finely muscled, powerful, lean.

She looked.

She was proportionate. Neither too small nor too big, although perhaps, it was all-relative when she was next to another being. She flexed her fingers, marveled as a thought caused movement in this body. It would take some time, adjustment to a body again rather than moving and being with only a thought. She lifted a foot, watching in move, still hovering in a physical form in the astral plane and looked at it, memorizing her form while feeling the energy flow along her muscles. She watched the foot, and the muscles in her lower leg contract and expand and thought this form would do.

Neither day nor night affected her now, only energy. Pure energy flowed over and around her. She bent. She molded. Something tugged at her ... a hint of warmth, fire, passion, heat. She used it as she crafted, and she honed. Cells re-stacked outside the shield as they disappeared from inside it. She was careful in her process, being as specific as possible with the minute details. She hovered, her head tilted, listened as the voices echoed around, over, and through her. It was different, hearing them both outside and within. Before, they simply were, as she was. Now, there was a dichotomy. A difference. Perhaps it came with the physical form.

Hearing the voices, she listened and absorbed, but she buried what information she could deep within her, ready to tap into it when and how she needed it. This was not the first time, nor the last, she'd recreated in the physical plane. It was the nature of her being. When called on by the forces, she descended. This time, she recreated herself. It had been so very long since she'd been called. This process, her re-creation, was new. The pain receded, and her body finished and formed still in the ether, cocooned in the warm mists. She would miss this other realm until she returned in pure essence. She wondered, briefly as her senses sharpened, what this realm would bring her to this time ... and then a hint ... a whisper, a knowing. There was another half of her out here. The fire within glimmered and flared in pleasure and beckoning.

It was the becoming she could do without. But this time ... there was something pulling her ... something like her, but it was not her.

The Powers that Be had formed her the first time. She was crafting ... no re-crafting herself in the image they'd created. She tweaked it a little because she could. And then, when it was done, she thrust her essence back into the physical form she'd created.

It hurt like hell. But the pleasure of it all as the harmony of another firepower ripped through her ... it blended it all out into an even and pure blaze. She needed to find the other that matched her, the energetic pull who'd helped form her re-creation.

Gaian's feet touched down on solid earth with a thud of satisfaction. Pure pleasure ripped through her when the steady hum of planetary energy washed though her. She was growing tired of this hunt, as much as she enjoyed it. As the scout among them, her job was to hunt, but this hunt grew long and weary. She wanted resolution.

She wanted to rip something to shreds. And she knew she was out of balance, and she wasn't surprised. The Goddesses of Air and Water had been murmuring incantations since the second planet. With one out of balance, the other three had to take up the slack. And as close as she was to Phyxe, the other two worked overtime to balance out her tiger nature. She took a deep breath and tried to focus, knowing a feral nature might only get the humans killed.

She glanced around with tiger-eyes at her sister Goddesses, each taking stock of their surroundings. She watched as Glacial wrinkled her nose at the sand stretching out before her. She knew the Goddess of Water was not fond of fire planets, of course. Wystin lifted her hand in an elegant movement and fluttered up a breeze to cool the night to a realistic temperature for her. Gaian smirked to herself. Welcome to the sheer heat and raw physicality of the realms, sister dears.

"Alternate form ladies. We hunt Phyxe's energetic signature," Zhanne's command rippled across them as she began to reform.

They each zeroed in on the sudden return pulse of their sister. A collective sigh of relief echoed through them. At Zhanne's nod, each transformed. Gaian focused and reached out to feel each and every molecule in her body. With a deep breath, she shifted them all in one sudden movement and rearranged. Her skin splintered and transmuted into fur. She stretched her body as the muscle of the tiger took over. A growl of appreciation leapt forth as the power of pure animal raced through her. She'd had practice these last few planets.

Beside her, Wystin followed suit, her body taking the split second hesitation as she reached within and did the same. With a cry, her hawk form took to the sky and circled while she waited on the others. Next, Glacial frowned a moment at the sand again. With a soft sigh, she closed her eyes, her molecules exploding outwards and streaming to the sky. Storm clouds hovered overhead. Gaian knew it had taken her far more effort than the others, as she sensed so little water in the balance of the planet's evolutionary cycle. She would make sure she stayed near the Goddess of Water in this realm.

Zhanne nodded her approval and chose to take the route of Earth. She shifted into wolf form without any hesitation. In a fluid movement, she set out across the sands, targeted, they all knew, on Phyxe. They followed and kept a pace that allowed them to work in synergy.

They would hunt Phyxe as One.

❧ TWENTY ❧

How do you battle a half-demon, half whatever-the-hell-he-was? Tru wasn't sure, nothing like learning on the fly. It had been centuries since he fought something other than human. He stood his ground when Rais used his wings to hit down hard through the air creating a rush of wind that would have sent lesser men sprawling. In the dark of night, the fire around them flared higher with the sudden surge in oxygen.

The planet rolled beneath his feet.

"I'd say your plans are starting to fall down around you."

Rais grinned as he palmed his own sword. "Not my plans."

Tru lifted his arm and arced his sword through the air as the demon rushed him. Their swords hit with a resounding metallic clang that could be heard in matching sounds around the courtyard. Desert battle cries swept into action on all sides. He sidestepped quickly as Rais' wing came down hard attempting a double strike.

"Sneaky, but I knew you couldn't fight fair." Tru got a close look at the demon's wings. His feathers were razor sharp.

The other man swung his sword around in slow, lazy circles off to his side as he started to circle Tru. The smile never left his face. "I'm a demon. You've got firepower. Who said the fight would be fair?"

Tru grunted in response. He didn't understand why the other man was taking such delight in dancing around.

Rais tilted his head, listening. His eye held a faraway look for a brief second before focusing back on Tru. His wings shivered slightly. "It sounds as though your men and women have finally figured it out."

"Women?" Tru started, and then he sensed them. Fire essence danced in fighting harmony around him. And

204

there, on the edges of his periphery, he sensed another flame build, embers starting to spark.

With lightening speed, Rais swung his sword out, aiming for Tru's head. Tru blocked, having sensed the energetic shift. He grunted in pain as Rais' fist landed a solid hit to his midsection. A rib cracked under the pressure. Flickers of flame darted through his body. He shoved his elbow in an upward sweep and watched in delight as Rais' head bent back. His body stumbled from the shot to his chin. The loud crack was rather satisfying.

Phyxe would be pissed that she hadn't been the one to deliver that blow.

The demon worked his jaw back and forth, rotating his head around as he tested its workability. Tru took advantage and swung. Vindication lit through his body as steel connected with feather and bone. Rais howled in pain, moving the injured wing back and out of the way as he swung in retaliation. But Tru was ready for him. He parried and kept up with a flurry of motion letting the fire fuel his fight. He ignored the rib and pivoted out of the way of a strike aimed at dissecting his shoulder from his arm.

He grimaced in pain as the tip grazed his chest. His skin parted enough for blood to drip from the wound. "Is that the best you've got, demon?"

"Oh, getting tired already, desert born? And here I thought you wanted to know the why and the how."

Tru bit down and swung, but Rais lifted himself up with a hard sweep of his wings, pulling further back out of Tru's range. He faltered a moment and then caught himself.

"Ah, so that wing hit hurt a little more than you let on." Tru smiled and stalked forward. The demon sidestepped him. "You're playing here. It's all a game to you."

Rais shrugged. "It was better than what I'd been doing. Hell is only tolerable for so long."

"Hell?"

The demon parried and surged forward, offering up another strike which Tru blocked before he swept himself backwards again. "You know, where the impure go to die. Demons, devil, the whole fire and brimstone kind of locale."

"More than happy to send you back there. Cause your permission for being on my planet has been revoked." Tru pulled the laser from its holster on his belt with his left hand while he swung hard with the sword in his right. The sword angled down, aimed to lance the other wing. The laser fired, and he watched the beam gleam brightly as it pulsated and ripped a hole in Rais' side. So the other could handle fire, but he could be slowed.

The demon howled in pain. His wings folded close into his body as he fought to keep his balance. Dark energy flickered around him, cocooning him. Tru took a step back with both his laser and sword at the ready. More magic. Rais' eyes lit with an unholy fire and the demon launched himself at Tru, his sword dropping to the ground. Tru took the hit full on. Tru's weapons fell to the side as he fought to pry Rais' talon-like hands from around his neck. He could feel the air being crushed out of him.

"You think you understand, but you don't. You won't find them. Not unless you look where I've been. Scour it all or you'll miss it." Rais hissed in his ear, so low he almost missed the words in the flapping of his wings and the gasping for air.

Tru struggled to get Rais to release his hold. Damned if he was going to die. Not on his watch. And why was the demon suddenly speaking in riddles. His vision faded.

Phyxe grabbed her sword and other weapons from the chair at the side of the room, stupid of the demon. Had he thought she'd be unable to figure a way around his magic? His conceit astounded her. She sent out quiet ripples of energy as she ran through the halls, sensing her sisters finally, and her priestesses. She could hear the sounds of battle outside.

A window. She leapt into it and peered out. Thank the stars for keeps of old, no glass, not that she wouldn't have gone through it, but she wanted some element of surprise. Warriors were everywhere. Desert robes mixed in with off-worlder uniforms. Here and there she caught glimpses of the women fighting, shields in place. Every so often, elemental fire flared out at the shadows.

It was then she noticed the shadows moving.

Firiea? She zeroed in on her priestess fighting and defending behind Devos.

You are finally back with us, m'lady?

In full fury. Do not let the wraith touch you.

Yes m'lady. We've got that part worked out, the girl said.

Phyxe grinned to herself. Good for her. An unholy cry of pain caused her entire body to tense. It turned of its own accord and her gaze finally found the one she'd been looking for. She watched as the laser fire ripped through the air, striking.

Damn demon. She barely hesitated when Rais flew into Tru and tackled him to the ground. In an instant, her body shifted to pure flame. She launched herself through the night sky at the demon. Energetic fire ripped through the night. All movement ceased in the courtyard as Phyxe narrowed her focus and angled the fire right through Rais' body.

The demon snarled and released Tru. Phyxe reformed and dropped to his side. Her hands ran over him checking and rechecking as he struggled to get the air back in his lungs. She sent small surges of energy through him, helping his internal fire heal as quickly as she could.

"I don't think so, demon." She saw him stumble away from them and start to tramp down the fire spreading through his body with his hands. With a flick of her fingers, she kept the flame burning.

The walls of the keep began to shudder. Men scrambled again to move out of the way as wind ripped across the already damaged gate's threshold. Shouts of shock crossed the courtyard as the largest tiger and wolf anyone had ever seen stepped over into view. A hawk swooped in. Clouds rolled in.

Phyxe smiled, feeling her sisters closer now, and never turned from staring at Rais. "I think you have a definite problem."

He tried to bolt to the sky. Energy crackled around him.

"Oh, no you don't, hell spawn." The fire rose as Phyxe focused. Her playful nature gone. Battle nature full force. Tru's essence flared with hers as he stood. The fire finally flowed back inside his body and added his energy to hers.

The demon cried out, the fire surrounding him before the energy could form. The energies shift behind her as her sisters resumed human form and began making their way across the yard towards her.

Gaian's energy flared first. The earth beneath Rais' feet trembled and surged forth, building a slow wall and creeping up his legs. Glacial came next, the blue white light of water adding to the rock and building a layer of ice above the rock. Wystin pooled her power. A vortex of air began to swirl, trapping and confusing the demon. Zhanne, last, cast the white light of pure energy in a cocoon about all the powers, and forced him to endure each and every one over and over again.

Phyxe smiled and then frowned. The elements caged him, but Rais' face held a smile of satisfaction. The demon was not showing signs of pain, but something else.

"Welcome, sisters. It's about time you showed up," she commented. Her attention split, part on Tru, part on the demon, and still threads checking the planet and the priestesses.

"Yeah, we thought you were taking a vacation." Gaian stepped up next to her and laid a hand on her shoulder, relief and strength radiating from her. Her body relaxed as her sisters formed around her. Power rippled in waves from every cell in each of them.

Wystin stepped forward, her voice whisper soft. "You should leave a forwarding address when you try to go on vacation."

"I thought about it, but where's the fun in that?" Phyxe's eyes never strayed from the demon. She varied the heat levels, playing, letting the other elements bend and recede. She toyed. She knew he was feeling the pain, but he smiled.

"I think time away is good." Glacial smiled as she took her place.

Zhanne tsk-ed them all. "All of you stopped focusing."

"Yes, you're doing all the heavy work." Phyxe cut her gaze to her elder sister. "He knows more than he should. I want to know how he bound me here."

Zhanne nodded. They all did. But before Zhanne moved her energy, the fire, water, earth and air snapped out of existence with a large and loud crack, and with it, so did Rais. Silence descended across the keep. Off-worlders laid down their weapons.

"Ah, Zhanne?" Phyxe turned and looked. The others looked as startled as she.

Shock flared in Zhanne's eyes before being quickly masked, but Phyxe knew all the sisters had seen it. "That was not my doing."

"What do you mean that was not your doing?" Tru stepped up next to Phyxe.

She saw Gaian tilt her head and sniff as she sensed movement and embers. Phyxe pressed a hand in her sister's shoulder before she twisted to pounce. She shook her head at the questioning eyes of the Earth Goddess.

"He is mine," Phyxe said.

Zhanne's gaze darted over at her in reproach.

"No arguments, sister. What's done is done. He is mine." Phyxe lifted a brow.

Zhanne faced Tru; distaste crossed her face. The others turned to look at the male, the human, entering their circle.

"If you didn't move him, where did he go?" Tru demanded.

"This is unacceptable," Zhanne snapped, energy flared around her. "I did not move your demon. And you, you are not supposed to be."

Phyxe's body went molten in a matter of seconds. "Power trip elsewhere, Blue. Your approval was not asked for nor was it needed. The universe decides our paths."

"You will not maintain your status." Zhanne's voice dripped of ice.

Phyxe growled, fire arcing across her body, and she did nothing to control it. Out of the corner of her eye, she noticed Gaian's eyes going wide with shock. She stepped away from Tru. "You do not decide our status. The Powers that Be do."

"I am our law."

Phyxe's eyebrow lifted. "No, you are our guide. We are the law, combined."

Gaian stepped to Phyxe's side and turned to face Zhanne. She lent her silent support, earth energy flared beneath them, lending stability to the fire. Wystin and

Glacial cast worried glances between them.

"Red, what is she so hot about?" Tru's arm curled about her waist. His fire flared subtly, enhancing hers.

"I shared the fire with you, without approval." She kept her gaze steady on the Goddess of Energy, ready to remove them both if need be.

"And this is more important than the demon causing all this hell being winked out of existence? As the Goddess of Fire, isn't it yours to do with what you will?" He tightened his hold.

"No, it's not more important. And, yes."

"No," Zhanne countered.

He tensed his jaw. "Let's try this again."

"You are not part of this discussion, human," Zhanne sneered.

The energy in him rippled enough for the sisters to feel it. Phyxe wanted to smile, but refrained as Zhanne's eyes widened.

"You pulled him completely over." She turned accusing eyes on Phyxe.

Phyxe shrugged. "It seemed like the right thing to do at the time."

"We have no mates. We have no Gods," Zhanne said.

"I have asked him to be neither. That is up to him. I gave him the gift of Fire. I have met no other so deserving."

"You had no right."

Tru's powers flared and fire leapt forth. Surprise lit the depths of her eyes. Zhanne countered in time with a shield of pure energy sweeping around her. She glared through the translucent film shimmering around her.

"He has no control," she said.

"Oh, I'd say he has control. He'd have toasted you otherwise. You'd have had to reform like you did when Phyxe got you the first time." Gaian laughed.

Zhanne blinked out of existence with a glare at them all. A loud pop surrounded them as she returned to the dimensional space.

Wystin shrugged. Her white hair fell over her face as she bowed and followed suit. "Welcome to our realm, warrior."

"Well, this is going to make for an interesting century." Glacial's smile reached all the way into the depths of her blue-purple gaze. "Welcome to the realm." Her going was softer as she winked and winked out of the realm.

Gaian turned to face Phyxe and Tru. "That went well."

Phyxe groaned at her sister. "That wasn't even a resolution. Where the hell did Rais go?"

"We'll figure it out, but not here. And, she can't do anything about your Fire God." Gaian grinned. "If the Powers that Be disagreed with you, they would have already done something."

Phyxe started as she realized it was true. If they hadn't wanted it to happen, it wouldn't have. She knew it. Zhanne knew it. Her sisters were quite aware of it. The question was, what now? She cast a glance at Tru who still stood scowling at Zhanne's empty spot. A frown marred his face. She tilted her head at Gaian who nodded and then quietly melted into the ground before phasing back into the dimensional portal.

"She's like that a lot," she offered up the only comment about Zhanne that she could.

He snorted and looked around, surprise showing on his face when he realized none of her sisters remained. "They're all gone?"

"For now."

"Happy bunch."

She shrugged. "We're used to things the way we know them."

"I am not comfortable with Rais disappearing if one of you didn't do it."

"Neither am I, warrior. But I can't track him from here. Gaian and I will follow his pattern. We'll get him. At least now, you can focus on getting your people back to their homes." She cocked her head in the general direction of the masses of off-world warriors, who'd been subdued by Devos and the priestesses. "I think you have some clean up to take care of."

His face finally registered that others milled about with shock and confusion marring their faces. "Correct."

"And Devos is about to come at us with a number of your warriors."

"Two hundred and thirty-six to be exact," he stated as he looked over her shoulder at his lieutenant.

211

"And the priestesses."

"Forty-three."

"I'd say they're going to need you to step up."

He glared at her. "And where do you think you're going?"

She sighed. "To hunt. And, I need to level set with one sister goddess."

"You'll come back?"

She nodded. "As soon as I'm able."

"I'll hold you to that."

She rushed forward almost knocking him over in her exuberance. "I expect you to do more than that, warrior."

He smiled as she landed her lips on his with a fierce kiss. His arms curled around her and trapped her to him. Hers wound around his neck. She didn't want to leave, but she needed to repair the rift with Zhanne. As much as she loved, lived even, to annoy the Goddess of Energy, she needed to check in with the Powers and make sure she hadn't made a huge mistake. She rather stay here and phase him to the nearest secluded space and rip his clothes off.

He growled at her as he caught the thought. A smile of agreement reached his lips as he pulled back. "This thought sharing, I can get used to."

She swatted at him. "Clean up your planet, warrior. I'll return as soon as I can."

"Yes, ma'am." He smiled a slow, sexy smile at her before turning to stride to the keep doors where Devos stood, warriors behind him armed to the teeth.

Duty called, for both of them.

❧TWENTY-ONE ❧

Tru stared at the screen in front of him as Zen ran scenarios across the holographic plane. Numbers, statistics, it all passed him by. He let it flow in and then right back out. He had his feet kicked up on the table, and he lounged in his chair. Bored. He'd returned to the palace in Tian. Once news spread of his return, his people began to move back into their homes, their jobs. The palace hummed with life and activity again.

Devos and his team had cleared out the off-worlders without issue once Rais' rule and power had been removed, thanks to Phyxe and the rest of the elemental Goddesses. Some had been returned to the Galactic Peace Council, others, only the records of their deaths. Tru held no pity when they were still missing so many of their own. The priestesses from the Haven cleansed and cleared the keep of the wraiths who'd stood no chance against the elemental fire, and then found the shield generators deep in the bowels of the keep. Once they'd been shut off and dismantled, the Ancient resumed her correct path in the galaxy. The shift from the planet rolled through his body and mind. The waters returned as she'd leveled out. Seasons began to shift back into balance, and the desert reacted the only way it knew how, resuming its proper path in evolution.

"If you're not going to listen to me." Zen's voice cut into his reverie.

He started. "I was listening."

"No, you weren't."

He sighed. No, he wasn't. He hadn't been listening to anyone for several days. He'd been focused on clearing out the planet and reestablishing trade routes and communications with the universal officials as they'd come back onto the radar. Now, he had all of it under control. It had taken months. Months. He still hadn't heard from Phyxe. Not even a glimmer of comment. He knew she was there. He could feel her on the faint edges of his consciousness, but he hadn't reached out. His body ached for her nearness. His heart ached for her smile. His soul ached for the other half of himself. He'd come to terms in the first few days of her absence that he'd fallen in love with her. He ranted at himself and railed, he'd finally given in.

What else was he going to do? She was a Goddess. And then, she was a goddess. Hell, even without the power of fire, he wanted her in his life. He wanted her here, damn it.

You know, you can easily follow her now, Firon said.

What? Tru bolted upright in his chair. If he wasn't used to the artificial intelligence helping him run things, he definitely wasn't used to the planet talking to him.

Focus and go get her.

I can't do that.

Why not?

Tru stared at the table in shock. He could follow her. What was holding him back?

Fear. He was afraid she didn't want him as much as he wanted her. That's what it boiled down to. She was over five thousand years old. She was used to this fire elemental thing. He was just getting started. She had no need of him. She was a Goddess. And she hadn't come back.

Time passes differently between dimensions, Lord Warrior.

Does it? Or is she so busy that she doesn't need me?

She will always need you. You are part of her now.

How can you be sure of that?

We are all part of the balance, Lord Warrior. For every action there is an equal and opposite reaction. For every masculine, there is a feminine.

But she hasn't even reached out.

Neither have you. It's only been the last few days that you've even taken time to breathe.

But she hasn't been far from me.

She never will. Focus. You can be with her in seconds.

Tru took a deep breath. Did he want to infringe, or did he want her to come back on her own? Hell, he wanted to follow and bring her back, where she belonged, at his side.

"Having an internal battle again, m'lord?" Zen asked.

Some days, he would like to kick the AI. Her personality evolved each time they interacted. Devos had found it amusing when he'd been introduced. But then, Devos found a lot to be amused about lately.

Tru ran a hand over his face. It was time he let the fire lead. He needed Phyxe beside him, wherever beside him was. The planet was running smoothly. Devos had most things under control. The Haven had the rest of it. There seemed to be a nice balance of power flowing. They didn't even need him now. The priestesses were setting up new educational centers. The warriors setting up training camps and helping those displaced to move back into homes or rebuild them. All he was doing was managing from a distance. And since he could hear all of them with a moment's focus, it was ridiculous being stuck in the command center staring at his boots.

"You're pouting," Zen said.

"I am not."

"Oh, good lord. Go after her already. You miss her. The priestesses miss her. It's not like it would be a BAD thing to have her here all the time." Most definitely evolved for an AI.

Tru laughed. Trust the AI to spit it all out. He rose. Time for fire to seek fire. He wondered if he could do it without her hearing.

Phyxe sat with her feet propped up on the table. It was her favorite position of late, especially when Zhanne decided to drone on about the state of affairs across the galaxy. She'd been caught up in getting herself resituated with her sisters. She'd checked in with all the planets that paid her homage, some for the first time in centuries. She'd even gone with Gaian to some of the Earth planets. She'd paced.

Now, she was antsy again, not that she hadn't been before, but she'd let the others sidetrack her. It hadn't worked. She missed Tru and missed him terribly. Zhanne had berated her for a few days. Phyxe ignored her. The

Powers that Be never answered her pleas. Silence was deafening on all fronts. At the edge of her awareness, Tru's continued actions kept her in remote touch with him. But she didn't reach out to touch. She let him deal with learning about his abilities on his own. She figured it would come far faster to him if she didn't intervene. He was never far from her awareness. She'd run out of things to keep her occupied. And now, she sat listening to Zhanne ramble on about whatever it was on her topic list. She was sick to her stomach.

"Phyxe."

She slid her gaze across the table. "Yes?"

"Focus," Zhanne said.

She shrugged. When something came up that required her full attention, she'd give it. Until then, she wanted to mope. And figure out the queasy feeling crossing her body. Cause it sucked.

Gaian kicked her hip under the table. Her dark eyes shot her a glance.

You know, I can tell you what you've been trying to ignore. Gaian commented.

Phyxe scowled at her.

You've been ignoring yourself.

Yeah, I want to pout. She refrained from sticking her tongue out at the Goddess of Earth. Barely.

Oh, great. A pouting Fire Goddess. You haven't done that since you were 312.

Phyxe sniffed and turned her head back to focus on Zhanne. She wasn't herself. She had no one to blame but herself. She was here hiding out rather than getting herself back to the planet and Tru.

Why are you hiding from him?

Because it seemed safer. She didn't bother to turn and face her. She took a deep breath.

You've never done the safe thing.

Yeah, well, somehow this is important.

Gaian snorted. Zhanne ignored her and kept on.

You might want to make your mind up soon and get moving.

Why? Time is relative to us.

You might want to do some inner searching, sister, and spend some quiet time with yourself and refocus.

Phyxe gave her a clipped nod and shut down the

telepathic chat. She knew she was behaving badly. It was to give herself time. If she wanted to return to Tru and the planet, she feared Zhanne and the Powers that Be were going to demand she give up her status. They would call a new Goddess into being and her powers would be stripped. She would be human. Tru would keep his gifts unless they stripped him of his, too. Sometimes this Goddess thing was overrated.

Zhanne dismissed them. "Phyxe, a moment."

She shook her head. "I've got a date with myself first. I need to figure something out."

Zhanne nodded and let her retreat without a word. Phyxe smiled slightly at the soft look of concern in her elder sister's eyes. She may bitch about the elder sister, but her heart was always in the right place. She was too business minded for the rest of them sometimes. She wouldn't want anyone else in battle except her sisters. She trusted them implicitly.

Now, if she could figure out how to trust herself.

I am fire. I am power. I am passion. I am strength.

Phyxe breathed in, up, and slowly back out again. She let the movement of breathing wash over her body. It swept through her chest, exploded gently into her ribcage, then collapsed, folded, and escaped with the clusters of knotted tension from the day. On the next breath, her spirit splintered from the casing of her skin. Separate, she was shattered, severed, and not quite whole. Another breath in, up, slowly, gently expanding, sweeping outwards. Life started to surge through her, crept up her toes, swirled around her ankles, arced around the muscles of her legs, coaxed them to release the tension. Let it go.

I am fire. I am power. I am passion. I am strength.

Coiled energy, tense, tight, retreated with each breath, a forced march of retreat up her body as relaxation settled and nestled in each cell. Heaviness weighed down her legs. The ashes from the flames burning around her cocooned her in warmth and serenity. She sunk and settled deeper into the fire. Another slow, controlled breath, she was no longer separate from the fire. Its fiery softness merged, became one with her physical form. The separateness battled valiantly, twitched along fingertips, and made a final show of defiance, threatening with glee to buck the focus, the concentrated effort to merge with the breath, the fire, and the force of life.

A deep breath, the heaviness, leaden across her pelvis and then spread up into her chest, blended her with the ash beneath. Edges blurred, a single swipe of pastels. No end. No beginning. No sharp jagged points. All one form, all one pulse. Her eyelids stopped twitching and lay feather light against the curves of her face. Each lash rested gently and found a home, a settling place. Only darkness painted the canvas behind her lids. Her spirit was no longer splintered in a multitude of directions. She was leaden. She was still. Cushioned in the warmth of peace, she was fire. She was breath, life, and the balance of nature.

The jungle of pain and pressure retreated; a path opened up. The darkness took on dimension. Life moved in the ink black sea. A break in the night ... a swirl of muted colors emerged. Subtle at first, they snuck up on the screen of her mind. Hues of blues and mauves arced into a dark rainbow, pulsating, cavorting, and dancing in the motion of breath. Like the spark of a candle flame, small flickers of white swirled into being. Entranced, relaxed, at one with herself, she knew nothing but the soft whoosh of breath, in and slowly back out, repeated as the stars shone in the night sky of her mind. Heartbeats slowed, measured, calm, un-pressured—the deeper the focus, the deeper the calm.

Peace, a feeling, a state of mind. She sensed it; she was it. Lashes swept upward, shifted the fabric of the universe, ebbed and flowed with the energy of space around her. Each cell merged with each cell of invisible force filling up what couldn't be seen. All was one. Peace radiated about her.

I am. I am the fire. I am the ash. I am the dance of life between the two, separated only by what is unseen, blended, born into each other by the same.

Her eyes opened, minute in the shifting focus. Everything merged together. There is no beginning where she began, no ending. Every object around her danced in a balance, a blending of motion and a movement of give and take. It is a shifting in the energies of the universe. When her energy stepped forward, the energy of another flowed into another. Nothing is empty; nothing is alone.

The firelight flickered in slow motion. The yellow gold of the flame twisted and turned, cajoling the eye, mesmerizing in its soft, sensuous dance of energy. It merged with the air. Nothing is separate.

Her breathing came slow, measured, inhaling the energy of the cavorting flames. Staring into it long enough, she lost her sense of definition about the room. The flame expanded. It is the sole focus of her intent. Definition of the external subsided; a blur of color encompassed what was once so well defined. And still her heartbeat slowed faint. It rested, its rhythm sustained and measured, in harmony with each breath. Nothing intruded on this sacred space. Outside of the flame, she sensed nothing. The beckoning light consumed her. She was the fire. The heat of the flame warmed her body as she continued to focus on it. Color surrounded her, consumed her in a motherly embrace. She was protected.

One last inhalation, one last breath, she pulled back from her intent of the flame. Slowly, gently, she expanded her vision to what lay outside the shell of the firelight. With increasing awareness, objects came back into focus. Definitions returned. Her breathing was slow, rhythmic, but the world expanded again. Ever so carefully, she allowed herself to focus on a single object. Bringing its edges in to clear sight, she defined them. A brush, a compact, a tube of lipstick. Her dressing table returned to its physical existence outside the subsiding flames of her fire basin. The hint of belonging still lingered about each item, but now they are separate, held together by an invisible stroke of cosmic energy.

And somewhere outside of herself a faint voice called her name and it reverberated through the cotton cloud setting of her mind, pulling her back from her shared connections. Peace hovered at the edges of her vision. Ever so gently, she moved her fingers and brought her body back to the physical plane, returning to existence with a calmness permeating her being.

She would return. Without Tru by her side, she was missing a piece of herself. She needed that piece back.

"How the hell did you get here?" Zhanne voice ripped out across the command room with icy precision.

Tru lifted an eyebrow at her tone. No wonder Phyxe talked about her sisters with both pride and loathing. He was certain he didn't want to remain in the blue-eyed one's presence any longer than necessary. Her gaze in its full color unnerved him. The others watched him with calm eyes. Well, not the dark-haired one. She seemed to be amused.

"I'm guessing the same way you did," he said.

"Impossible."

"No, not really."

Zhanne lifted a single eyebrow. The sister's eyes all flew open wider in shock. The dark-haired one's smile got bigger.

"You are not permitted here."

"Oh, I'm thinking I am, since I managed to even get here." He'd faced tougher fights than the one she could bring on.

"He has a point, Zhanne," the dark-haired one drawled.

Zhanne cast her a stony glare. "I'd recommend that you not help him in this matter, Gaian."

The one called Gaian shrugged and proceeded to check out her nails, a smile still gracing her face. She shot him a look through lowered lashes.

"What have you done with Phyxe?" he asked. His Fire Goddess was nowhere to be seen. He could sense her, but she hovered on the very edges of his awareness, withdrawn and removed, as if she were hiding.

"We have done nothing with her. She is our sister."

Tru watched Zhanne. The fire flared to life within him. It would be so easy to let loose, but he hadn't done so, yet. He'd been in control and testing his abilities in a safe manner. Something about her icy tone and condescending look make him want to toss a fireball her way to see if she could outmaneuver him fast enough.

"I wouldn't test her, warrior. She has fire power, too," Phyxe's husky voice swept over his shoulder. "She's also got a few thousand years of practice on you."

"I'm a quick learner, Red." He turned towards her.

She'd stepped quietly into the room behind him. His eyes devoured her. From her glistening red-gold hair down the long, lean lines of her body. He hadn't seen her in months, and he wanted to drink it all in at once.

"I'm surprised you managed the dimensional jump."

He lifted a shoulder. "I was determined."

He stepped closer to where she hovered in the doorway. Her eyes held an unusual calmness, a peace. He wasn't quite sure what had changed, but something had.

"You were too far away. And since you didn't seem to be coming back, I came to get you."

She smiled. "Fire getting antsy?"

"I was getting antsy, the fire can be controlled. You were too far away, and I wanted you near." He heard a few sniffs behind him and chose to ignore them. Her sisters could think whatever of him. He wanted Phyxe's sole attention.

"I missed you too, warrior." She stepped away from the door and darted into his arms, hers locked around him.

"I realized when you disappeared in the keep and then reappeared that I wasn't going to be able to do this without you. I want you in my life. However long that ends up being."

She tilted her head up at him. "We live a long time, warrior."

"Well, then, you're going to get tired of me in a few hundred years."

She grinned. "I doubt that. You may get fed up with me first."

"It's a good thing I love you and can overlook your flaws."

"Ooh." She swatted at him. "Nice and mean to me all in once sentence."

He laughed and looked at her expectantly.

"And yes, I love you, too." She wound her arms around his neck and pulled him into a deep kiss. Her lips locked on his, and they winked out in a burst of flame leaving a very surprised Zhanne, a deeply touched Glacial and Wystin, and one highly amused Earth Goddess.

It was all about the exit.

Phyxe: Goddess of Fire

Language
I figured I'd sneak this in here. I had such great fun researching and trying to figure out curse words I thought I'd give you the short list, only those I ended up using.

Krite - christ (made up)
Tovel - bastard (made up) based on Swedish
Ubilin - Gothic for Evil one
Thahts - focus
Taujan - Good

Keep a look out in Book Two, *Gaian: Goddess of Earth*. I'm sure I'll be adding in more!

Phyxe: Goddess of Fire

Stay Tuned for more in the Goddess Chronicles Series

Coming Soon

Gaian: Goddess of Earth
Glacial: Goddess of Water
Wystin: Goddess of Air
Zhanne: Goddess of Energy

....
And don't miss out on the Urban Samurai Series!

Keep up to date
Visit
www.sybir.com

Stacia D. Kelly

ISBN: 978-0-9852837-1-1
PHYXE: GODDESS OF FIRE
Copyright© 2012 by Stacia D. Kelly

For questions or comments, please contact us at: info@catklaw.com.

www.catklaw.com

A sneak peek at Gaian: Goddess of Earth....shhh, don't tell I shared ;)

Chapter One
"Tiger. Tiger. burning bright / In the forests of the night, / What immortal hand or eye / Could frame thy fearful symmetry?" ~William Blake

Kiet Dracen tensed as the fist connected to his stomach for the third time. He exhaled, wanting to curse. As heavily muscled as he was, that one was gonna leave a mark. This was getting old, or he was. Same thing day after day. Get thrown in the pit or ring, fight, take damage, met out damage, get thrown back in a cell and be left to heal overnight. Maybe get food, if someone remembered to dole it out. Then, repeat.

He'd lost track of the days.

He blocked a hit coming with his forearm wincing at the bone on bone crunch and took a hook to his ribs. He winced, but this time, there was no pain. Shock passed over and through him as he realized only surprise lanced through his body. He must be adjusting to the hits. The scar laden warrior trying to kill him snarled when Kiet lifted an arm to block another strike. This block and move method didn't seem to be slowing the other man down. He continued to stalk him around the arena and refused to let up whether he pulled his punches or used full force. Kiet was trying not to kill, but the glazed look in the other man's grey eyes gave every indication of drugs or inducement of an alternate nature. His ribs hurt, and he knew there would be more than one broken one.

He sighed. He was being a baby. He'd suffered far worse sparring with his brothers.

If he hadn't spent all these past years in more priestly pursuits, he'd have offered up one of his brother's favorite, more blatant, curses right then and there. Instead, he inhaled deeply. He didn't need the curses...he needed pure power. Warrior Priest. His skills might be rusty, but he did have them. He stood his ground and summoned what energy he could through the dirt floor and his bare feet. Goosebumps broke out over his skin, and his muscles tightened in anticipation. He allowed the energy to pool and let his attacker come to him. Too many times, they used up all their force in rushing. Thank the Goddess this arena floor was actually the surface of the planet. It gave him some power. The power of the planet wound up his legs, earth energy, his energy.

When the other man caught up to him and swung at him again, his large fist aiming for Kiet's jaw, Kiet countered with a solid block, a current overtook him and solidified his arm. Channeling as much power as he could, his other arm arched up and caught his attacker firmly under the rib cage. The crack reverberated around the arena. The force left the man as he struggled to catch his breath. Continuing forward, Kiet followed with an elbow strike to the jaw. He reached his hand around his attacker's neck, pulling him down and forward, driving his knee into the man's face.

When the man fell, gasping for air, Kiet knelt next to him. He hit the nerve point in the man's arm to incapacitate him, and then hit one on each leg to keep him from standing. Pressure points were a godsend. Of course, his brother's always protested it as unfair battle tactics. Whatever worked, and it hadn't involved snapping the other man's neck.

Satisfied, he stood and tried not to grimace as his ribs reminded him of exactly why he'd finally retaliated. He hadn't been able to phase in the manner he'd wanted, instead, he'd been stuck in the physical realm, unable to allow things to pass over and through him as much as he'd like. The limited access to his shamanistic nature was taking some getting used to.

The bruises and broken parts would take healing on his part, if they let him have the time.

He didn't even allow it to startle him as the body on the ground before him disappeared. Nothing in this place held the power to do so anymore. Instead, Kiet listened and waited for another door to open, allowing him to leave. The door opened, and another being strode in to do battle. He bit back a groan. How many bodies were going to have to hit the floor before he could find a quiet space to sit down and heal? He needed to make sure it wasn't his own.

The new warrior drew a sword, a lethal grin crossing his face. Goddess, this was gonna hurt.

She landed, both feet forming on something solid where moments before, was nothing but ether. The world materialized inch by inch. Energy vibrated around her as she hummed under her breath in frustration. It needed to be here, faster. She'd been scouting and planet hopping for the better part of a week, but this time, the shift wasn't of her doing. She solidified, crystallized. Her head still spun. The dimensional shifts were disconcerting when she was the one doing the shifting, being transported by something other than her own power was worse. Heavy, her muscles thick, denser, not the normal heaviness from traveling through dimensions, but tied. She tested her feet, the heaviness settled with a metallic snap around her ankles. She glanced down, knowing what she'd find.

Thick silver anklets with strange glyphs gleamed back at her, taunting her. The images were far too familiar. She'd seen the ones on the Goddess of Fire's wrists. Hers had been golden, larger, and smoother. Gaian rotated a foot. The foot moved fine. She tried to shift. And nothing…contained. Earth energy swirled up within her and then stopped as if hitting a wall. She frowned, and her displeasure deepened as she tried it again.

Oh, someone needed a lesson in manners. She growled deep in her throat.

She leaned over to test the shackle with her hand, knocking her knuckles against it. Metal, metal reverberated under the tap. *Halja*, damn it to the ninth dimension and back. They'd just gotten Phyxe out of this situation. Here she was stuck in the same predicament when moments before she'd been on her way back to Sanctuary to start tracking the demon who'd captured her sister and then disappeared off the face of the fire planet, Firon.

What the creation was going on in their universe? And who the hell hadn't been paying attention?

Her skin along her jawline twitched. She itched to switch forms. She refrained from muttering another Old

228

Earth curse that wanted so desperately to burst forth. She needed shoes if she were going to have to traipse around the planet. Whatever pulled her had pulled her barefoot and barely dressed. Moments ago, she'd been decked out for full battle, a sword on her back, lasers in her boots. There would be hell to pay for taking her weapons. She loved her sword. Now, she wore some sort of skimpy grey tank top and skintight black shorts. Some one had the wrong idea of appropriate clothing for traveling. Her only other adornment were her newly acquired anklets. Jewelry was one thing, the shackles created a whole new realm of reality.

"They don't come off."

She stilled then turned her head. The Voice. She knew that Voice. That soft, hypnotic, calming drawl and then, she noticed the cell. She twisted her entire body, turning in a complete circle and slowly took stock. Metal floor, one solid wall to the back, finely meshed bars on three sides. Shadows moved on either side of her. A bed melded to the floor. The same with the chair and the table. A small vestibule at the back she would guess to house the toilet, a sink, and water. A cell. Her heart rate threatened to increase. She tramped down on a momentary sense of panic. She'd been in worse situations and survived. Whoever pulled her would not be able to contain her for long.

But a cell? Her right eye twitched once before she forced her body and her breathing under control.

She lifted her head and flipped her hair over her shoulder. She ran a hand through it and took a deep breath in, steadying herself. Her nose wrinkled at the scent of fear and hunger mixed in with the cold bite of metallic, processed air. She would have preferred the clean fresh air of the open plains if she were going to be stuck in a prison. Soft keening sounds came from a few cells over and wailing from somewhere beneath her and to the right. Her heart rate accelerated. Only metal vibrated around her, where was the earth?

"Calm." The Voice soothed.

She turned back to the Voice. "You do not belong here, Priest."

He shifted forward, closer to the fine metal mesh wall separating them. She bit back a gasp of surprise as his form crystallized through the mesh. That beautiful, calming, hypnotic voice belonged to a mammoth of a man. When she'd seen him last he'd been a dark figure resting against the trunk of a tree halfway up the thick greenery, sheltered from the rain beneath a large, leafy branch. His body had been relaxed, quiet and watchful. Now, his massive, tattooed, muscular form towered over her from the cell beside hers. She bit the corner of her lip. She hadn't realized he would be so, well large.

He had to be over six and half feet tall. And stars above, he was built like the side of a mountain. It would take an army to move him.

Strength and power radiated from him. He stood quiet and still, as strong as the tree he'd been taking shelter in. A faint aura of green and gold shimmered around him. She studied every inch of him. His chest broad, bare, was lean and muscled. His torso chiseled to perfection as if he spent his days in physical labor. On his right shoulder an image pulsed with an eerie white on white light, a tiger tattoo wrapped around his left arm and flowed into his torso, stalking something across his chest. She looked closer, in the lines of fur, a dragon and an eagle glimmered in and out, and tiger stripes stretched from the end of the tiger's body down his arm to his wrist. The image pulsed as if alive, but iridescent. Her gaze lowered, down, over his stomach. She bit back a gasp as her body heated up. The muscles in her stomach tightened. The dark pants, loose and slung low on his hips, only accentuated the leanness in his body. Her fingers curled as she realized she was leaning closer, wanting to feel the heat of his skin. She shook herself mentally and noticed his feet were as bare as hers and planted in easy confidence, tanned and perfectly balanced on the floor beneath them.

He shifted on his feet, and her gaze traveled back up his body. A fresh wound slashed from the edge of his right eyebrow, across the bridge of his nose and ended just above the left corner of his lip, the only flaw on his sculpted features. Irrational anger swept through her at the sight of the wound. Who had dared to hurt him? She started and realized her body betrayed her to a human. It was no concern of hers if he was hurt. She needed to focus on what pulled her here.

Goddess, who was she kidding? She wanted to pounce him, and the universe be damned. She bit her tongue and winced at the pain tasting the tangy hint of blood.

Focus. Focus. Focus…and then he moved again, and she was entranced by the play of muscles across his chest.

"You know me." He stated. His eyes traveled over her body as she'd done to his.

"I know your Voice, Priest." She bit her tongue again for good measure, hoping the minute pain would get her mind out of the gutter. Him, she knew him. Yes. She'd been in tiger form, hunting her sister. She let her gaze slide over him again, drinking in his physicality. She couldn't get enough of looking at him. The power in his form had her body humming in synchronicity. She wasn't a small woman by any means, and he dwarfed her. This was surreal, trapped in a cell and her body betraying her need to hunt with a need to touch. Humans did not affect her so. She was a Goddess. Yet, she dreamed of his voice since she'd left his planet when she'd been hunting Phyxe. She'd vowed to return at some point soon if only to see if the energy in his voice matched the vibration in his body. She hadn't seen him before, only hazy features in the rains, a glimpse of dark eyes, which were actually a sapphire blue, a hint of his black spiky hair. She'd remembered the voice, and its ability to make her heart race, to make her body hum.

"Kiet Dracen, Lady." He bowed his head in greeting. "But we have not met."

"We have, in alternate form." She'd wanted, no needed, to be closer to him then to test that hint of power. She stepped nearer, transfixed on his gaze, ignoring the cold metal beneath her bare feet in the cell. She hated cages, but him, him she could almost reach him through the open spaces. She didn't stop herself from reaching out to touch his arm, the nearest part of him. She wanted to trace the contours of the tiger. Her image. His skin twitched as her fingertips made contact. He tensed, but didn't pull away. A hint, a knowing passed between them. His eyes widened as if in realization and then, as quickly, he shut down, his gaze blank.

She frowned and tilted her head. She didn't understand why he was ignoring the knowledge. "Kiet. I am Gaian. You know me."

He'd closed his eyes as her fingers touched his skin. His jaw tensed. His body coiled as if ready to move away yet unwilling to disrespect. "I see a golden tiger when you speak, lady."

She trailed her hand over the edges of the tiger stripes, wanting to touch more, but satisfied with where she could reach, for the moment. Power pulsed beneath his skin. She heard as his teeth grind down. "You'd see more of one if I weren't bound by these shackles."

His eyes snapped open, and his nostrils flared as he lifted his head. "You do not belong here."

She laughed, the sound at odds with their surroundings, removing her hand from the heat of his skin and tapped on the metal between them. "I'm pretty sure, with all these cages, no one belongs here."

His mouth clamped shut, and he stepped away from her when the sound of metal on metal echoed down the hall. Gaian twisted her head, remaining close to the bars that separated them. All sounds, all movement from around her stopped. The level of fear heightened, and she sensed Kiet's body transition to complete stillness.

"Quiet. They come to find a new toy to play with."

She cut a glance at him, but remained facing the sound of footsteps. Her Voice was turning out to be far more than she expected. Nian'ian was not known to produce psychics among her people, or she was further along her evolutionary path than she'd anticipated. She had a feeling with him; there would be more than a few surprises.

"Toy?" This kept getting better and better. She would hate to have to reset the planet. She didn't have time for this. She needed to track the source of these bonds, not play in the ridiculous game whoever had going. If she had to, she would destroy it all and resume her tracking. And, if that damn demon had anything to do with all of this, she was going to rip the wings off his back the first chance she got. Phyxe would get over it even though she'd claimed first rights on demon punishment.

"Here's the new one, as he said she'd be here." The horrid creature who stepped before her cell reeked of alcohol and some scent she couldn't place. She sniffed harder and wished she hadn't. She should have relied on the visual clues. Her stomach rolled. She'd smelled a lot of putrid things in her lifetime, but this creature…his partner wasn't much better. "He wants her."

"Careful, they deal in death." Kiet began to pace. Gaian wondered how hard he'd have to hit the wall to go through it. He was contemplating it. His large body drew their attention for a moment.

"Don't worry, warrior. They're still clamoring for you, but this one needs to be tested." The guard swung a large metallic staff against the bars of Kiet's cell as if to drive him back. The ringing of metal on metal would have sent most people running. The priest stood his ground without flinching. Diamond hard eyes glittered back at the guard who stepped back a few paces from his cell.

"I am death." She lifted an eyebrow. Death was hers to deal. She did not tolerate threats. She destroyed cities, planets for disrespect from the people populating it. She'd rebuild and reawaken the planet. The people. Well, their energies would eventually resurrect, if they passed the tests. She tolerated no disrespect for that which she'd built to care and shelter them. Her planets were her children.

She stood to her full height, knowing without a doubt that she radiated strength and power. Her body had been perfected through centuries of sheer physical training and mental stamina, a finely honed weapon. She knew she was impressive, even more so in this half dressed state they'd pulled her in. The woman in her wanted some shoes, and the warrior in her wanted her weapons, but she'd get over both. She would adapt, hunt, and deal. She'd deal death with her bare hands and be happy doing so.

"Apparently, someone needs to learn some summoning manners." She murmured eyeing the guards. They would be easy kills, a single leap and twist of the head to the one, a roundhouse kick to the jaw of the other, both too stupid and slow to respond to her speed.

The guard grinned eyeing her up and down. His gaze lingering on her chest, and he waved a hand out. "Well, we didn't know yer majesty would be joining us."

"Careful." The deep baritone commented. Anger rolled off him, and then he took a deep breath as if to calm himself.

"Catch a tiger by the tail…" She refrained from rolling her eyes. *"They cannot harm me, warrior. Be calm."*

"You will lead, thank you." She said, sweeping out of the cell. Let them think, for a moment they even held an ounce of the power. She would fix that soon enough.

They mocked her. Rude. Humans. Some days, she wondered why they'd been created. They caused the most trouble in the universe. All drama. She'd dealt with worse, human or not. Her jaw tilted up, and she flashed her canines at him, licking, and grinning. She opened her eyes wide and inviting. The larger guard stepped back, allowing her space to move out of the cell on her own.

Eyes weighed on her from the others cells and forms huddled in the dark, hoping to remain unseen. She waited until the guard closed the door and stepped in front of her. No need to show off for them yet, at least, not too much. She wanted to know their plans. She didn't even have to test even the topmost layer of the mind of the nearest guards thoughts to know he wanted to slam her head against the bars before leading her to her calling. She repressed a growl as she picked up hints of memories in their mind of other women, other fights. A painful, slow and torturous death would be suited for these two. She would take them apart piece by piece and then, let Phyxe roast their pieces while the others of their kind watched.

She shook herself and focused. This was the hunt. When in doubt, fake it. She'd be damned if she were at a disadvantage because she couldn't shift or tap into most of her powers. And, the men here, if they could even be called that, true men didn't hunt and debase others…these, creatures, required a lesson in feminine power. She shut out the millions of tumultuous thoughts descending on her from the beings in cages around her as they passed. She obviously still maintained a large portion of her powers…her ability to track thoughts…and use her powers of suggestion.

Before she stepped away, she dipped her head and winked at Kiet, her Voice. *"This should be an interesting ride. Remain safe, Priest. I'd hate to have to hunt here before I'm ready."*

"You will be the hunted, lady. Be careful."

"Hunted? Riddles and games…this space is going to

be a hell of an education for someone. I am always the hunter."

Her Voice remained silent. Kiet Dracen. She let the name roll around her head as she followed the guards. Strong. Sculpted. Earthy. Hell, she even liked his tattoos.

She almost purred. Play time.